"With *The Names of the Stars*, Ann Tatlock has hit another home run. Her keen understanding of both history and character makes for a poignant and powerful novel that will live in the hearts and minds of its readers for years to come. It's no wonder she has such a devoted and loyal readership."

—Aaron Gansky, author of *The Bargain, Who is Harrison Sawyer, Heart's Song,* and the Hand of Adonai series

"Ann Tatlock has been one of my favorite authors for many years, and I was delighted see her new novel, *The Names of the Stars*. She never disappoints, and this story provides an extraordinary experience of intriguing characters, realism, surprise, drama, and emotion. Tatlock again works her creative magic. She, and her books, are stars in this writing profession."

— Yvonne Lehman, author of 59 novels and 15 non-fiction Moments series

"Seamlessly woven, *The Names of the Stars* is as unique as it is masterfully composed. By using symbolism from Charles Dickens' beloved *A Christmas Carol*, Ann writes with wisdom and compassion about a time in history that holds similarities to our current era."

—Alice J. Wisler, award-winning author of *Rain Song* and *Still Life in Shadows*

"There are people who can tell a story and then there are people who are story weavers. Ann Tatlock is a story weaver. In this multi-layered novel *The Name of the Stars,* page after page uncovers yet a deeper story, a new desire, another thought-provoking moment of realization for her characters and for me. Tatlock's ability to draw the reader in and engage them in every facet of each character leaves them clamoring for more. I am not disappointed. Yet another amazing opus by Tatlock."

—Cindy K. Sproles, best-selling and award- winning author

"Ann Tatlock has long been one of my favorite novelists, and with *The Names of the Stars*, she does not disappoint. From Vaudeville tours in 1918, complete with a glimpse into the Spanish flu epidemic, to the world of the rich and famous of Broadway in the 1930s, the story centers around Annalise Rycroft, a young girl with an amazing voice who is forced to use it for another's glory. Jealous and determined to prove her own worth, Annalise eventually finds fame with its accompaning heartache and emptiness. Tatlock's pitch perfect prose resonates throughout as Annalise, with the help of a dogeared edition of Dickens' *A Christmas Carol*, ultimately learns the value of every life, those discarded as worthless as well as those idolized and worshipped. An entertaining, thought-provoking, and hopeful novel, not to be missed."

—Elizabeth Musser, author of The Swan House Series:
The Swan House, The Dwelling Place, The Promised Land

"I've slept in seedy hotels. I've rattled through the Midwest on night trains. I've seen the audience trough flickering stage lights. I've lost and loved. In short—I have been to Vaudeville. And I loved every song and step. Well done, Ann Tatlock! You are truly the cream of the crop."

—Buck Storm, author

THE NAMES OF THE
Stars

Ann Tatlock

NEW HOPE®
P U B L I S H E R S
Imprint of Iron Stream Media

An imprint of Iron Stream Media
Birmingham, Alabama

New Hope Publishers
An imprint of Iron Stream Media
100 Missionary Ridge
Birmingham, AL 35242
NewHopePublishers.com
IronStreamMedia.com

Iron Stream Media serves its authors as they express their views, which may not express the views of the publisher.

This book contains references and quotations from *A Christmas Carol* by Charles Dickens, first published by Chapman and Hall, London, December 19, 1832. Public domain.

Scripture quotations from The Holy Bible, Douay-Rheims 1899 American Edition Version. Public Domain.

Library of Congress Control Number: 2020946398
Cover design by Hannah Linder

ISBN-13: 978-1-56309-422-4
Ebook ISBN: 978-1-56309-423-1

1 2 3 4 5—24 23 22 21 20

DEDICATION

To EJ
with thanks

PART I

1918

CHAPTER I

A knock came at the dressing room door. "Ten minutes, Miss Rycroft."

That sound, the knock on the door, reaches me even now, sliding down through the years and filling me with that thrill of anticipation and no small amount of nervous energy. The audience is waiting, and what they are waiting for is you. Or, as on that long-ago day, they were waiting for my mother.

"Thank you, Mr. Timms," Mother called. She took one last look in the mirror to make sure her beauty was intact, then rose from the dressing table with arms outstretched. "Well, darling," she said to me, "wish me luck." She said this always with such theatrical flair I felt as though she weren't speaking to me at all but simply reciting another bit of stage dialogue.

Of course in the theater, we never wished anyone good luck because that was considered bad luck. But I was already well rehearsed in my own line, and now repeated it dutifully, "Break a leg, Mama."

She nodded, then patted her upswept hair and smoothed her frilly dress along the contours of her slender hips. A small smile played across her lips as she moved across the narrow confines of the dressing room. I followed her into the dimly lighted backstage hall where the smells of greasepaint and cheap perfume gave way to the more acrid smells of must and mold and human sweat.

We had landed in another small-time Vaudeville theater somewhere in the Midwest. I can't remember now exactly where we were. St. Louis, maybe. Or Omaha or Des Moines. To my eyes, all the theaters and all the towns and all the decaying hotel rooms looked the same.

Mother's cue meant Uncle Cosmo was still on stage, trying to reel in the matinee audience on the strings of his violin. As the opening act, his job was to entertain the masses while they straggled in and stumbled over one another to find their seats. His was a "dumb act" that involved no words because the audience wasn't ready to pay attention. Uncle Cosmo stood on the small strip of stage in front of the curtains, a lone and sorry figure, the harsh spotlight glancing off his glasses as he played songs that no one really cared to listen to. I could hear the men and women even now, the whole of them a restless creature out in the house, impatient with the notes my uncle was casting at their feet like so many wilted petals. I always felt sorry for old Uncle Cosmo; he had the worst spot on the bill. Maybe that's why all the songs he played sounded so sad.

My mother stood beside me taking deep breaths. After all these years on the stage, she still got nervous in the moments before her entrance. That's why Mr. Stanley, our troupe's manager, always showed up at the last second to offer his standard fare of encouragement. "Knock 'em dead, Bernadette."

Mother's sole response was to lift her chin another notch. Though we couldn't see him, I knew that even now Uncle Cosmo was backing off the stage while playing out his final notes. The thought of him walking backwards always left me clenching my fists and bracing against the shattering crash of him falling into the orchestra pit, just as he had done a year or so ago. Since his accident had garnered the greatest laughs of the night, Mr. Stanley had spent weeks trying to get Uncle Cosmo to repeat it, but in light of the fact that the fall had bent his glasses and shattered his kneecap, my uncle refused.

Also out there in front of the curtain, stage left, someone was changing out the cards that announced the acts. Probably Mr. Timms, the assistant stage manager at this theater, a little man who made his living knocking on dressing room doors and herding show people from one place to another like a dog herding sheep. Surely by now he had withdrawn the first card and cast it aside, the one that read "Cosmo Turlington, Consummate Violinist." (He was actually a Rycroft, twin brother of my late grandfather; Turlington was his stage name.) In its place, another card appeared, introducing "Rex and Bernadette Rycroft, the Singing Sweethearts," although in truth they weren't sweethearts at all but brother and sister who, as far as I could tell, didn't even like each other very much but kept the act together in their mutual pursuit of fame. Both had been abandoned by their spouses long ago—Uncle Rex, twice—which spoke of how difficult they could be to get along with.

Mother, Mr. Stanley, and I stood side by side. We could see Uncle Rex on the far side of the stage from which he would make his entrance, meeting Mother in the middle. The house grew quiet. From the orchestra pit came the opening notes of a familiar tune, and the curtain began to rise. Mr. Stanley laid a hand on Mother's naked shoulder (her dress being an off-the-shoulder style that daringly displayed both collarbones) and offered once again his tired platitude, "Knock 'em dead, sweetheart," to which Mother quietly and calmly replied, "Touch me again, Mr. Stanley, and I'll knock *you* dead."

And then she was sashaying her way onto the stage, opening a parasol that a stagehand handed off to her just as she was stepping into the spotlight. Before the parasol was fully open, I heard Mr. Stanley chuckle to himself and then, without taking his eyes off Mother, he said to me, "Yessir, Annalise, your mother's got it." I didn't like what he said, though I didn't fully understand it, and I didn't like the way he looked at Mother, but then again, all the time we'd been with this troupe—for more than a year now—I'd never liked Mr. Stanley very much.

I moved away from him and a little closer to the stage itself to watch Mother and Uncle Rex sing and dance.

I always thought it a magical moment when Mother first opened her mouth and began to sing, as she really did have a fine voice, like an angel, I thought, though admittedly I'd never heard an angel sing. That voice had followed me all my life, had calmed my fears, sung me to sleep, been the background music to all my days, and though I loved Mother, I believe it was her voice that I loved most. Mother's character—her temperament, her emotions, her affections—all were changeable. Her voice was not. Her voice was a constant, and it was beautiful.

She believed it was going to carry her to stardom one day, and so in every show, in every theater in every town, she gave the act her all. She and Uncle Rex both performed not only for the "peasants," as they called the theatergoers, but more importantly, for that one unexpected someone who could change everything. After all, you never knew when a talent scout might be in the house, someone who would at long last lift the Singing Sweethearts from small-time to big-time to legitimate stage all with one swift flick of his magic wand.

The audience here in St. Louis or Des Moines or Omaha or wherever we were warmed to the Sweethearts at once, and that was a good thing, I knew. You didn't want a cold audience, one that sat on their hands, because then the talent scout might leave before the end of the act. If the audience sighed at the romantic songs, which this one did, if they laughed at the occasional jokes, as this one did, if they tittered at the sexual innuendos and clapped at the elegance of your soft-shoe routine, that could only up the ante that the scout would be impressed. If he was out there.

> My heart, once sad and lonely,
> Has found its one and only
> In you, dear,
> In you, dear …

I sang quietly along with Mother and Uncle Rex, a shadow hidden in the wings. Some months before, they had tried to make me part of the act. Uncle Rex, who was diligent and ruthless in teaching me how to sing, claimed I had a golden set of pipes so powerful they could shoot a song from here to Timbuktu and back again without a hitch. He said that one day my voice was going to make us all rich, and that it wasn't too early to get started.

The problem, though, was that the golden pipes were encased in a vessel of dubious clay, as my little girl body seemed reluctant to grow and take on shape. Though I was thirteen, I looked no older than ten, and I was so small, skinny, and angular that Uncle Cosmo once said God had forgotten to put flesh on my bones. Still, Uncle Rex smelled money, so decided to pass me off as even younger, like child prodigies Lotta Crabtree or Elsie Janis or even Baby Gladys, who eventually became known as Mary Pickford. All of them had been entertaining audiences long before they reached double digits.

And so Uncle Rex wrote a song for me that we practiced for months and finally debuted in a theater in St. Paul, Minnesota. Billed as Little Miss Honeycomb (*"Sweetest thing to ever sing!"*), I was all dolled up in a yellow taffeta dress and black patent leather shoes, my hair in ringlets and ribbons. On opening night, Uncle Rex gave me an encouraging shove onto the stage, certain he was sending me out to become the next America's Sweetheart.

I wanted to please him, and Mother, and the audience, and myself. I had practiced the song hundreds of times, and I knew I could sing it well, but as I stood there center stage, fancying myself Baby Gladys and attempting to sing my heart out, I felt my knees weakening from the weight of too many eyes, and even as I struggled to hold myself up, my nerves began to unravel. Somewhere in the middle of the second stanza, I discovered I couldn't breathe. As I struggled to push the notes up from my lungs through my throat and out my mouth, what came out instead was a monstrous hiccup. Followed by another. And yet another. The orchestra played on, but I could accompany them only with these hideous noises. In desperation, I looked toward the wings from where Uncle Rex and Mother were watching my disaster of a performance. Mother was wringing her hands, and my uncle was waving his arms at me as though to say: *Just keep singing! The show must go on!*

I looked back to the audience, who had begun to titter. A small wave of laughter rolled in from the back rows. I tried to pick up where I left off, but only hiccupped once more. The laughter grew louder. Finally someone in the audience hollered, "She's only a kid, leave her alone," and someone else called out, "Just start over, sweetheart, you're doing fine." The latter statement was followed by a smattering of applause, and I knew that moment was the crossroads: I could try again, or I could give up and leave the stage. The orchestra quieted, and I tried to quiet myself. Several seconds passed in which my chest was mercifully dormant. The conductor looked at me and nodded. I nodded back. The music began again. I opened my mouth and, to my dismay, hurled upon the audience the loudest explosion so far.

In spite of the fact that I exited the stage in disgrace, Uncle Rex and the stage manager allowed me to try again the next night. The same thing happened. When my performance repeated itself yet a third time, that was it. I had struck out. That third night, as the curtain lowered on my erupting form, I ran into the wings, trembling with rage and shame. The unchained laughter of the audience followed me.

Alone in the dim light off-stage, I discovered that humiliation can pierce a soul with actual physical pain. I lifted a hand to my chest. Beneath my ribs, my heart beat wildly. The hiccups had stopped, but I still struggled to breathe. Feeling weak, I dropped to my knees and wept a bucket of tears all over the front of my yellow taffeta dress. It was Uncle Cosmo who came and comforted me, who lifted me into his arms and carried me back to the dressing room.

Mother never said a word after that third performance, preferring to pretend I hadn't embarrassed her. Uncle Rex simply pulled me from the bill before the stage manager could.

There's an old adage in show business that says, "You don't need talent, just courage." Uncle Rex lectured me that my talent was no good because I didn't have the courage to use it. He actually wagged a finger at me as he sputtered, "I'm putting you on hiatus until you grow the spine you need to be on stage without making a fool of yourself. You'd better hope it's soon, young lady, or else you'll end up excess baggage, and the last thing our troupe needs is more excess baggage."

So now I watched from the wings, hoping and praying my spine would somehow grow, maybe even in spite of myself.

> My life, once solitary
> Is now made ever merry
> By you, dear,
> By you, dear ...

Across the stage, in the far wing, I could make out the well-endowed figure of Uncle Rex's stepdaughter Georgina Slump. She had shown up some months before when she turned sixteen and her mother, my uncle's second ex-wife, finally allowed her to join us on tour. Gina was in love with the limelight and she, too, wanted to be a star. Since it was Uncle Rex who had introduced her to showbiz, he felt obligated to write her into the act. I had already washed out by then, so my uncle figured maybe Gina could expand the act and bring in the money I'd failed to bring in. After all, with her hourglass figure, her delicate features, her full head of dark curls cascading to her waist, who wouldn't welcome her presence on stage?

But there was one problem: she couldn't sing. Not even her considerable courage could make up for the sour notes and the ill-timed starts and finishes that characterized her routines. One stage manager commented that Gina was an act that only a deaf man could fully appreciate. She was easy on the eyes but hard on the ears, and not even a vaudeville audience could be forgiving of her faults. She, too, was put "on hiatus" till Uncle Rex could "figure something out." I once suggested that they pawn her off on a burlesque show, since her singing wouldn't be heard over the catcalls and whistles of the men, but my suggestion didn't go over very well, especially with Gina.

> Because of you, dear,
> I'll never be blue, dear,
> Because of you
> My heart is gay ...

Mother and Uncle Rex slid into the final chorus of their first song, and the audience was drinking it up. From out of the dark came the occasional sharp whistle, the hollers of approval, the cheerful laughter of acceptance and finally, a thundering applause, a solid bridge of admiration upon which Mother and Uncle Rex could walk confidently from their first song into their second.

In the wings, I watched as they bowed demurely, and as they bowed, I pinched the hem of my plain cotton dress and bowed deeply. I bowed to the left, bending at the waist, head down and hair falling forward until, with a dramatic upward toss of my right arm, I rose, swiveled, and bowed deeply to the right. The air throbbed with applause; I felt it pulsing through my whole body. With my eyes closed, I could easily imagine the adoration was all for me, and it was wonderful, wonderful!

Only when I straightened up did I hear the laughter. Somebody was laughing at me. I turned and looked up into the amused face of Mr. Stanley, his mouth so wide with glee I could see the shiny redness of his gums where several teeth were missing. "Oh, that's rich!" he cried, reaching into his pants pocket and pulling out a handkerchief. He dabbed at his sweaty brow. "You taking a bow, of all things. Face it, Little Miss Hiccups, no one will ever clap for you!" He laughed again at the thought, then turned and, chuckling still, walked away, leaving me there in the back-stage gloom, all joy gone in one fell swoop.

CHAPTER 2

U ncle Rex stuck his head in the dressing room door and settled his gaze on me. "You're on in fifteen minutes. You almost ready?"

"I don't want to do this, Uncle Rex."

"Too bad, kiddo. Until we can get you back on stage, you have to be good for something. And look at you, skinny as you are, you make the perfect poor little waif with prickly heat." He laughed at that as he retreated, leaving me frowning at the back of the dressing room door.

I stood at the dressing table with Mother who, using greasepaint and a wedge of sponge, colored my left cheek a pale pink.

"Hold still, Annalise," she chided, "I'm almost done. And stop frowning. You'll get permanent lines between your brows before you're twenty. There, now look at yourself in the mirror and tell me what you think."

I hesitated, not wanting to turn to the mirror. I often felt that way, not because I didn't want to see my reflection, but because I was afraid there'd be no reflection there for me to see. Since I was a nobody, how could somebody be in the mirror looking back at me? But I did as I was told, and there I was, a plain-featured kid with limp blonde hair and a face half-covered in pretend prickly heat. The pinkish rash started on the left side of my neck, climbed up over my jaw, and spread out across my cheek.

To supplement our income, Uncle Rex had taken to selling snake oil out in the alley at night after the last show. He paid a kid a nickel to hand out flyers during the day and, much to my amazement, folks showed up outside the stage door promptly at nine o'clock to see whether Rex's Tonic might cure what ailed them. It was nothing but sugar water with green food coloring, but Uncle Rex managed to pawn off bottles of it for twenty-five cents each. He convinced the crowds of the tonic's effectiveness by using Gina and me as plants, two girls healed of their ailments right on the spot.

Of course, he could only pull it off the last two or three nights we were in a city. By the time folks figured out the tonic was useless, our troupe had long ago pulled out of the station, and we were already peddling the stuff somewhere else.

I hated the whole affair. I hated tricking people into thinking sugar water would stop their headaches or cure their coughs or drive away demons of despair. Something about it seemed wrong and I wanted no part of it.

Gazing at myself in the mirror, I narrowed my eyes. "No one's going to believe that's a real rash," I said, though experience had already told me otherwise. And Mother did too.

"Sure they are," she said cheerfully. "Most people are fools, Annalise, and a fool and his money are soon parted. Good thing for us, too, because we need the money."

I looked at her and felt my jaw muscles tighten. For one swift moment, I envisioned myself spilling the beans on Uncle Rex that night. Right in the middle of his snake oil show, I'd holler at the crowd, telling them the tonic was only sugar water, and the rash on my face was only greasepaint, and the man who was trying to make them think otherwise was only another charlatan. *Don't be taken for fools!* I'd say. *Take your money and go home!*

But just as quickly as the vision came to me, I knew I wouldn't do it, because we did need the money, and I did have to do my part so I wouldn't become excess baggage.

"Go on, dear," Mother said, giving me a little shove. "Hurry up or you'll be late."

The night air outside the theater was warm and bitter. Twilight was giving way to darkness. I lowered my head, walked the block to the corner, turned and walked to the alley that led to the stage door. A crowd of a couple dozen had already gathered. Mostly old folks. A few young women with children. A sprinkling of curious adolescents. Many of our young men had gone to war, were even now fighting and dying in trenches all over France, which meant they weren't here to protect the vulnerable from the likes of my uncle Rex. While I was still a distance away, I saw my uncle make his grand entrance from the stage door, saw him pause there on the back steps, greeting the crowd like he was about to perform his greatest show. And I guess he was. Because he was able to make this audience think what was only pretend was true.

"Ah, my dear ladies and gentlemen," he said. "I'm delighted to see you here, and you'll be glad you came, I can promise you that. I am Rex Rycroft, singer, dancer, and star of a traveling show, but I'm also a man with an intense interest in medicine and a man who wants to help you." He made his way to a table one of the stagehands had set up for him for a dime. On it sat the various bottles of Rex's Tonic that he hoped to unload that night. He waved a hand over the bottles. "What I have here for you, ladies and gentlemen, is something the likes of which you have never seen! You will be astonished! You will be amazed! I call it Rex's Tonic, and as its name suggests, it will make you feel like a king."

A small sigh of delight rose from the crowd. The group tightened into a small knot as everyone stepped closer to the table, wanting to view the bottles of shiny green substance glittering in the dim light of the lamp outside the stage door. I stood at the edge of the crowd, awaiting my cue. I heard footsteps behind me and knew they belonged to Gina. She, too, was getting ready to play her part.

"That's right," Uncle Rex bellowed. "You will feel like a king! I have toiled for years to perfect my tonic, working day and night, experimenting, researching, testing, trying and trying again until I came up with just the right formula, the special prescription I have here for you tonight. What is it that ails you right now, ladies and gentlemen? Is it the gout? Angina? Dropsy? Do your bones ache and your lungs rattle? Whatever it is, dear folks, this tonic will help. You can drink it to bring relief to an ailing stomach. You can dab it on cuts and burns and rashes. That's right, use it outwardly on the skin or ingest it for internal use—either way, Rex's Tonic is guaranteed to cure what ails you. And, folks, at only twenty-five cents a bottle, it's a steal."

"How can we be sure it really works?" came a voice from the crowd, an old man's voice.

"Good sir!" Rex cried dramatically, one finger pointed skyward. "I'm glad you asked that. Now let's see." This was the point when his eyes moved over the crowd, settling finally on me. "You there. Little girl."

That was my cue. I was on. Lifting a hand to my chest, I tried to sound both shy and surprised. "Me?"

"Yes, you, dear. What's that on your face?"

My fingers traveled up to my face. "On my face, sir? Why, it's a rash, sir."

Uncle Rex leaned forward and squinted. "It looks like this unusually hot May sun has left you with a bit of prickly heat, darling."

"Prickly heat, yes, sir." I nodded.

"Well, come on up here and let's see what Rex's Tonic can do for you." He motioned me up to the front of the crowd with a wide sweep of his arm.

I stepped gingerly through the crowd and took my place by the table. I dropped my eyes, not wanting to see the faces gathered around. But it was too late. I had already seen them. The woman holding the child whose nose dripped with mucus and whose chest heaved with cough—her face was filled with anticipation. And the old man bent over a cane—his eyes were filled with a hesitant hope. And the young fellow—a schoolboy—whose arms were mottled with red patches of eczema—he stood silently, slack-jawed, waiting for the miracle that would make him like everyone else. In that moment, I hated myself and what I was doing. I tried to tell myself these people were simply fools, as Mother had said, and nameless peasants, as Uncle Rex called them, but I didn't believe it. Tears pushed at the back of my eyes and a lump formed in my throat.

Run! Run while you can! I wanted to yell. *Haven't you ever seen a charlatan before? Haven't you ever been visited by a traveling medicine man? They're all liars! Every last one of them!*

But I said nothing. I remained purposely expressionless and waited.

"Now then, darling," Uncle Rex went on, "don't be afraid. I'm just going to dab a little of Rex's Tonic on that rash, and we'll see how well it works."

He picked up a bottle of the tonic and poured some out on a rag, of which he had a pile on the table. He was just about to touch my face with it when another voice rose from the crowd. "Wait a minute! I want to see this for myself!"

It was Gina. She was already pushing her way through the crowd when Uncle Rex said, "Come on up here then, little lady. You're more than welcome to see for yourself." What the assembly didn't know, or didn't notice, was that Gina's interruption allowed my uncle to change out the rag for another one, one that had been dipped in lard. Lard was what we used to remove greasepaint because it was cheap.

Gina reached me and pretended to examine my face. "That's prickly heat, all right," she said knowingly. "So, let's see what your tonic can do."

Uncle Rex acknowledged her challenge with a chivalric nod of his head, then proceeded to wipe gently at my cheek with the lard-laden rag. Gina's hands flew to her mouth. "It's going away!" she cried. "The rash—it's going away!"

"Is it true?" the bent old man hollered.

"Can it heal my baby's cold?"

"Can it make my skin clear?"

"Can it take away the pain in my hips?"

Questions flew at us faster than shots from a Gatling gun, and Uncle Rex's smile spread ear to ear. He raised both hands over the crowd like a preacher bestowing a blessing. "Good people, yes and yes and yes, my tonic can do all those things."

"But wait," Gina cried, again right on cue. "Can it get rid of this awful wart on my thumb?"

Uncle Rex pinched her digit between his own thumb and index finger and pretended to examine it. After a moment, he bowed slightly at the waist. "Of course, my dear. Be my guest. Just dab a little of the tonic on that wart and see what happens."

Gina did as she was told. Several seconds passed while everyone waited. Anticipation hung thick in the air, and Gina milked it by drawing out the time, turning her head this way and that as she stared at her thumb held up before her. At length, Gina screamed so loudly the whole assembly jumped as one. "It's gone!" she cried delightedly. "The awful old wart is gone. Oh, thank you, Mr. Rex. No girl as beautiful as I should have a wart!"

As expected, and as had been the case in every other town, that was when the bottles started flying off the table and the nickels, dimes, and quarters into Uncle Rex's pocket.

In the midst of the havoc, I quietly slipped through the stage door. I wasn't supposed to go back into the theater that way. I was supposed to slip back down the alley since I was pretending to be just another little girl from the town. But I didn't care if I got in trouble with Uncle Rex. At that moment, I hated him.

Back in the dressing room, I grabbed a rag from the dressing table and scrubbed hard at my face. Mother sat in a wing chair in the corner, fanning herself with a prop fan from one of her acts. "Well, how did it go, dear?" she asked languidly. "Did we make some money?"

For a long moment, I didn't answer. Finally, I said, "I don't want to do this anymore."

Mother stilled the fan for a moment and sighed. "And so, dearest Anna, what *do* you want?"

What did I want?

She had to ask, as though she knew nothing about her own daughter?

I wanted to sing without getting hiccups. I wanted to get on stage and impress people with my golden pipes that could throw a song all the way to Timbuktu and back. I wanted to impress large audiences and I wanted them to clap for me, because then I would know that they knew I was alive. I wanted to be able to look in the mirror and not be afraid there'd be nobody there. I wanted to believe it was a good thing I had been born and a good thing I was here, and I wanted to know I wasn't just part of the surplus population in this wide world. I simply wanted to be seen. Because if I was seen, then maybe it would be possible to be loved.

In the end, as Uncle Cosmo would say, I had more wants than I could carry in my pockets at any one time. That's a whole lot of wants, especially when you're not sure you'll ever get any of them.

Mother looked at me, shrugged at my silence, and sighed again. "See, you don't know what you want. Let's go back to the hotel and go to bed. Uncle Rex intends to start rehearsal early in the morning."

CHAPTER 3

That night I had the dream. It always started out happy. I'm sitting in a sun-soaked room, holding a baby in my arms. We are in a large rocking chair, so large my feet don't touch the floor, and yet the chair is rocking gently. The baby is wrapped in a tiny quilt, white with pink and blue lambs embroidered on it. Tucked into the quilt with the baby is a small velveteen bear with black button eyes and a sewed-on smile. I can't stop gazing at the baby's face. I'm in awe of his perfect miniature features, the downy brows, the little bump of a bridgeless nose, tiny lips through which pokes the tip of a little pink tongue. His eyes, when open, are a mesmerizing blue, clear as two glass marbles. He is the most beautiful creature I've ever seen, and I'm content to stay right there till the end of time.

But then the dream takes a strange turn. Voices rise up behind me. I can't understand the words being spoken, but the voices are angry. And sad. And scared. One of them belongs to my mother, the other to a man I do not know but who nevertheless seems familiar.

I'm afraid they'll wake the baby. I want to hold him closer, to protect him, but as I try to squeeze him to my chest, I find my arms encircling an empty quilt. The bear is there, lost in its folds, but the baby is gone. The room has grown dark, as though night has fallen suddenly, without warning. A shiver of fear runs through me. I have lost the baby. He was in my arms and I was supposed to take care of him, but I've lost him and it's my fault.

There was a time when, at this point in the dream, I'd wake up screaming. My cries would bring Mother to my bed. Through my tears I'd tell her about the baby, about how he'd been there in my arms but I had lost him, and I needed her help to find him. She'd shush me and tell me it was all a bad dream. Just forget it, she'd say; think pleasant thoughts and go back to sleep.

I tried to forget, but couldn't. The dream became my recurring nightmare. After the sixth or seventh or eighth time I told my mother about the dream, she grew angry and told me I was being silly and stupid and she never wanted to hear about this dream of a baby again. And so I never again told her. But the dream kept coming back. Always the same. Haunting me like a story yearning to be told and begging to be believed.

This time I simply awoke with a start, my wide-eyed gaze taking in the still unfamiliar hotel room in this now forgotten city. I felt my heart thumping against my ribs and listened to the blood rushing in my ears. How was it that my mother, lying next to me in the twin bed, didn't hear the beating in my chest and the whooshing wind blowing through my brain? Surely it was loud enough to awaken even Gina in the other bed across the room, but she, like Mother, went on sleeping deeply, the sleep of exhaustion that was part of our wandering life. Beyond Gina's bed was the door adjoining our room to the room where Uncle Rex and old Uncle Cosmo slept. I was sure I was the only one of us awake. I was the only one of us looking for the lost baby who refused to be found.

***

In the morning, we learned that Uncle Rex had finally "figured something out." That is, he decided what to do with Gina and me.

We sat on chairs in a rehearsal room at the theater—Gina, Mother, Uncle Cosmo and me—while Uncle Rex stood to lecture us. He was wildly excited, pacing the floor and waving his arms as he bellowed to his bewildered audience, "I don't know why I didn't see it before! It's perfect. It's been right under my nose this whole time!"

Mother tried unsuccessfully to stifle a yawn. "Well, Rex," she said, "are you going to tell us, or would you rather we guess?"

Uncle Rex barked out a laugh and clapped his hands together. "It's just this, dear sister." He put his hands behind his back and rocked up on the balls of his feet. "You'll call me a genius."

I rolled my eyes and fidgeted in my chair. If this had anything to do with selling anything and if I had to feign illness or madness or otherwise pretend to be something I was not in order to separate men from their money, I was turning in my resignation.

My uncle pointed an index finger at Gina. "Beautiful, isn't she?" he asked. Gina smiled happily as Uncle Rex looked to the rest of us for a response.

"Uncommonly so, yes," Mother said.

"She's lovely," Uncle Cosmo agreed.

I nodded reluctantly.

"I mean, they don't make them like that very often, do they?" Uncle Rex went on. "She's got curves in all the right places." Gina giggled in delight as Uncle Rex once again waited for our replies.

"She's built very well," Mother said.

"I suppose you might say that," Uncle Cosmo offered timidly while dropping his eyes to the floor.

I narrowed my own eyes and said nothing.

"I mean, what man wouldn't want to gaze upon her loveliness?"

"Oh, Daddy Rex!" Gina said, using her nickname for her stepfather.

"No, really, Gina. You're the kind of young lady a man dreams about. You're the stuff of fantasy. You're—"

"What's your point, Rex?" Mother interrupted.

"I'm getting there, Bernie." He was the only one who could get away with calling her Bernie rather than Bernadette.

Mother sighed. Uncle Cosmo coughed nervously and adjusted his glasses on his nose. I glared at Uncle Rex and waited.

Now he pointed his long narrow finger at me. "And Anna here, well, she can sing like nobody's business, right?"

Mother, in the chair beside me, turned her gaze to me. "Except for the hiccups," she said.

"She's certainly got the voice of an angel otherwise," Uncle Cosmo offered.

"Not just the voice of an angel," Rex countered. "The voice of an entire angelic choir. She's got the most powerful pipes I've ever heard"—Mother looked up sharply—"next to you, Bernie. She's her mother's daughter, a chip off the old block, a rich vein of gold just waiting to be tapped."

"So what do you intend to do about her hiccups, Rex?"

"I'm getting to that, Bernie. Listen, when does she get the hiccups?"

He looked at us, palms turned out, waiting for an answer like a schoolteacher.

"When she's on stage?" Uncle Cosmo ventured hesitantly.

"Exactly!" Uncle Rex cried. "She only gets the hiccups when she's on stage, when she sees the faces of the audience and feels all those hundreds of eyes on her. *Then* she starts with all the hiccupping."

"So?" Mother asked.

"So …" Uncle Rex paused and smiled. "Let's let her sing *off* stage."

"*Off* stage? What are you talking about? What kind of act is that?" Mother sounded more annoyed with Uncle Rex than usual.

"A great act," my uncle shot back, "because here's the plan. *Gina* will be on stage. Gina, all dolled up in a fancy dress with the hourglass figure and just the right amount of cleavage and—"

Uncle Cosmo snorted. Gina clapped and bounced in her seat. Mother's jaw came unhinged and her mouth fell open.

"And," he went on, "we'll plan to add a stable of hoofers to the act, four or five good-looking young men who can dance around Gina while she sings—"

"But she *can't* sing, Rex," Mother said wearily. "That's the problem."

"I *know* that, Bernie, but ..." And here Uncle Rex went mute and held out both hands toward me. For a long moment he stood there satisfied, as though his gesture explained everything.

And it did. I finally caught on. "You want me to sing for her!" I cried.

"Bingo!" Uncle Rex's outstretched arms flew upward. "Isn't it great? Between the two of you we have one whole perfect entertainer!"

I jumped from the chair. "I won't do it!"

"What?"

"I said, I won't do it!"

Mother tugged at my dress and pulled me back into my seat. "You'll do it, Annalise. Rex is right. This just might work."

"But how's it going to work when she's in the middle of the stage and I'm singing in the wings? No one's going to believe it's Gina singing."

"I've already thought of that," Uncle Rex said. "When Gina is dancing with the boys, she can be in the middle of the stage. But whenever she's singing, she'll be either stage left or stage right, and you'll be right behind her. No one's going to catch on. It's going to be perfect. It's going to be big!"

"All we have to do," Mother said, "is come up with an act."

"I'm way ahead of you, Bernie." Uncle Rex pulled a piece of folded paper from his shirt pocket. "I've been working on a signature song, and I finished it last night. Listen!" He strode across the room to the upright piano and placed the piece of paper on its music stand. Before he began to play, he turned back to us and explained, "Now listen, the first thing you need to know is that that little lady over there is no longer Georgina Slump."

"I'm not?" Gina squealed.

"No. You are now"—he played a few notes on the piano by way of introduction—"Georgia Snow."

"Georgia Snow," she repeated breathlessly. "Oh my, Georgia Snow!"

Mother sat nodding her head. Uncle Cosmo snorted again. I fought the urge to run out of the room.

Uncle Rex rolled out a few more notes. "Okay, folks, so here's the song." And with that he proceeded to play and sing.

> They call me Little Snow Angel,
> Pretty as can be.
> Skin so white and smile so bright
> You'll want to be with me.

Gina jumped up from her chair, still squealing, and made her way over to the piano.

> They call me Precious Snow Angel,
> Come to me, make haste,
> I'll spread my wings and keep you

(Here Gina opened her arms as though spreading her wings.)

> Warm in my embrace.

(Here Gina hugged herself.)

> I stand demure, my soul is pure
> As the driven snow.
> But when you come to me, dear,
> I'll never let you go.

(Gina twirled around the room, still hugging herself.)

> They call me Pretty Snow Angel,
> Halo for a hat.

(Gina pretended to put on a hat.)

> But when my lips touch yours, dear,

(Gina shuts her eyes and puckers up.)

> You may question that!

Was Uncle Rex kidding? I couldn't believe it! What a stupid song! What a lousy idea for an act. No wonder we had never got out of small-time vaudeville. For once, I realized that my mother and my uncle were maybe not so all fired-up talented as they thought they were. And I realized, too, that my own train to stardom was riding on shaky rails.

Uncle Rex and Gina went through the song two more dreadful times. Finally, Rex played the final notes and stood. He held out a hand toward Gina and said with a flourish, "Ladies and gentlemen, I give you Miss Georgia Snow!"

Gina smiled broadly and bowed deeply. Mother and Cosmo applauded. I clenched my jaw so fiercely I could hear my teeth grinding together, uppers against lowers, like two large millstones crushing wheat.

CHAPTER 4

Mother wrestled with the train window until it finally slid open, letting in a whisper of warm air. She would have to close it again before the train left the station or we'd be covered with soot and ashes long before we got to wherever it was we were going now.

She dropped onto the crushed-velvet seat beside me with a thud and an exasperated sigh. Snapping open a folding fan, she vigorously beat the air in front of her face. Her hair was matted across her forehead, and tiny beads of sweat broke out on her upper lip.

"This heat is intolerable," she grumbled.

Gina sat in the seat facing ours. "We'll be underway soon, Aunt Bernadette," she said.

"Not soon enough." Mother closed her eyes, leaned her head back against the seat, and went on fanning.

I peered out the grimy window, watching the jostling busyness of the platform. I didn't know where we were going or how long it would take to get there. Mother might have told me, but if she had, I'd already forgotten. I didn't care. One place was exactly like another to me, and for all I knew our life was one of going around in circles, traveling ceaselessly through the same few tired towns.

I did know, though, that we would play only one or two more engagements before the summer break. The stifling heat of July and August left theaters deserted, so managers simply closed them up until the fall. Big-time vaudevillians went off to their summer homes at one of the resort colonies; the rest of us made do. Once the hiatus ended in September, our troupe would reconvene and continue our journey eastward toward the coast.

Getting an entire troupe loaded onto a train was no small feat. All in all, with performers, non-performing spouses and children (the excess baggage), stagehands, personal assistants, an agent or two, and of course Mr. Stanley and his personal secretary, Miss Alice Withers, we numbered somewhere around seventy-five total. That made for a great pile of suitcases and steamer trunks to be loaded onto the baggage car, not to mention boxes of props, scenery, and costumes.

Our troupe was an ever-changing creature, with acts coming and going all the time. A few acts moved up to the big time, some shifted to other small-time circuits while many burned out or got fired. Some acts followed the same circuit for years and years, spending their entire lives in a relentless cycle of smelly trains, cheap boarding houses and hotels, and dumpy theaters. These were the folks who made just enough money to survive. This was where we were now, my family and I. But not forever, we thought. Mother and Uncle Rex considered themselves rising stars, and for that reason we didn't much fraternize with the other acts in our troupe. We weren't like them. We were only passing through—though to me, the passing seemed interminable.

"Gina, dear," Mother said without opening her eyes, "do you happen to know whether Rex was able to secure us some berths for the night?"

Gina nodded. "He got one for you, one for me, and one for Anna. He and Uncle Cosmo, though, will be sitting up tonight."

"Again? They never get much sleep that way."

"Daddy Rex says he doesn't need sleep, and Uncle Cosmo can sleep anywhere. We might as well save the money."

"Oh, money, money, money," Mother said wearily. "It always comes down to money, doesn't it? Or the lack of money, as the case may be."

"Daddy Rex does his best to take care of us," Gina said defensively.

More than once I had heard Mother complain that Rex was simply tight-fisted. He even served as our own agent, not wanting to give a cut of our earnings to everyone else. Mother sometimes questioned whether we might not be in the big-time even now, if only we had a real agent.

"If that stubborn brother of mine wants to suffer," Mother said, "that's fine. But Cosmo is simply too old to sleep sitting up."

Uncle Cosmo sat across the aisle from us, his violin case on his lap. He rarely let the instrument, his life's blood, out of his sight. He did look old; in fact, to me he appeared ancient, though he was at that time only somewhere around sixty. He listened intently to Mr. Meriwether, a loquacious fellow who sat in the seat facing him. In the seat beside Mr. Meriwether was his singing toy poodle, Troubadour. A fairly new addition to the troupe, they had so far managed to bring in the big laughs, which translated into money in Vaudeville. Dressed in matching costumes, Mr. Meriwether sang, chatted up the audience and cracked jokes while the dog managed to bark, yelp, and howl in all the right places. While Mr. Meriwether danced and turned somersaults and did handsprings, Troubadour pranced across the stage, walked on his hind legs, or otherwise chased his tail in circles. Animal acts were almost always a hit, and Mr. Stanley was glad to have them.

Also in our troupe was a magician and his daughter-assistant, a brother comedy team (one brother performed in blackface, which always got a laugh as the men professed to be twins), a contortionist whose handle was The Astonishing Mister Twister, a monologist who recited patriotic poems (during those war years, he was generally followed by the stage manager making a pitch for Liberty Bonds), a couple of tap dancing twin girls, a team of jugglers, a variety of singers and one-act performers, and a family of unicyclists from Russia who went by the name of The Sensational Cycling Sokolovs.

There were others, of course, but from a distance of years, I don't remember them. Many of the acts were simply forgettable. Most have merged into one huge variety show in my mind, a stage full of desperate people singing, dancing, juggling, cycling, and contorting their way to a perceived immortality, one that could be achieved only by the approval of the people who were willing to watch.

For it was the audience who would make or break you. That's what I saw from the wings, what I learned from the sidelines. I saw the performers when they came backstage after their acts, saw the glow of triumph on their faces, saw, too, the despair of defeat, depending on how the audience received them. Without an adoring audience, the entertainer is nothing.

Most performers, like my uncle Rex, had complicated relationships with audiences. Rex Rycroft was on the stage because he didn't want to be like those in the house—the common people, the people consigned to the dark, with neither names nor faces. While he was performing, he acted as though he were doing it for them, to entertain them and give them pleasure. He acted as though he loved them. *Thank you! You're a truly great audience, a truly great audience!* But that wasn't true at all. He was doing it for himself, to secure for himself a place above the masses. The irony in all of this was that Uncle Rex held in contempt the very people he believed could make him a god.

Beside me, Mother sighed deeply again. "Oh, where is Rex?" she asked. "And when will this train ever get underway?"

As though in answer to her biding, Uncle Rex came down the aisle toward us, moving in quick strides and waving a letter in the air.

"Bernie!" he hollered. "I just got this from Stanley. Postmarked New York. We got our date!"

Mother sat up abruptly, eyes wide. "You mean, the Palace?"

Uncle Rex nodded as he slid into the seat beside Gina. He offered the letter to Mother with a flourish. "See for yourself."

Mother dropped the fan to her lap and grabbed the envelope eagerly. She pulled the letter out and held it in trembling hands. Her lips moved as she read.

Gina leaned forward in her seat. "Well, what does it say?"

Mother slapped the piece of paper to her heart and took a deep breath. "We're to be there on the seventh of November. The theater opens at nine a.m. sharp."

Gina clapped and squealed in that way of hers. Uncle Rex's chest puffed out as though he had done something wonderful. Mother still clutched the letter to her chest, her face lifted to the ceiling and her eyes closed as though she were praying, though I knew she wasn't the praying type. I was bewildered, clueless as to the cause of their rejoicing. I pulled on Mother's sleeve. "What's it mean, Mama?" I asked. "Are you and Uncle Rex playing the Palace?"

My heart started racing at the thought. Playing the Palace in New York was the pinnacle of success, the dream of every vaudevillian. The theater was the best on the Keith Circuit, built by B.F. Keith himself, the founder of American Vaudeville and the man who, though he was dead, still wielded his considerable influence over every aspect of show business.

Mother opened her eyes and looked at me. She folded the letter and slipped it back into the envelope. "Not exactly, dear," she said. "Not yet, anyway. It's the tryouts. You know, I've told you before. Every Thursday they open up the theater so acts can come in and audition. There's all sorts of scouts there, looking for new talent. Plenty of big names have been discovered that way, of course. And now Rex and I will have our turn."

"Oh, Aunt Bernadette, you're going to be the next Sarah Bernhardt!" Gina cried. "And Daddy Rex, you're going to be … well, whoever's the greatest, you'll be just like him."

Rex shook his head and said with a glint in his eye, "Oh no, Gina, dear. No use comparing me to anyone. I'm going to be Rex Rycroft, and that will be the greatest of all."

Gina leaned over and kissed her stepfather's stubbly cheek. "Of course, Daddy. You're so right."

Rex patted her hand. "Thank you, my dear."

"Do you think Mr. Albee himself will be at the tryouts?" Gina asked, referring to the man who had owned the Palace since Keith's death.

"Maybe, if we're lucky," Uncle Rex said. "And if he knows what's good for him."

"Rex!" Mother said abruptly. "Do you have the itinerary from Stanley? Where will we be in early November?"

"We should be right there in New York, or close," Uncle Rex said. He pulled a sheet of paper out of his breast pocket and unfolded it. He mumbled for a moment, then finally enunciated more clearly as he said, "Erie, Pittsburgh, Harrisburg, Philadelphia, New York. Yes, it's perfect. Perfect. Just as we wanted. We will already be in New York on the seventh."

"Oh, Rex, I can't believe it's finally happening." Smiling broadly, Mother snapped open her fan again and went back to beating the air.

"It's happening, Bernie, and it's about time. We've been paying our dues for far too long, and it's time to bid Stanley and the small-time farewell."

"What about me, Daddy Rex?" Gina asked.

"What about you, dear?"

"If you make it on Broadway, can you get me a place too?"

Rex patted Gina's hand again. "We'll see."

He was dismissing her, I could tell, as though he didn't need her anymore. Gina frowned, but I grabbed at the straw of hope the news had given me. "Do we still have to do the Georgia Snow routine?" I said.

Say no! I pleaded silently. Say we can drop the whole idea and place our bets on the Palace audition. If Uncle Rex and Mother made it into the big time or, better yet, on the legitimate stage, I wouldn't have to be Gina's voice. We wouldn't have to scratch out a living with dimwitted acts and useless tonics. We'd be living on easy street! And maybe, just maybe, once I grew my spine, I could finally step out from the wings and into the spotlight myself.

But Uncle Rex smashed my hopes like a man crushing a bug. "Of course you do, Anna," he snapped. "The Georgia Snow act can be a really big draw if we do it right. I've already called ahead to Chicago and asked Ben Stubbing to find four dancers and send them on to us in Maysville. If they can sing, all the better."

"Ben Stubbing?" Mother raised a brow.

"You remember, we worked with him in Milwaukee a few years back. He's a talent scout in Chicago now and he owes me a favor."

"Oh yes." Mother nodded.

Uncle Rex turned back to me. "I expect you and Gina to be performing the act the moment we open after summer break. We have a lot of work and a lot of rehearsing to do between now and then to be ready."

"Oh, we'll be ready, Daddy Rex," Gina said. "I already know my part."

Her part? All she had to do was pretend to sing. Maybe wiggle her hips a little and toss a few kisses to the audience to bring in the catcalls.

The dancers and I would be the ones doing all the work, making her look good for doing nothing. We hadn't even played to an audience yet, and I already resented the act. I hated Gina and wished she had never joined the troupe.

I looked across the aisle at Uncle Cosmo, who stared intently at us from behind the round lenses of his wireframe glasses. Mr. Meriwether was still chattering away, but Uncle Cosmo had obviously tuned him out and was listening to our conversation instead. Something in his eyes told me he understood how I felt. He had always been kind to me, though as a rule he was aloof and solitary, a man who had, as Mother said, rolled up into himself when his wife died a dozen years before, leaving him a childless widower, a man alone and without roots. Even when he was playing happy songs on the stage, his eyes were sad. His round face was a moon that reflected only twilight. Even his gentleness seemed to spring from a deep melancholy, as though his acts of kindness to me were an attempt to apologize for the fact that I had to live in this world.

He was my grandfather's twin brother, and though I'd never met my grandfather—he had died before I was born—I knew exactly what he looked like because the two had been identical in appearance. But not in temperament, Mother said. The way she described it, when the egg split in the womb to form the brothers, one got all the boisterousness while the other all the melancholy. Split evenly right down the middle. No matter that Grandfather drank himself to death. He'd been a happy drunk, singing his bawdy songs and telling his ribald jokes right up to the end. Uncle Cosmo never touched a drop. Rex said it was probably a good thing old Cosmo didn't drink; if the old man were to drown his sorrows with liquor, he'd simply disappear like melting snow. There was nothing besides sorrow inside to survive the deluge.

But I loved him and turned to him often when I wanted comfort or simply company. I felt the need for his company now. I moved across the aisle and sat down in the window seat beside him. I gave Troubadour a pat on the head, nodded at Mr. Meriwether, then leaned back and tucked my hand into the crook of my uncle's arm.

He smiled down at me, though the smile didn't reach his eyes. "Hello, dear. So you're not so keen on the Georgia Snow routine, are you?"

"I hate it," I replied grumpily.

"I see. Well, it gives you a chance to sing, and maybe you'll be able to perform without the hiccups."

"Maybe. But I don't want to sing for Gina. I mean, I don't want everyone to think my voice is hers when it's mine."

Uncle Cosmo nodded. "I understand. But maybe you won't have to do the act for long, if things go well at the Palace."

I thought about that a moment. Then I said, "Uncle Cosmo, what if Mama and Uncle Rex do get their big break and end up on Broadway? What will you do then?"

My uncle sighed, and his eyes became even deeper pools of distress. "I don't know, Annalise. Stay with Mr. Stanley, I suppose, for as long as he'll have me. Perhaps I'll fall off the stage again, only this time I'll break my neck and that will take care of everything, won't it?" He gave me a wink and a fleeting smile.

I leaned my head against his shoulder. He patted my hair. I didn't like thinking of the world without Uncle Cosmo in it.

The train whistle blew. The conductor called one last, "All aboard!" In the next moment, with a jolt and a hiss, the train rolled slowly out of the station, and we were on our way to ... wherever.

CHAPTER 5

We spent two weeks in one southern Illinois town and one week in another before the troupe disbanded for the summer break. From there, it was a short hop for my family to get to Maysville, where we always stayed during the hiatus. Maysville was another small Illinois town, not far from Springfield, and about two hundred miles south of Chicago. It was also the home of a man named Albert Littleworth who, like Ben Stubbing, owed Uncle Rex a favor, one he was apparently incapable of ever fully paying off.

Uncle Rex and Mother had grown up with Albert Littleworth in Joliet—where we still had family but none of whom was willing to take us in. Thankfully, though, Mr. Littleworth was obliged to give us a place to stay during the summer breaks. As the story goes, when my uncle and Albert were both thirteen, Rex saved the diminutive Albert from drowning in the Des Plaines River. The river, swollen with rainwater, might have washed the boy from its relatively narrow banks into the larger Illinois River into the great Mississippi River and finally out to sea at the Gulf of Mexico had Rex not courageously jumped in and pulled his friend to safety. Ever after, Rex held Albert hostage to this act of bravery. No doubt some summers Albert wished Rex had left him to die rather than having to open his doors to a homeless troupe of vaudevillians, but I never heard him say as much. I surmised it by the words he didn't say, two of which were "Welcome back."

Albert Littleworth was a small, timorous man, but nevertheless surprisingly successful in business. He lived with his family in a large Edwardian house on the edge of town. It was a three-story brick structure with a mansard roof and plenty of room for the host of people who inhabited it for the months of July and August. In fact, the third floor had once been a ballroom and still housed a grand piano, making it the perfect place for rehearsals.

Ben Stubbing was good to his word, and shortly after we arrived at the Littleworth house, four male hoofers showed up on the doorstep ready to join the act. They were just boys, really, with the youngest at fourteen and the eldest at seventeen. They'd been taking singing and dancing lessons from a certain Mr. Allred in Chicago and were ready to get the experience they needed in the competitive world of show business. Experience was all we could offer, as Uncle Rex had no intention of paying them. But it wasn't a bad deal, really—experience, room, board, and travel in exchange for joining our show for a year. They and their parents agreed to the arrangement, and they arrived eager to work.

Their names were Ray, Luther, Willard, and Eddie, and before they so much as had their suitcases unpacked, Uncle Rex had us all in the ballroom for our first rehearsal together. He had spent weeks working on two more songs to lead up to Georgia Snow's signature song, "Little Snow Angel." Just the day before, he had put the finishing touches on "Do You Love Me?" and "You Warm My Heart." Now that the boys had arrived, he was keen to get the show on the road. Uncle Cosmo was there to help with the choreography. Mother gave input on music and lyrics, and by the end of the day, we had a creditable version of our new act, "Miss Georgia Snow and her Winter Wonder Men."

Also before the end of the day, those same Winter Wonder Men had all fallen head-over-heels in love with Gina. They would spend the next weeks and months mooning over her like panting puppies, drinking her up with their eyes. I, on the other hand, was scarcely noticed and rarely acknowledged by the boys. Not that they were unkind; they were a friendly, gentle bunch in their own way. They were simply too distracted by Gina and starry-eyed about the stage to notice a little kid like me. They didn't even seem to realize that I was the one doing all the singing.

One afternoon at the end of rehearsal, Ray—the eldest boy and the tallest, a handsome fellow with thick dark hair, rich brown eyes, and dimples that dotted his cheeks when he smiled—cornered Gina by the piano and said, "You know, you surely have a beautiful voice, Miss Georgia. The most beautiful voice ever. It's a privilege to be able to sing with you."

Gina nodded demurely and smiled. "Why, thank you, Ray. That's very kind of you."

There I stood right behind them, not quite believing what I had just heard. Neither one of them acknowledged who the voice actually belonged to! At that moment I was quite certain that if I looked in a mirror, there would be no one there.

Uncle Rex toiled that summer like he'd never toiled before, pulling the rest of us into his whirlwind of anxious preparation. We spent hours rehearsing every day, singing and dancing, and singing and dancing some more till we thought we'd drop dead from exhaustion and heat stroke. For my part, Uncle Rex decided I should sing while standing mid-way up a six-foot folding ladder so that my voice would ring out over Gina's head, rather than be lost behind her. Because he wanted me to become used to the feel of singing at a height, my days were spent with the ladder rungs digging into the arches of my feet while I clutched the uppermost rung with sweaty palms. More than once I felt lightheaded, dizzy from the heat and the height, until I actually began to sway. I was afraid I might fall, tumbling off the ladder just as Gina spread her snow-angel wings in an inviting gesture of fleshly affection. I didn't want to be the one to fall into those waiting arms. Noticing my distress, Uncle Cosmo suggested I might sit atop a four-foot ladder instead, but Uncle Rex dismissed his suggestion by saying that one's diaphragm enjoyed the greatest freedom when one was standing. I hoped at least my diaphragm was enjoying something because the rest of me was patently miserable.

Rehearsals were bad enough, but even in our off hours there was little rest for the weary. We were expected to help with the sewing of costumes, the choosing of props and wigs, and the designing of posters for all the theaters that would naturally want to feature our show.

To help keep a few coffers in the grouch bag, Uncle Rex sometimes borrowed Albert Littleworth's car to sell tonic in surrounding towns. I had to go with him and Gina the first few times, but I eventually wiggled out of that hated task when the four boys took turns being the victim with the rash. They were happy to do anything to spend a few extra hours with Gina, even if it meant separating fools from their money.

That summer I shared a bedroom on the second floor with Mother and Gina, the floor where Albert Littleworth, his wife, and their four children also slept. Uncles Rex and Cosmo had cots on the sleeping porch at the back of the house, and the boys slept on mats on the floor of the ballroom. It was the best Albert Littleworth had to offer, but far better than most of the hotels where we stayed. At least here we didn't have to place each bedpost in a dish of oxalic acid to keep the ants from crawling between the sheets with us.

At the end of each day when I laid down in bed, I was so tired my bones ached. I can still remember how it felt to lie beneath the open window, enjoying the cool night air on my skin, and listening to the night songs rising up from the yard below. Those were moments of peace, sandwiched between the dreaded hours of rehearsals and the dreaded hours of sleep. I didn't want to rehearse because I didn't want to sing for Gina, and I didn't want to sleep because of the dream.

The dream of the lost baby was more insistent now, knocking on my slumbering brain and demanding to be given center stage. I didn't know what it meant. I knew only that it left me feeling sad and on edge when I awoke, as though I had left something vital undone, and someone was suffering because of my negligence.

***

One Saturday morning toward the end of August, I awoke from the dream. As always, it took a moment for my heart to quiet and my mind to return to the realness of the room around me. Once my breath had stilled, I sat up and looked around. The other two beds were empty. I must have slept late.

I slid off the bed and padded over to the desk where I kept my collection of books. I had never gone to school, but Mother taught me lessons while we were on the road. Dressing rooms were my classrooms, and the first words I ever read were from an ad in *Variety*, the vaudeville trade publication and the showman's bible. My little library included six books: *McGuffey's Fourth Eclectic Reader*, *McGuffey's Fifth Eclectic Reader*, a book on world geography, *Tales from Shakespeare* by Charles and Mary Lamb, a new and still crisp-paged 1916 edition of *The Fairy Tales of the Brothers Grimm*, and, my favorite book, *A Christmas Carol* by Charles Dickens.

I pulled this one from the pile and ran my fingertips lightly over the cover. The book was a first edition, published in 1843, old and somewhat yellowed, made more fragile by my constant turning of the pages. Though a Christmas tale, I read it all year round, again and again. I loved the story of Ebenezer Scrooge, Jacob Marley, Tiny Tim, and the three Christmas ghosts. As a very young child I'd named my stuffed bear Mr. Fezziwig after Scrooge's kind and generous boss who showed up in the vision of Christmas past. I was enchanted by how the three ghosts showed Scrooge the things he couldn't see for himself, and how the Christmas Eve visitation changed him from a selfish old man to a kind-hearted benefactor. I don't know how many times I had read the Dickens story, but I knew several passages perfectly by heart and was close to perfect on several more.

The book had belonged to my father when he was a child. Opening to the title page, I saw once again his name, Charles Cullen, written in a childish script. Beneath his name was the date December 25, 1885, which made me think it had been a Christmas gift to him. It was the only thing of his that I had. I didn't even carry his name, Cullen, but went by my mother's name of Rycroft. I was Annalise Rycroft, as though my father had nothing to do with my being here.

And in fact he was hardly a memory to me, little more than a vapor that rose in my mind on occasion but swiftly disappeared. I didn't know what he looked like or what his voice sounded like. I didn't know where he was now and why he had left us in the first place.

I carried the book to the bed and looked out the window. At the center of Maysville was a town square, a wide strip of green with benches, a gazebo, and plenty of shade trees. It was my favorite place in town, and I had been there many times this summer and in summers past. I would go there again this morning, I decided, far away from the noise and confusion of the crowded Littleworth house. And far away from the haunting residue of the dream.

But first, breakfast. I dressed and, with the book tucked up under one arm, descended the stairs. At the bottom, I paused long enough to look into the parlor. Mr. Littleworth sat in a red leather, button-seated wing chair by the hearth reading the newspaper. His feet, like two brown sock puppets, were propped up on a footstool and crossed at the ankles. His small round face was overshadowed by a pair of dark-rimmed glasses—the lenses of which were as round as his face. His bald head reflected the light given off by the fringed lamp beside him. When he realized I was there, he lifted his eyes toward me over the top of his glasses and cleared his throat. "Good morning, Anna," he said.

Why, oh why, had I stood there staring when I should have scampered off before he noticed me?

"Good morning, Mr. Littleworth," I answered reluctantly.

"You slept well, I trust."

"Yes, sir."

From beyond the open window, I heard the shouts of his four children playing in the yard. The youngest dancer, Eddie, was out there with them. All the boys, when we weren't rehearsing, often joined the Littleworth kids in a game of tag or dodge ball. Sometimes I did too, but not often. I felt shy and awkward around others my own age.

"I suppose you're hungry." He rarely ever asked me a question, but rather spoke mostly in statements.

"Yes, sir."

"I believe your mother's in the kitchen. She'll get you something to eat."

"Thank you, sir." I turned to go, but then remembered I ought to be polite. "I hope you had a good night too, Mr. Littleworth."

Albert Littleworth's eyes rolled upward from the paper once again. "Mrs. Littleworth and I slept very well, once we brushed the bits of plaster off our bed."

For several weeks now he'd complained that all our dancing in the ballroom had cracked the ceiling in his bedroom below. He pointed out the damage to Uncle Rex, who promised to re-plaster the entire ceiling himself, but so far hadn't acted on his promise.

"Gosh, I'm sorry about that, sir."

"Yes, well …"

"Maybe it would help if you moved your bed," I offered.

He stared at me a moment, his eyes unreadable. "I'll take that under advisement. Thank you, Anna."

"Yes, sir."

I slunk away to the kitchen, a large airy room at the back of the house that smelled always of bacon grease and overripe fruit. Mother sat at the kitchen table, drinking coffee from a floral teacup. Some of the coffee had spilled over into the saucer, and every time Mother took a sip, a drop slipped off the bottom of the cup and onto the bodice of her dress. She seemed not to notice, or else she didn't care.

"Good morning, dear," she said wearily when she saw me. Her hair looked as though it had been pulled back from her face without first being brushed, and there was a distinct shadowy moon under each eye.

"Hi, Mama. Where's Uncle Rex and everyone?"

"Well, let's see. Rex, Gina, and Ray are off selling tonic somewhere. Mrs. Littleworth has gone to the market, and Luther and Willard went with her to help carry the sacks, as Rex has the car. Cosmo, he's—well, I don't know where he is." She shrugged and gave me a wan smile.

"You look tired, Mama."

"I was up late working on an order for Mrs. Sellers." Mother was an excellent seamstress, and every summer she picked up piecework from Mabel Sellers who owned a tailor shop downtown. She squeezed in the work between the cracks of everything else she had to do—making our own costumes, rehearsing new routines for her act with Uncle Rex, and generally overseeing the care of the boys, Gina, and me. "You want something to eat?"

I nodded. I sat and laid the book on the table. In another moment, Mother set a bowl of corn flakes and a glass of milk in front of me. I poured most of the milk over the cereal and sprinkled it with sugar from the sugar bowl. Mother poured herself some more coffee and sat down across from me. She was facing my direction, but her eyes seemed to be focused on something far away.

The crunching of the cereal as I chewed seemed particularly loud in the silence of the kitchen. Not knowing what to say to

Mother, or whether I should say anything at all, I let my eyes wander about the room. Kitchens were not a regular part of my life. I was more at home in theater wings and rail berths than in the solid, unchanging structures that were most people's homes. The floor was a pale yellow linoleum, the same color as the cabinets. The wallpaper was a floral pattern of roses and wisteria, and above the table hung a needlework picture of a white clapboard house in a meadow with the words *Home is where the heart is* stitched across the sky. A window above the sink was framed by white eyelet curtains that lifted vaguely whenever there was a breeze. The primary features of the room were a dainty white ice box and a black behemoth of a gas stove with a wood-burning oven. A cast iron kettle and a variety of pots and pans cluttered the stove. All in all, it was a pleasant room, and I thought Mrs. Littleworth must have rather enjoyed stepping into it every morning.

At length, my eyes landed again on the book I'd brought downstairs with me. Impulsively, because I sometimes did things without thinking, I said, "Mama, do you have a picture of my father?"

Her gaze snapped back from wherever it had been and settled firmly on me. "Your father?" She looked as though I had just offered her something putrid to eat, like one of the dead mice the Littleworths's cat was always dragging in.

I slunk down in my chair and nodded.

"Why are you thinking of him?" she asked.

"Well, I ... I'm not thinking of him, really, I ..." I reached for the book and opened it to the title page. "I just saw his name in my book, and it got me to thinking, well, not really thinking but just wondering ..."

Before I could finish, she stood and carried her coffee cup to the sink. When she spoke, it was toward the open window, as though she wanted the whole world to know what she had to say. "I don't have a picture of that man, Annalise, and as far as we're concerned, he's better left forgotten."

***

Maysville was a pretty little town with residential streets spread out like spokes from the hub of the central business district. If I turned left from the Littleworths's house, I'd soon end up in country meadows and cornfields. If I turned right, which I did, I was heading straight toward town and the park where I planned to sit and read.

I walked contentedly with *A Christmas Carol* clutched to my chest, looking right and left, from one side of the street to the other and back again, trying to take it all in. The houses were neat homes of either brick or clapboard, some of them large like the Littleworths's house, most of them more modest. All were well maintained, with flower boxes in the windows or larger gardens fronting the porches. Babies slept in carriages under shade trees on the front lawns; girls played hopscotch on the sidewalks and boys played kickball in the streets; men read newspapers on the porches, or gardened, or cut the grass; women hung up laundry, or congregated by fences to chat, or walked to town carrying their shopping baskets. Neighbor called to neighbor; children laughed and sang ditties; from the open windows of one house came the sounds of someone playing the piano. "Yankee Doodle Dandy" gave way to "Over There"—tunes that were popular because of the war. I also noticed the blue star banners hanging in a number of windows, meaning the families that lived in those houses had a father or brother or son fighting in the war. There were gold star banners too, though thankfully not as many, as that meant the father or brother or son was never coming home.

Before long, the residential streets gave way to Main Street and the heart of town, where several blocks of false-fronted brick buildings housed the town's businesses: the Maysville Café, a millinery, Mrs. Sellers's tailor shop, a general store, a lawyer's office, a dental office, the offices of the *Maysville Gazette*, a bakery, a bank, a library. Downtown was busy this

Saturday morning, the sidewalks bustling, the streets noisy with the clopping of horses' feet and the rattling engines of the various Model Ts and other motor cars. Women walked with parasols to keep the sun off their skin, and men wore straw hats or black bowlers that they lifted toward the ladies in passing. I walked among them, feeling like a spectator who had slipped unnoticed onto the stage of their lives. I wondered who they were and where they were going on this summer morning and where they had been all the years I had been living out my life on the ever-turning wheels of the Vaudeville circuit. Had they been right here all along, living and loving and working and growing up and growing old?

Uncle Rex called this kind of life "a humdrum existence" and said he wouldn't be caught dead living where Albert Littleworth lived and working where Albert Littleworth worked and what good was it to toil at a desk all day and to be so unimportant that the only time your name appeared in the papers was the day you were listed on the obituary page. I thought Uncle Rex just might have a point. I, for one, wanted to see my name in the papers long before I was dead. I smiled dreamily as I tried to imagine it: *Annalise Rycroft Plays the Palace! Thousands Flock to Hear Those Golden Pipes! She Throws a Song to Timbuktu and Back Without Even Trying!*

At the corner of Main Street and Rose Avenue was the moving picture theater. It was closed—had been closed for a couple of months as even the cinemas shut their doors during the worst of the summer heat. But now there was new lettering on the marquee. I stopped in the middle of the sidewalk to read it: "Charlie Chaplin Revue! Starting September 7!" A poster hung behind glass by the door with more details.

Don't miss the
Charlie Chaplin Revue!
Coming to the Maysville Theater, September 7, 1918!
Four pictures from the world's most famous comedian!

Three hours of non-stop entertainment!
Tillie's Punctured Romance
The Floorwalker
Easy Street
Shoulder Arms

Suddenly I was thinking in exclamation points: How I wished I could see those pictures! I had to see those pictures!

I had seen only one picture show in my life because moving pictures were a threat to Vaudeville, and Uncle Rex refused to support them. But Mother, I knew, would occasionally sneak away and put her quarter down for a show. I memorized the titles of the pictures to tell her when I got home. Maybe she would like to come to the revue, just as a last fling before we got back on the road.

I moved away from the theater and on down the street to the park at the center of town. Finding an empty bench beneath a large red oak, I sat for a time and watched the couples strolling, women pushing baby carriages, a young man walking a dog, and children playing in the gazebo. I liked the laughter and the low murmur of voices all around me. I liked the birdsong in the trees, and the way the sunlight slanted through the branches of the oak and touched the ground, melting there into soft buttery pools in the grass. I even liked the sounds of traffic, a policeman's piercing whistle somewhere off in the distance, the occasional "Arruuu-ga!" of a motorcar's horn. It was noisy here; yet quiet in a way that life on the circuit was never quiet, for on the circuit there was always the clatter of train wheels followed by the brazen din of banging props and yelling stage managers and nervous, bustling troupe members as we traveled from one town to another.

After a while, I opened the book on my lap and began to read. I had placed a bookmark near the beginning, and that was where I started now. It is Christmas Eve day, and Scrooge is at work in his counting-house with his clerk, Bob Cratchit, in an adjoining room. Scrooge has just turned down an invitation to spend Christmas with his nephew, who has left the counting-house dejected but determined to keep his Christmas humor, unlike his uncle Ebenezer who seems to have no humor or gladness at all. Just as the nephew leaves, two portly gentlemen arrive and Cratchit, who has been trying in vain to thaw his frozen hands by the flame of a candle, lets them in. The gentlemen, hats in hand, tell Scrooge they are raising funds for the poor and destitute. "Many thousands are in want of common necessaries," they explain. "Hundreds of thousands are in want of common comforts, sir."

Scrooge asks them whether there are no prisons. Oh yes, plenty of prisons. And Union workhouses? Yes, those too. But such places "scarcely furnish Christian cheer of mind or body to the multitude."

The two portly gentlemen are endeavoring to buy the poor some meat and drink, some means of warmth. How much can they put Scrooge down for?

Nothing! is the angry reply. The poor ought rather to go to the prisons and workhouses and find help there!

But! the horrified gentlemen respond. "Many can't go there. And many would rather die."

And then I come to the words of the story that haunt me and send a shiver down my spine whenever I read them—no, not just whenever I read them but whenever I remember them, for they are seared on my brain the way a brand is seared on a cow's hide.

"If they would rather die," says Scrooge, "they had better do it, and decrease the surplus population."

The surplus population. I knew exactly who Scrooge was talking about. Me. And all the people like me, who were poor and nameless and unknown and insignificant. More than anything, I didn't want to be a surplus person, because if I were doomed to live out such an unnecessary life, how would

I ever find moments of happiness? How would I ever feel myself worthy of love?

Though Scrooge's words terrified me—would it really be better for me to cease existing?—I turned repeatedly to this story and cherished it. Maybe because, in my trembling, arrogant little heart, I believed I could lift myself from surplus to star, and that one day I would be both loved and adored by millions, and I would be happy.

I stopped and lifted my gaze from the book. Not far away, a family with a picnic basket was spreading a blanket on the grass. A young man and woman strolled arm in arm, talking and laughing quietly together. A trio of boys knelt on the sidewalk, playing marbles. A little girl sitting on the grass beside them turned her face up to the sun and smiled.

I saw each one with my eyes, but my heart took no notice at all.

Chapter 6

A week passed, another week of searing heat and tiresome rehearsals and lost baby dreams and falling plaster. Now it was Saturday again, but at long last it was also September, and on that morning when I came downstairs for breakfast, Albert Littleworth was able to cast a tenuous smile in my direction, knowing that by the next afternoon, we'd be back on the road and far away from his house in Maysville.

I myself was getting more and more nervous about rejoining the troupe, fearful of actually performing the Georgia Snow act on stage. I wondered whether I could pull it off or whether I'd end up getting hiccups, even though I was behind the curtain. A single hiccup would incur the wrath of not just Uncle Rex but Gina too, and Mother, and the four boys, and probably even Uncle Cosmo, who had been working hard on the intricacies of the dance routines right along with the rest of us. I wondered, too, whether we could *all* pull it off, me and Gina and the Winter Wonder Men. The boys were talented singers and dancers and had their part down pat, and I knew Gina's songs backward and forward, had found my balance on the ladder, and had never once hiccupped during rehearsals, but could we really convince the audience that Gina was singing when she was only mouthing the words? I feared we would be found out, would be booed off the stage, even become the target of tomatoes and other rotten fruit. If we failed, what would become of us then? We had better hope Mother and

Uncle Rex were discovered at the Palace so the show—and our lives—could go on.

I was eating a bowl of cereal at the kitchen table when Mother sat down beside me, a cup of fresh coffee in hand. "You mentioned the Charlie Chaplin Revue is playing at the cinema downtown, starting today."

My mouth was full, but I nodded.

"I thought we might go to the matinee showing this afternoon."

I quickly finished chewing and swallowed. "Really?" My eyes widened and I sat up a little straighter. "You and me?" I asked.

She shrugged. "We haven't seen a picture in a long while. I thought it might be fun."

Excitement bubbled up in my chest and spilled out in a squeal. "You mean it, Mama?"

"Of course."

"Can we afford it?"

"I've got enough for two tickets."

"So we don't have to go with anyone else? Like Gina and Uncle Rex?"

"No." She shook her head, hooked the handle of her coffee cup with an index finger and lifted the cup to her mouth. After taking a sip, she said, "No, it would be better if they didn't come."

I didn't quite know what she meant by that and didn't care. An afternoon at the picture show with my mother was a rare treat. Doing anything at all with my mother just for fun, and just the two of us, was almost unheard of. In fact, for a little while that day, I felt as though she *was* my mother and not just a distant performer or another member of the troupe.

***

The Maysville Theater was small and crowded and smelled musty and vaguely of the O-Cedar Polish that Mrs. Littleworth used to clean her floors. I followed Mother as she chose our seats halfway down the aisle and to the left. At the front of the theater on the right was an upright piano with a round swivel seat. A thin, narrow-hipped man wearing a checkered shirt and suspenders sat at the keyboard, playing a peppy tune as the audience filed in.

I was so excited I could hardly sit still. Snapping open my fan—for almost all the women had hand-held fans—I batted at the air furiously in a release of nervous energy. The one film I had seen was *Esmeralda* with Mary Pickford, and while I had loved every minute of that show, it had long been my secret desire to see Charlie Chaplin on the screen. Chaplin had once played Vaudeville, had maybe even tread across some of the stages we had played, and now—now he was the undisputed king of comedy, known and adored around the world.

"When's it going to start, Mama?" I asked impatiently.

"In a minute, I'm sure," Mother said. She too was fanning herself, though not quite as vigorously as I.

A family turned into our aisle and filled the remaining seats. To my right was a girl about my own age, then next to her, a boy a couple years younger, and beyond him, a middle-aged man and woman I assumed to be their parents. The girl and I exchanged a tentative smile but didn't speak. I turned in my seat to watch the last few stragglers making their way down the aisle. At last, every seat in the theater was taken. A feverish murmuring whirled around the room on the competing currents of air created by the fluttering fans. In the next moment, the piano player paused. The lights grew dim. The curtains down front were drawn back, the piano player jumped back into a spirited tune, and the light of a projector sliced the darkness above our heads, casting flickering images on the screen.

The girl beside me clasped her hands to her chest in anticipation. She didn't have a fan but no matter; I was making enough of a breeze for the both of us, maybe even for the whole row. The words *Tillie's Punctured Romance* appeared on the screen, and a whisper of approval rose up from the crowd.

Then, there he is! Charlie Chaplin as a gentrified version of the Little Tramp, wearing a neat straw hat instead of a bowler, a well-fitting dark jacket with Western bow tie and cummerbund. He twirls a cane as he shuffles along a country road in his signature oversized shoes. He's "The City Guy," a nameless man in search of someone to swindle. Conveniently, he comes upon Tillie, the apple of her papa's eye, the homely, oversized, aging spinster from Yokeltown, who is throwing bricks for her dog to fetch. Alas! One of the bricks hits our Little Tramp and he is down and out!

The audience snickered and laughed in the way that warmed any performer's heart, though Charlie Chaplin and Marie Dressler weren't really there on stage to hear us. Never mind that. They pulled us into their world and we were there with them, howling when big Marie Dressler stepped on little Charlie's foot, uh-ohing when Charlie discovered Papa's stash of money, hissing when The City Guy tried to talk Tillie into taking her father's money and eloping. When at first she balked at the suggestion, the audience had some suggestions for Tillie: "Don't do it!" "Run away, Tillie!" "Throw another brick at the cad!"

But Tillie doesn't listen. Instead, "Her hitherto untouched girlish heart throbs in answer to the call of love." And so she takes her papa's purse and off she goes with the man who wants her money, not her heart, the man who already has a girl in the city who happens to be his partner in crime. That woman is the beautiful Mabel Normand, who callously laughs at Tillie from afar and calls her one of Ringling's elephants. Like Charlie, what Mabel wants is money, and she'll allow her man to entertain any charade to get it, even that of pretending to elope with an elephant.

The whole show was a tangle of pratfalls, exaggerated expressions and gestures, a few swift kicks to the seat of the pants, and through it all, Tillie preens like a plucked peacock who doesn't know its tail feathers are gone.

There was hardly a break in the laughter, a hilarious blend of snorts and chortles and chuckles and childish giggles, which filled the theater and threatened even to overtake the best efforts of the tireless piano player. I myself hadn't laughed so hard in a good long while, and I was happy to be in this place with these people at this time—not in the theater but in the imagery city, not with the audience but with Charlie and Tillie and Mabel, not in the present time, but in a timeless now in which even the criminal act is funny and the bad guy is the one who makes us merry.

As I watched, my own life became the *un*real, my own worries a small affair, not worth noticing. All I wanted was for Charlie to get the money and to live happily-ever-after with the beautiful Mabel.

But all the fantasy was broken about twenty minutes into the movie when Mother leaned toward me and whispered, "In this next scene, keep your eye on the piano player." I shook my head slightly, as though to brush her suggestion away. I didn't want anything interrupting the story I had entered, to stop the realness of it and the laughter, no matter how briefly.

Charlie leads Tillie into a restaurant and, yes, there is a piano player and a violinist and a few couples dancing, but all that is nothing, just the backdrop to the scene, just props for the moment when Charlie orders drinks and gets Tillie tipsy so that she gets up and dances. That is the real scene, that is the action, the hilarity. That's what I want to see, Tillie dancing and falling and unable to get up even when four men try to pull her up, including the piano player.

"Do you see him?" Mother asked.

"Who?"

"The piano player."

I sighed. "Yeah. So?"

"He's your father."

"What?"

"He's your father. Charles Cullen."

My fan stopped fluttering. My body seized up as though gripped by a vise. I couldn't move and would have thought I had shut down completely except for the wild banging of my heart against my chest. My father? My *father*? My face burned, not just from the heat but from something else. Shock? Fear? Anger? The room seemed to spin, and I thought I might be sick.

I turned my gaze to Mother's profile; she had simply gone back to watching the show. It took me a moment to gather my wits, but finally I asked, "Are you sure?"

She leaned toward me again. "Of course I'm sure. Do you think I don't know the man I was married to?"

She straightened up and I looked away. That man ... up there ... playing the piano. A vaporous memory floating in my brain slowly took on shape and form, took on a face, and I knew that what she was telling me was true. I knew that man. I remembered him. He was indeed my father.

"Mama?" I said, my voice choked and ragged.

"What?"

"Can we go home?"

"Of course not. I paid good money for these tickets."

And so we stayed. But there was no more laughter. Not for me. I was surrounded by it, but I scarcely heard the gaiety as I sank down into a place that felt something like grief. Tears rolled down my face and I let them fall, unchecked. I didn't know for certain why I was crying, except that I was suddenly aware of the crack in my heart, left there when my father left me.

I could no longer follow what was happening on the screen, didn't care if Charlie and Mabel got the money, didn't care if Tillie's romance was punctured. My own afternoon had abruptly and unexpectedly been deflated by a few words from my mother, and by the moving picture of a man I had once known long ago.

For two more hours and longer, the images on the screen were simply a blinking distraction to my own thoughts and feelings. I saw and heard only moments from my own life, rising up in ghostly form as though coming back from the dead. My father tap dancing on stage while I watched from the wings. My father in the seat beside my mother on the train. My father holding me in his lap while reading to me from *A Christmas Carol.*

Bah! Humbug!

Spirit! Show me no more!

God bless us, every one!

His voice was right there, his lips were close to my ear as I snuggled against his chest. I could hear him, just as he had been.

God bless us, every one!

The next movie played, and the next, and in between reels, before the final show, the theater owner got up and made a pitch for Liberty Bonds while the piano man played "Over There" and Stereopticon slides of patriotic scenes flashed on the screen. *We must remember our brave boys who are defending us overseas, fighting and getting wounded, and sometimes dying in this war to end all wars. They need our help! They need our support! Are you doing your bit?* But not even the images of young men dying could bring me out of myself. Battlefields, muddy trenches, fallen men—I caught snatches but just as quickly let them go. I couldn't be bothered by something an ocean away when my own heart lay wounded here on the home front.

My tears eventually stopped, but my mind went on racing. I wanted only for the whole revue to be over so I could get away from this place that had unexpectedly given me back memories of my father. I had so many questions I wanted to ask Mother, but they were falling away even as I was trying to gather them together and put them into some sort of order.

At long last, it was over. The house lights came on. The music stopped; the piano man stood and wiped his brow. The audience rose stiffly and began to shuffle out. Mother and I, unspeaking, joined the flow. Up the aisle and through the lobby and out the front doors onto the sidewalk where we stood squinting and blinking against the late afternoon sun. We turned toward home and, for several long moments, we walked without speaking.

Finally, I said, "Mama?"

"Yes, Annalise?"

"Why did you take me there?"

"You said you wanted to see your father. Now you've seen him."

True. I had wanted to see my father, and now I had seen him. "How did you know he was in that picture?"

"I saw it when it came out a few years ago. When I went that first time, I had no idea he was in it, but there he was."

I wondered whether she'd stopped breathing, like I did, when she recognized him on the screen. What had she felt? Surprised? Confused? Sick? Had she cried? "Is he still out in Hollywood?" I asked.

"As far as I know."

"Is he famous now?"

She shook her head. "No, he isn't famous. I've never even seen him in anything else. Not that I go to a picture show very much."

I slowed my pace, not wanting to get back to the house too quickly, as there was so much I wanted—needed—to learn.

"Why did he leave us, Mama? What happened?"

"I've never really been sure. It was all kind of sudden ... and strange. One day just before a show, he was hit on the head when a wooden prop fell over on the stage. It knocked him unconscious, and he stayed that way for two days. When he woke up, he announced he was going to Hollywood."

"That's it?"

"That's it."

"He didn't tell you why he was leaving?"

"Not in so many words."

"But didn't he love us?" I looked up anxiously at Mother. When she didn't answer, I tugged at her sleeve. "Did he love us, Mama?"

She answered my question with a question. "Is he here?"

I didn't have time to consider that before Mother stopped abruptly and took a deep breath. She turned to me and gazed intently at my face, as though trying to read what was there, or as though she was looking for signs of a lost husband. Maybe I was the only proof she had that he had ever been a part of her life. Finally, she said, "Yes, he loved us once. He probably still loves you, in his way." And then she went on walking.

I wondered what it meant, that he loved me in his way. He didn't even know me. How could he love me? We were almost home when I said, "Did he really play the piano?"

At that, she laughed a little, as though remembering something pleasant. "Oh yes. Your father could play the piano like nobody's business. He was a very talented man."

I smiled and for a moment even felt a little proud. But then, I remembered the last title card from "Tillie's Punctured Romance," the words of the final scene. It flashed through my mind just as it had flashed on the screen. Charlie is being carted off by the police, and Tillie and Mabel have bonded in the knowledge that they neither need nor want him, that he has in fact done both of them wrong. The two women embrace in their newfound friendship while Tillie says to Mabel, "He *ain't no good to neither of us.*" And that's it. That's the way the story ends.

Mother and I walked the rest of the way home in silence.

CHAPTER 7

The next day we packed up our bags, our costumes, our few props, my six-foot ladder, and we left the Littleworths's house. Albert Littleworth drove us to the train station in shifts—first Uncle Rex, Mother, Gina, and me, and then Uncle Cosmo and the boys. He shook Uncle Rex's hand cordially, thanked him for the last-minute re-plastering of the bedroom ceiling, and bid us safe travels. He lost no time in exiting the station, and I thought I saw his shoulders rise and fall in an immense sigh of relief.

We met up with our troupe in a town called Edgemore, just south of Bloomington, where we were booked into the Starlite, a theater so small it didn't even have seats, just benches for the audience to sit on. No balconies either. And no orchestra pit. Just a three-piece band, as we called it in Vaudeville: a piano, a piano player, and a stool. Oh, and sawdust on the floor to catch the men's spittle, those sticky little shafts of tobacco juice some men were so fond of shooting forth at inopportune moments.

Mr. Stanley purposely chose this small house so he could vet the new folks: a three-hundred pound ventriloquist named Mr. Dapper and his multi-lingual dummy Mr. Danny Do-good, a family of pantomimes who had just brought their act over from Liverpool, and an all-girl ensemble of plate-spinners. Opening in a small house also allowed the rest of us to work out the kinks of whatever fresh routines we'd developed over the summer. I, for one, was glad to start small with the Georgia

Snow routine. Better to be laughed at by a few dozen people than hundreds.

From Edgemore we'd be going on to play three days at the Colonial Theater in Chicago, a large and rather stately theater that could seat 1,700 people. The place had once been a legitimate theater, but in recent years had been given over to Vaudeville, burlesque, and motion pictures. Still, it was a far cry from the pitiful houses we usually played, and Mr. Stanley wanted to make sure we were ready. We had a couple rehearsal days at the Starlite and then at last, to my trepidation, came opening day: Wednesday, the eleventh of September.

That day happened also to be Mother's birthday. Every year Uncle Rex gave me a few coins to buy a present, and this year, as usual, he handed them over somewhat grudgingly at the last minute. After scouring the local five-and-dime store in the heart of town, I settled on a small bottle of toilet water that smelled vaguely of lavender. Dropping the change on the counter, I hurried along the crowded sidewalks until I reached the stage door in an alley off the town's main street. A wall clock inside the stage door told me it was almost noon; we were on for the matinee at two o'clock.

I arrived breathlessly at the door of our dressing room. My simple drop waist dress had no pockets, so I hid the bottle of toilet water behind my back, unlatched the door and burst into the room.

"Happy birthday, Mama!" I cried merrily.

She looked at me from the dressing table where she sat clutching a small page of ivory-colored stationery in one hand, a torn envelope in the other. In front of her was a large bouquet of flowers, red roses and white calla lilies, the same arrangement Uncle Rex sent her every year on her birthday. Where he got the money, I didn't know. We scarcely had money for food and lodging, let alone luxuries like roses and lilies that served no real purpose and then withered after a few days or a week. But it wasn't my place to ask, so I never did, though the empty spot in my stomach always felt larger whenever I looked at the flowers.

"I see Uncle Rex's flowers arrived," I said.

Mother nodded. "Yes. Aren't they lovely?"

Even now, my stomach growled. "Sure. They're nice, I guess."

She folded the letter and slipped it back into the envelope, then picked up a handkerchief from the dressing table and dabbed at her eyelids and cheeks. She tried to pretend she was only preparing to put on her makeup, but I could tell she was wiping at tears. She cried every time she had a birthday.

"What's wrong, Mama?" I asked.

"Nothing, darling." She smiled at me wanly, the corners of her mouth trembling.

"You've been crying, though. Did Uncle Rex say something in his note to make you cry?"

"Oh no, no. Nothing like that." She took a deep breath and looked at herself in the mirror. "I guess I'm just being silly, dear."

"About what?"

"Oh, you know." She moved her eyes to me again and tried to smile once more. "Or, I suppose you don't, of course. It's just that, every time I turn another year older, the dream seems to fade a little more. I don't think I will ever really make it to the legitimate stage."

"Don't say that, Mama!" I said, "You'll make it. I know you will. You're still young and beautiful and anyway, you have the appointment at the Palace. They'll see how talented you are, Mama, really they will!"

We weren't used to being demonstrative in our affection, but I couldn't help rushing to Mother and throwing my arms around her. To my surprise, she held me close, and I felt her tremble as a sob escaped her.

"Don't cry, Mama," I went on. "It's your birthday. You should be happy today. And this is the year you'll make it to the big time. I just know it!" I drew back and cradled the little bottle of toilet water in both hands. "This is for you. I hope you like it."

Mother lifted the gift from my hands and ran a finger over the label. She untwisted the cap and held the bottle to her nose. "It's lovely, Anna," she said. "Thank you."

As she settled the bottle on the dressing table, the door burst open and Gina flew into the room. "I'm so nervous I could die!" she cried.

"What are you nervous about?" I asked.

She stared at me wide-eyed. "The show, silly. What do you think? We're performing Georgia Snow for the first time and you ask me what I'm nervous about?"

"But why should you be nervous? All you have to do is stand on stage and pretend you're singing."

"That's not true! I have dance steps to remember, and besides, if you mess up the songs, I'm the one who'll look like a fool."

"I'm not going to mess up. I know the songs better than you know the dance routines—"

"But what if you get the hiccups and everyone thinks *I've* got the hiccups—"

"Girls!" Mother interrupted. "That's enough. Neither of you will do well if you're all worked up like this. Now try to relax. You've rehearsed the routine a thousand times, and you both know what you're doing, so everything is going to be fine." She pushed the chair away from the dressing table and rose. "I have a few questions for the stage manager, but I'll just be a minute. Try not to kill each other while I'm gone." She took a step, then turned back, picked up the letter, and slid it into the pocket of her dress.

We watched in silence as Mother moved across the room. When the door closed behind her, Gina narrowed her eyes at me and said, "You'd just better make me look good, or else ..."

I crossed my arms. "Or else, what?"

Instead of answering, Gina stamped a foot, then slipped behind the dressing screen to wiggle into her costume and begin the laborious transformation from Georgina Slump to Miss Georgia Snow.

***

We were number seven on the bill of ten acts, sandwiched between the plate spinners and the family of pantomimes from Liverpool. Uncle Rex had talked Mr. Stanley out of playing us as the final act, the act that got the least respect, the act that was "playing to the haircuts" because the audience was by then already filing out of the theater. Mr. Stanley—upon learning that the person of Georgia Snow was comprised of two people, one the body and one the voice—had turned a startling shade of red and said our scheme would never work. Uncle Rex begged him to sit anywhere in the house and listen while we rehearsed.

"It's a great act, Stanley," Uncle Rex assured him. "Just give us a chance. We've been working on it all summer, and I can tell you we're going to go big with this one. Just wait and see if we don't."

By the end of the second day of rehearsals, Mr. Stanley relented and said we just might get away with it. He moved us up to number seven. The last spot was given to the tap-dancing twins, a couple of unremarkable girls who were too young and unsophisticated to care whether they were playing to the backs of people's heads.

The matinee that afternoon started as usual with Uncle Cosmo and his mournful violin, followed by "Rex and Bernadette Rycroft, the Singing Sweethearts." Both acts were well received, as were The Sensational Cycling Sokolovs. But after the Russians exited the stage, everything started to fall apart. Mr. Meriwether's dog Troubadour got spooked by the shrill, two-fingered whistling of an intoxicated man in the front row and started howling in all the wrong places. Then Mr. Dapper the ventriloquist was just working up a good rapport with the audience when his three-legged stool collapsed, casting the portly gentleman to the floor and hurling his dummy, Mr. Do-good, across the stage. The unintended flight decapitated the little mannequin before both body and head finally rolled to a stop somewhere just short of stage left. The plate spinners, newcomers to show business, were so undone by the tragic death of Mr. Do-good they couldn't keep their plates in the air. The three of them ended up ankle deep in shards. Mr. Stanley had their pink slip written even before the curtain began to fall on their failed performance.

To gain some extra time for sweeping up the broken plates, Mr. Stanley sent The Astonishing Mister Twister out of turn to do his contortions in front of the curtains. Surely, he couldn't fumble his act as badly as the others, unless he twisted into a position from which he wasn't able to unravel himself. While he was out there doing his show, Gina, the hoofers, and I wrung our hands nervously backstage, waiting to go on. We heard laughter and applause greeting the antics of Mister Twister, so we hoped he was winning back the audience. Still, we all believed the series of disasters among the earlier acts didn't bode well for our debut of Georgia Snow.

Shortly, the Starlite stage manager told us to position ourselves as the curtain would be rising on our act in five. Gina, who really did look stunning in her layered dress of white tulle and white organza bowler hat, took her place on stage. The boys, dandy in dark suits with cummerbunds like snowflakes, lined up ready to file out shortest to tallest. Uncle Rex hurried to the floor to take over the piano. I climbed my ladder, recently situated by a stagehand just out of sight in the wings. I would be only a couple of feet behind Gina, though unseen.

Nor could I see the audience, and I didn't want to see them. I hadn't even peeked through the crack in the curtains to glimpse the sea of faces beyond. The drunk on the first row had been escorted out by the theater manager, so that was one less unruly person to worry about. But I could only imagine what this sampling of Edgemore's population was like. Undoubtedly not the best representatives of this little town, though I knew there were women and children among them, this being the matinee. Also among them were Mother and Uncle Cosmo, who had slipped out to watch our act from the back of the house.

I took a deep breath to calm myself. If my hands hadn't been clutching the ladder rung, I would have clutched them to my chest and petitioned the heavens not to let me to break out in hiccups. As it was, I breathed a silent prayer that we would make it through the act without mishap or embarrassment. I didn't like being Gina's voice, but I didn't want to be humiliated either.

The final applause for Mister Twister broke out abruptly and loudly, then slowly faded. The house became quiet. One or two people coughed. A child's voice cried out, then sounded muffled, then stopped altogether, as though a hand had been clamped over his mouth. My heart beat wildly in my chest. I suddenly wanted to be somewhere else, anywhere else but here. I had half a mind to flee, even took one step down on the ladder, but in the end I couldn't do it. Mother, Uncle Rex, Gina, the boys—they all expected me to sing. Our performance was our bread and butter. I had no choice.

I took one more deep breath and watched as the curtain began to lift. When it was halfway up, high enough to reveal Gina standing in the spotlight, Uncle Rex played the opening bars of our first song, "Do You Love Me?" This was it; it was now or never.

I closed my eyes and told myself we were in Albert Littleworth's ballroom where I had sung these songs a thousand times. I opened my mouth and hoped that Gina was opening hers. And then I began to sing. "Does the sun rise at the break of day?" To my own surprise, the words came out clear and strong. Below me, the boys began to march on stage. "Do buttercups always bloom in May? / Do the rivers roll down to the sea? / And please tell me, do you love me?"

"Yes, yes, yes, and yes, we love you!" the boys sang. They doffed their straw hats at Gina one by one as they danced by her in a line. I sang on.

> Do the stars twinkle at night?
> Does the moon fill the heavens with light?
> Does my kiss fill your heart with glee?
> Please tell me, do you love me?"

"Yes, yes, yes, and yes, we love you!" Ray took Gina by the hand and fairly floated with her out to center stage for the dance routine. Gina twirled, pivoted, and promenaded with each of the boys by turn, acting shy and demure one minute, blowing kisses to them the next.

By now the house was cheering wildly, the air sharp with the various hoots, hollers, and whistles coming up from the floor. Even I had to admit that Gina was enchanting, as beautiful as any star, as tempting as any siren. How could an audience not be drawn to her?

Ray led her back to the side of the stage for the final stanza. I was on again.

> Do you smile at the touch of my hand?
> Do my whispers leave you feeling grand?
> In a crowded room, am I the one you see?
> Oh please tell me, do you love me?

As the song wound down, the audience wound up again with wild applause, catcalls, and one persistent declaration coming from somewhere out on the floor, "We love you, Georgia Snow! You bet we do!"

Over on the piano, Uncle Rex slid into the opening notes of "You Warm My Heart." We were on to song number two, and by now I was feeling good. Confidence flowed through my veins, and I was ready to knock 'em dead. The audience might think they were in love with Gina, but it was my voice that was drawing them in. It was me they loved, though they didn't know it.

On I sang, while down below, Gina and the boys danced and flirted and blew kisses to each other and to the audience, and for the next quarter hour, through "You Warm My Heart" and on through "Little Snow Angel," it was a virtual love affair going on right there in the Starlite Theater between Georgia Snow and her Winter Wonder Men and the good folks of Edgemore, Illinois. I'd never quite experienced such magic, never felt such goodwill from a crowd as I was feeling then, and, for the first time in my life, I felt a rush of approval, the keen and piercing joy of admiration.

The final notes of the last song were met with more thunderous applause, and I watched from atop the ladder as Gina and the boys joined hands and bowed low before the audience. Up they rose, clasped hands reaching toward the ceiling, then down again as the applause went on and on.

At last, the curtain fell, and Gina and the boys moved off stage where Mr. Stanley waited to congratulate them. "Fabulous! Great job, all of you," he said as he shook each boy's hand and demurely kissed Gina on the cheek. Cheeks flushed with excitement and chests heaving with exertion, Gina and the boys hugged each other and patted each other on the back and laughed together in triumph while I watched from above. In another moment, Uncle Rex and Mother joined the festivities in the wings. No one glanced up or said a word to me. When the next act was ready to go on, Gina and the boys moved off together as one great love fest headed to the dressing rooms, and still I stood atop the ladder unwilling to come down. I was up there even as the curtain rose on the pantomimes from

Liverpool, and I might have stayed there all night and into the next day, nailed to the rungs by an overwhelming sense of unfairness, if someone hadn't tapped me on the foot.

I turned and looked down, and there was dear old Uncle Cosmo, smiling up at me. "Well done, Anna," he whispered. "And not a single hiccup."

I managed a smile in return. "Thanks, Uncle Cosmo," I said. "Really. Thanks for noticing."

CHAPTER 8

On the train from Bloomington to Chicago, Uncle Rex couldn't stop talking about how Georgia Snow had been successful beyond our wildest dreams. After the first show at the Starlite, every performance was standing room only. The whole troupe began to get good reviews in the local paper, but it was Georgia who was bringing them in, Georgia and her Winter Wonder Men. As a result, Mr. Stanley was giving us top billing in Chicago.

The more Uncle Rex prattled on, the angrier I became. Maybe Georgia was bringing them in, but it was my voice—my talent—that was keeping them there. Perhaps it was an oversight, but Uncle Rex failed to say anything about that. As the miles rolled beneath us and Chicago loomed, I felt I might burst with fury. I refused to look at Gina and the boys, who sat across the aisle, but kept my face turned toward the window. Only slowly did I realize Uncle Cosmo, beside me in the aisle seat, was talking to me.

"Oh yes, I can assure you that the place is quite haunted," he was saying.

I shook my head, as though to clear it. "What place?"

"The Colonial. Where we're headed. Don't you know the story behind the theater?"

I shook my head again. "No. What happened at the Colonial?"

"Well, it was called the Iroquois when it opened, back in oh-three," he said. "It had been open only a month, maybe six weeks, when there was a terrible fire. The irony, of course, was that even their own playbill boasted that the Iroquois Theater was absolutely fireproof. Not once but twice, in all capital letters. 'ABSOLUTELY FIREPROOF!' As though there was not one speck of doubt, not one iota of uncertainty. How safe the audience must have felt, reading those words while they waited for the house lights to go down and the curtain to go up. How lovely, they must have said to themselves, to know we won't burn up tonight while we're enjoying the show. Why, it says right here in the playbill in all capital letters that the place is absolutely fireproof—"

"But what happened, Uncle Cosmo?" I asked again, interrupting him.

"Oh yes, well, you see, Eddie Foy was there, appearing in 'Mr. Blue Beard.' He wasn't playing the part of Mr. Blue Beard, though. He was playing the part of Sister Anne—"

"Sister Anne?"

"Yes, that's right."

"Why would he want to play the part of Sister Anne?"

"Well, I suppose it was better than playing one of Mr. Blue Beard's six ugly wives."

"Six ugly wives?"

"Yes, and he had six beautiful wives too. But that's beside the point. The point is, Eddie Foy was so popular that on the night of the tragedy—it was a winter night, sometime right after Christmas—around two thousand people crowded into the theater, far more than the place could hold. The second act was just beginning when some canvas backdrops caught fire backstage. It seems nobody noticed quickly enough to put the fire out before it could do any damage. Or perhaps somebody did notice and said to himself, 'But of course it can't spread. This theater is absolutely fireproof.'

"But spread it did, to the stage first, sending the performers straight for the stage door in a panic. Their quick escape was fortuitous for them, but you can imagine how the blast of cold air only fed the flames inside. Eddie Foy was the only actor to stay behind, and he stood there on stage quite bravely, trying to calm everyone down. But even as he assured them that everything was under control, the fire jumped out to the auditorium and up into the balconies and soon the place was almost entirely engulfed in flames. People ran to the exits in a huge stampede, so that some were trampled to death. But the doors ... well, you see, the doors opened inward rather than outward. They couldn't be opened for the crush of people clamoring to escape. If only the doors had hung on their hinges the other way, the story might have ended quite differently."

Uncle Cosmo paused for a moment and gazed out the window at the passing landscape, as though his telling the story had left him too sad to go on.

"So," I prodded hesitantly. "I guess a lot of people died."

He turned back to me and nodded. "More than six hundred, all told."

"Eddie Foy too?"

"Oh no. He managed to get out. None of the performers was killed. No, only the audience. Men and women ... children too. They had gone to be entertained, to laugh, to briefly escape the monotony of their lives, and before the show was over, six hundred of them had perished in a giant inferno. It was the worst disaster in all of Chicago's history. Not even the Great Chicago Fire of 1871 left so many dead."

"How did anyone survive at all, Uncle Cosmo?"

"I'm not sure, though many did get out. There were fire escapes available from the upper balconies, and some fled that way. But as the fire worsened, many ended up leaping to their deaths from those same fire escapes, falling from three or four stories up above Randolph Street. Eventually, it was either jump or burn."

In the seat facing us, Mother stopped fanning herself long enough to huff out a sigh and roll her eyes. "Oh, Cosmo," she said. "You do have a flair for the dramatic, especially when it's morbid."

Uncle Rex, sitting next to Mother, added, "Well, you know how the macabre always lifts his spirits. Uncle Cosmo relishes the stuff."

"He does not," I said in the old man's defense, though I wasn't so sure he didn't. Uncle Cosmo seldom dabbled in pleasantries. Tugging his sleeve, I said, "So if the place burned down, they must have rebuilt it, right?"

"Oh yes," said Uncle Cosmo. "They rebuilt it right away and renamed it the Colonial."

"So if it's a whole different place, then maybe it isn't haunted."

"No chance of that. It's a well-known fact that the place is inhabited by spirits."

"Are you telling me people have seen ghosts there?"

He shook his head. "Not seen so much as heard. You see, it's been said that when the theater is empty, that's when you can hear the cries of those poor people trying to get out. The screams, the wailing—it's quite terrible. All those lost souls, mourning the lives they didn't get to live."

"If the theater is empty," Uncle Rex said, "how does anyone hear them? Seems a pretty good trick if you ask me."

"Well," Mother said, "perhaps there's a mouse in the theater that tattles to the manager and complains about the ruckus. After all, it would be difficult to raise a family of little mice with all those dead people carrying on so."

She and Uncle Rex shared a laugh, but I didn't find anything funny. I was stricken by Uncle Cosmo's words: *All those lost souls, mourning the lives they didn't get to live.* Those people—they must have been part of the surplus population that Ebenezer Scrooge held in such disdain. All those hundreds of men, women, and children must have been disposable, that they could be stamped out so ruthlessly. Like unnecessary furniture on a stage. Props and odd bits of scenery. Little more than the canvas backdrops that had started the fire in the first place.

Mother must have noticed my distress. "Oh, don't worry, Anna," she assured me. "There's no such thing as ghosts."

But I wasn't afraid of ghosts. I was afraid of the surplus population, of being counted among them. Six hundred nameless props destroyed because there was no place for them on the stage, no need for them in the show.

I leaned toward Uncle Cosmo and put my lips close to his ear. "I believe you, Uncle," I whispered. "Anyone who died like that would naturally go on crying forever and ever."

The old man winked at me and patted my hand. "Smart girl," he said. "When we get there, we'll listen very closely and see if we can't catch some of the echoes."

***

We were booked into a shanty of a hotel on Madison Street in the Loop downtown, but I expected nothing else. The worst rooms in the worst hotels were reserved for vaudevillians. We referred to it as being relegated to "Soubrette Row," so called for the light, romantic comedies common to our trade. So far as cheap lodgings go, we had seen and experienced it all, and we were used to seediness in all its permutations: peeling wallpaper, lumpy mattresses, broken chairs, ants and bed bugs and cockroaches, windows that wouldn't open, windows that wouldn't close, windows that had no shades, windows with broken glass, pipes that rattled with steam, radiators too hot or too cold, elevators that didn't work or that rattled loudly when they did, and down-the-hall bathrooms with faucets that perpetually dripped, leaving ugly brown stains in the sinks. To me, such rooms held all the comforts of home because, aside from our time at Albert Littleworth's, they were the only home I knew.

What I wasn't used to was the excitement with which our troupe anticipated our upcoming engagement. The Colonial, also in the Loop on Randolph Street, would be the largest, most beautiful theater we had ever played. For the past two weeks I'd heard words like opulent and luxurious being bandied about, along with the question of how on earth Mr. Stanley ever managed to get the likes of us booked into a place like that. Even though it was largely used for Vaudeville shows and motion pictures, it was a far cry from the sorry houses where we usually performed.

Upon our arrival, our troupe entered through the stage door in the back alley and gathered around the call board to get our dressing room assignments. The theater's stage manager was there to greet us, clipboard in hand, pencil tucked behind his ear. So far the place was like any other, dimly lit, sterile, with scattered props in the hall and the scent of must in the air. Tacked to the board were various lists and announcements, including the standard warning about the use of profanity and vulgarity. The manager, a tall, lanky fellow with dark close-set eyes and an alarmingly large nose, introduced himself to us as J. Edgar Pettigrew. He then lifted the pencil from his ear and used it to point to the "Notice to Performers."

"Please note," he announced loudly, "that vulgarity will not be tolerated. Not in word, not in action, not in costume. Certainly not in *this* theater."

As his eyes rolled over the crowd, his monstrous nostrils flared, as though to sniff out any odor of impending vulgarity among us. "I could read this notice to you," he continued, "but I'm sure you are all familiar with it."

Oh yes, we were familiar with it. We practically knew it by heart. These notices were the same everywhere. "Such words," it advised, "as Liar, Slob, Son-of-a-Gun, Devil, Sucker, and any and all similar words unfit for the ears of ladies and children, as well as any reference to questionable streets, resorts, localities, and barrooms, are strictly prohibited under fine of instant discharge." This welcoming memorandum was unfailingly signed with the anonymous *nom de plume*, "General Management."

We had seen it a thousand times in a thousand places until we simply didn't see it anymore. Many acts were determined to get away with whatever they could—a little skin, some suggestive gestures, even what might pass for a double entendre—without actually stepping over the line. It was the drive to be daring for the sake of engaging the audience. Even Georgia Snow hinted at promiscuity, but no general manager was going to instantly discharge us for that, so long as the money was rolling in.

If we hadn't already known, our first clue that this theater was different from others we'd played was that it offered thirty-six dressing rooms. Thirty-six! Mother and I still shared a room, but Gina had her own. After the stage manager assigned the rooms, the troupe broke up and wandered off. I told Mother I'd meet her in our room in a few minutes. I wanted to take a look around first.

"Don't get into trouble," she said, "and don't go anywhere you know you're not supposed to go."

"I won't, Mama."

I just wanted to see the stage, to stand on it and look out over an auditorium that held almost two thousand people. Too, I wanted to listen, in case I might hear the echoes of the dead that Uncle Cosmo was so sure inhabited the place.

From the back hall it wasn't difficult to find my way into the wings and onto the stage. I simply followed the dim glow of the ghost light that was ever burning onstage when a theater was empty. The curtains were open. The house itself was dark, save for a solitary light shining somewhere in the far back reaches of the auditorium. A small shiver ran up my spine, and for a moment, I was afraid. I listened to the dark, and heard nothing more than silence. No whispers, no moans or cries, only a quiet that seemed somehow filled with anticipation.

Then, suddenly, oddly, the house lights came on and the whole place opened up before me in all its glory. I couldn't help but gasp. I was looking out over a big, beautiful shiny world of reds, greens, and gold. Row after row of plush red velvet folding seats with gilded armrests stretched for what seemed miles, ending in a series of stately columns that supported the two balconies. My eyes moved up to the balconies and on up to the pale green ceiling that seemed as far away as heaven, where the cut glass of the chandeliers sparkled like stars. A large orchestra pit lay at my feet, and to the right and to the left were ornate box seats where the wealthiest patrons could enjoy their own company.

I felt very small, yet very large with possibility. This place spoke of grandeur and magnificence, and as I stood there on that stage in front of that empty auditorium, I didn't hear the echoes of the dead but the applause of the living, the thunderous approval that my young heart longed for. I knew beyond a doubt that I wanted to sing in the spotlight, right there where a thousand eyes could see me, not behind the curtain where I was hidden and unseen. I wanted my voice to ring out over these hundreds of seats, and I wanted to take a bow at the end and hear this whole wide glamorous world applauding me. I wanted to prove Mr. Stanley wrong when he said no one would ever clap for Annalise Rycroft.

I knew now I had the talent and the voice. But I didn't yet have the stage presence. If only my girlish body would fill out like Gina's. If only my face would acquire a beauty it so far lacked. If only I could sing on stage without getting hiccups. If only I could grow that all-important spine.

So many "if onlys." How would I ever get beyond so many hurdles? Given time, would they all take care of themselves? I had to believe that they would. I had to believe that someday, everything wrong would come around right, and I would be a star.

CHAPTER 9

We opened at the Colonial on Friday night, September 20. For hours before, the troupe flitted about backstage in a nervous frenzy, and Mr. Stanley repeatedly dabbed at his sweaty brow with a crumpled handkerchief. He snapped so often at his hapless assistant, Miss Withers, she finally threatened to take the next train home to Hoboken if he didn't apologize. He must have made amends somehow because she didn't go back to Hoboken.

Shortly before showtime, Uncle Rex called us all into his dressing room to give us a pep talk. Gina was there, as were Ray, Luther, Willard, and Eddie. Mother too, though Uncle Cosmo was off spending time with the dog Troubadour, his favorite member of the troupe and the only one, he said, who never complained about the harsh life of the traveling performer.

Uncle Rex sat on his dressing table with his stocking feet on the accompanying chair. He held several newspapers in his hands, and I knew without even looking that they were last week's editions of the *Edgemore Daily Chronicle*. He had already read us the reviews of our show a dozen times, but apparently he was going to read them again.

We seated ourselves on chairs, trunks, and in Eddie's case, on the floor. The tension in the air was palpable. Gina sat fanning herself as though to fend off a fainting fit. The hoofers were pale and rigid, their eyes darting about like trapped moths searching for a way of escape. For my part, I was so tense I thought my hastily eaten supper might just as quickly come back up, so I sat with one hand over my mouth and the other over my stomach.

"Now listen, everyone," Uncle Rex began. "I know you're scared. Of course you are. That's normal. Even the greatest performers experience stage fright. But the only difference between the Colonial and the Starlite is the size of the place. That's it. And all that means is that there are going to be even more folks out there who are going to love Georgia Snow." He paused a moment and waved the newspapers in the air. "Don't forget: You killed them in Edgemore. The audience was going wild over you. The newspapers were singing your praises."

I thought briefly about Edgemore, that rinky-dink town and its tiny theater with the sawdust floor, and I wasn't encouraged. Even the newspaper was less than impressive, having dropped the "i" in Georgia twice, and misidentifying Mr. Dapper's dummy (who had been resurrected with some wire and a rubber band) as Mr. Goody-two-shoes rather than Mr. Do-good. Yes, the reviewer had called us swell and sensational and enormously talented, but I wasn't sure that meant much coming from someone who couldn't even spell correctly or get his facts straight. That was a small-time newspaper in a small-time town. The Starlite couldn't compare to the Colonial and Edgemore was hardly Chicago.

"But Uncle Rex," I whined. "What if they figure it out?"

"Figure what out?"

"You know that Gina's not really singing. That I'm singing for her. What if the audience finds out?"

My uncle shrugged. "So? You think they really believe that dummy Do-good is talking? 'Course not! They know it's Dapper doing the talking and that's the whole point."

"But—"

"Not to compare you to a dummy, sweetheart," Uncle Rex added, looking at Gina.

Gina nodded and offered a tenuous smile.

"But Uncle Rex," I protested, "our act is different."

"How?"

"Gina's *supposed* to be singing."

"Yeah, but she *can't* sing."

"But everybody thinks she can."

"Listen, Anna, this is show business and show business is filled with illusions. People come to be entertained by those illusions. So just do your part, and everything is going to be fine. Better than fine—it's going to be *great*. Just keep telling yourself that."

With my fears dismissed out of hand by Uncle Rex, I clamped my fingers back over my mouth. I felt more nauseous than ever. As my uncle jabbered on, I let my mind drift back to the day before when I stood alone on the stage. Looking out over that sprawling auditorium, I was so sure I could do it, so certain I could impress the audience. But now, just before showtime, all my confidence was gone. What if I forgot the words? What if I hit a sour note?

"It's Anna we have to worry about," Gina said, interrupting—and echoing—my thoughts. "I know my part and the boys know theirs. If anyone's likely to mess up, it's Anna."

"I haven't messed up yet!" I protested. "I've done nothing but make you look good."

"Yes, and you'd better not mess up tonight, that's all I can say," Gina shot back.

"Why do you threaten me every time we go on?"

"I don't threaten you—"

"Yes, you do, Gina!"

The room fell silent. Heads swiveled this way and that, and all eyes finally settled on Eddie, the youngest of the dancers. For he was the one who had hollered, "Yes, you do, Gina!" He was someone who scarcely ever spoke, and now he was standing up for me. I eyed him with wonder. The silence continued as everyone seemed to be waiting for him to explain his sudden outburst.

He looked around sheepishly. Then he sat up a little straighter and said, "Every time, right before we go on, you tell Anna not to mess up, like if she does you're going to kill her or something. And then where would you be? Just think about it, will ya? None of us would be anywhere without Anna's voice."

Eddie looked at me and smiled slightly, and I felt tears burning at the back of my eyes because that was the first time anyone recognized my importance to the act, outside of Uncle Cosmo. I smiled at Eddie in return, my face growing warm and my breath quickening at the thought that I wasn't completely invisible. Someone had seen me!

Before I could thank Eddie, Gina's head swung back toward me and her narrowed eyes locked with my own. In that moment, I came to fully realize one thing: I was the one with the power. Eddie had made that point quite clear: *None of us would be anywhere without Anna's voice.* He was right! I could make Georgia Snow look good or I could make her look like a fool. Georgina Slump's future was in my hands, and she had undoubtedly known it from the beginning—and now I knew it too.

As though she knew what I was thinking, Gina said, "Yes, but where would Anna be without me? She can't get out on stage without hiccupping. Even if she could, how could that flat-chested homely little twit be Georgia Snow? The audience would think it a joke."

"Girls!" Uncle Rex said. "Listen to me. Didn't I say from the start that the two of you together make one great entertainer? That's the whole point. Both of you make up Georgia Snow. And according to the reviews"—Uncle Rex shook the newspapers in the air—"Georgia Snow is a marvel, a great sensation, a marvelous act. So let's get out there tonight and break a leg!"

In another hour, the audience was seated, and Uncle Cosmo was in the spotlight, playing his tunes. In spite of all our fears, something magical happened that night for the entire troupe. We connected with the audience like never before. They laughed, sighed, gasped, and applauded in all the right places. Mother and Uncle Rex exited the stage feeling adored. Mr. Twister, the Liverpool pantomimes, the Sokolov cyclists all held the audience in awe. Mr. Do-good kept his head, making Mr. Dapper proud. Mr. Meriwether and Troubadour elicited howls of laughter. One after another, each act was ushered off-stage by enormous applause. Mr. Stanley sweated all the more profusely for the joy of it all, and Alice Withers was seen shadowing him with a hard-earned smile.

And then the curtain rose on Georgia Snow. The familiar opening notes of our first song gathered and blossomed in the orchestra pit. In the next moment, Gina glowed in the spotlight in her white tulle dress. I couldn't see the audience, nor had I peeked beforehand to see what those rows and rows of red velvet seats looked like now they were filled with people. I didn't want to get the hiccups and ruin the show. Though as I looked down on Gina, just a few feet below me there on stage, I was filled with a curious mix of fury and envy. If we were both Georgia Snow, why was she alone getting all the recognition?

I knew how easily I could ruin the act for her, making her a laughingstock and knocking her down not just a peg or two but all the way to rock bottom. One bad note, one forgotten line ...

It was tempting, but something in me wouldn't allow it. Everyone—the whole troupe—was counting on me, and I couldn't let *them* down. I took a deep breath, found the words that had long since been seared into my brain, and sent them out through my vocal cords as powerfully as I could. And there must have been some sort of power at work that night, because as Gina and the boys did their bit on stage, the audience responded with sighs of praise, gentle laughter and, in the end, a whirlwind of applause that sent Georgia Snow and her Winter Wonder Men back out on stage three times for bows and more applause.

The next morning we gathered again in Uncle Rex's dressing room, this time with a whole new set of newspapers. Chicago's newspapers.

"Listen to this, everyone. Just listen to this," Uncle Rex announced from his perch on the dressing table. He opened one of the papers, scanned the columns and found his place. "The *Chicago Tribune* says, 'Miss Georgia Snow is simply stunning. Seldom does one see such beauty, charm, and talent all wrapped up in one person.' So what do you think, huh? Didn't I tell you from the outset that Georgia Snow was going to be big?"

Gina squealed and the boys cheered. For my part, I was stuck on the words "one person." That was wrong! Just yesterday Uncle Rex had emphasized himself that Georgia Snow wasn't one person, but two. And yet, of course, we couldn't let on. No one outside the troupe could know the truth.

I knew this much, though, and appeased myself with the thought: Gina had the beauty and charm, but I had the talent. And that was the more important piece.

Mother, too, was strangely quiet, looking like a wax figure, her face pinched and pasty. I recognized the look of envy, and I wondered whether she was beginning to abhor Georgina Slump as much as I did.

"And wait, there's more!" Uncle Rex went on. He opened another paper. "This is from the *Chicago Herald-Examiner*. 'The entire show was top-notch but rising to the top of the top was Miss Georgia Snow and her Winter Wonder Men. One could do nothing other than sit mesmerized by the charming Miss Snow and her talented young hoofers. Theirs is an act one could easily watch again and again without growing weary.'"

More squeals. More cheering. More silence from Mother. More mixed emotions roiling in my own chest.

"And from the *Chicago Daily News*," Rex continued, "'Miss Snow's voice has those dueling qualities of both strength and tenderness so rarely encountered on the stage. It is a voice of perfect pitch and clarity, one that is sure to carry the young and beautiful Miss Snow onto stardom.'"

I gasped at that, knowing the reviewer was talking about me. It was his opinion that my voice could make me a star.

My nemesis and I looked at each other across the room. Gina's brows were raised haughtily and her lips curled up in a snide smile. Her eyes told me she saw herself as the luxury liner ready to be pulled into the port of success, and I was the little tugboat that was expected to guide her there. But did she really think this was how it was going to be for the rest of our lives? That I would be content to stay behind the curtain while she glowed in the glory of the stage?

That night, after our second performance at the Colonial, I dreamed again of the lost baby. When I awoke the next morning, a pale light seeped in through the tattered window shade and lay across my bed. I propped myself up on my elbows and gazed about the homely little room there in the Loop, the dismal dwelling that so characterized the meanness of my life, and for the first time I wondered whether the lost child of my dreams could be me. Maybe the dream meant that I was lost in that place where the nameless wander the earth without purpose, like the souls who perished in the fire and who ever after mourned the lives they never got to live.

I couldn't let that happen. I had to grow a spine, and quick.

CHAPTER 10

Success followed us as we moved eastward to Ft. Wayne, Cleveland, and Pittsburgh. In this last city, we didn't stay in a hotel with the rest of the troupe, but in a boarding house on North Negley Avenue owned by an old acquaintance of Uncle Cosmo. Edith Tuck, a long-time widow, had been sheltering transients in her great behemoth of a brick house since before the turn of the century. She had room enough for the eight of us during our week-long run in Pittsburgh, and it was in her somewhat garish parlor that Rex and Mother's plans for the future began to unravel.

Late on the morning of October 3, I sat in a wing chair by the empty hearth, my legs tucked up beside me. Cradled in my lap was a book Mother had found among Mrs. Tuck's own sparse collection. In one of her usual uninspired attempts to educate me, Mother had opened it, pointed to a section on Custer's defeat at Little Big Horn and instructed me to read. But I was tired and the text itself was pulling me toward sleep when Uncle Cosmo, in the other wing chair, said quietly, "Good God in heaven."

It seemed a bit blasphemous of the old man, very close to taking God's name in vain, something he never did. When he looked up from the *Pittsburgh Post-Gazette* in his lap, his eyes were two dark moons, wide and unyielding. Whatever it was he had read, it had to be bad.

Uncle Rex, on the couch with another section of the paper, mumbled, "What's the matter, Uncle? More stories of hauntings? Ghosts right here in the theater in Pittsburgh?"

"No, no, not ghosts." The old man shook his head. He seemed to be searching for the right words. "It's right here on the front page. Didn't you see it, Rex?"

"I don't suppose I did." Uncle Rex sighed. "Is it above the fold or below the fold?"

"Below."

"See there? The really important news is always printed above the fold, so what you're reading can't be anything earth shattering now, can it?"

"But I rather believe it might be—"

"If it's war news, I don't want to hear anything about it, unless you're going to tell me Germany surrendered."

"No," Uncle Cosmo said, "Germany hasn't surrendered."

"Well then, you can spare me anything else. I have just finished reading our latest glowing review, which I will happily share with everyone at rehearsal today. Other than that, what else matters?"

"Well, perhaps this matters to us since it has to do with the city we're traveling to next." Cosmo snapped the paper open so it was no longer doubled over at the fold, but hung in front of him like a full banner of bad news. "Within two days' time, it says here, Philadelphia has reported more than a thousand new cases of the plague. More than six hundred cases reported yesterday alone. The hospitals are so full they can't handle all the sick."

"The plague?" Mother echoed. Like me, she had been drifting off to sleep. She yawned and rubbed circles on her forehead to push the sleep away. "You mean that Spanish flu that's going around and that's got everybody all up in arms?"

"Well, people are certainly beginning to be up in arms now, my dear, and with good reason," Uncle Cosmo said. "Government officials knew the flu was especially dangerous this year, and yet in Philadelphia they went ahead with that confounded Liberty Loan parade in spite of it. While folks should have been taking precautions, the parade brought two hundred thousand of them together and gave the flu the perfect opportunity to spread. But it's not just in Philly, of course. It's everywhere and it's extremely deadly. Listen to this. It says here that in a number of cities, including Philadelphia, people are dying so fast the bodies are piling up at the mortuaries and there aren't enough coffins in which to bury them all."

Mother gasped and turned pale. I closed the book in my lap and sat up straighter.

Uncle Rex uncrossed and re-crossed his legs. "Well, the coffin-makers will just have to up their production," he said. "That's all there is to it. Dead bodies simply can't be left unburied for any length of time."

"But Rex," Mother whined, "as Cosmo said, Philadelphia is where we're going next. If there really is an epidemic, it sounds like we'll be walking right into the worst of it."

"Maybe things will be better by the time we get there."

"But that's only a few days off."

"Don't worry, Bernie. Every year there's flu, and every year the papers make a big to-do about it. Sells papers, you know."

"And yet," said Uncle Cosmo, "in some states, officials are closing public places—schools, churches, theaters. I wonder whether our circuit might be shut down for a time."

Uncle Rex frowned. "It doesn't say there that the theaters are closed in Philly, does it?"

Uncle Cosmo shook his head. "No, not in Philly. Not so far."

"And certainly not in New York?"

"No, there's no mention of New York."

"I can't imagine they'd shut down the theaters in New York for anything. Not even for death."

"Do you suppose so, Rex?" Mother asked. "What if all the theaters are closed when it comes time for our audition at the Palace?"

"That's weeks off yet, Bernie," Uncle Rex said. He turned the page of the paper and appeared to be scanning the headlines. "Surely this whole thing will have passed by then."

Uncle Cosmo looked incredulous. "My dear Bernadette," he said, "people are dropping like flies, and you're worried about the audition? And you, Rex—I should think you would take this seriously."

"Oh, I am, Uncle. I'd consider it a real setback if we have to postpone the audition, but as I say, that's weeks away and between now and then, the medical community has plenty of time to get a handle on the situation."

Uncle Cosmo sighed and shook his head. "Am I to believe you two callous creatures are really my brother's offspring? I wonder whether you might not have instead sprung from the loins of, say, Jack the Ripper?"

"You're your usual amusing self, Cosmo," said Uncle Rex without an upward glance, "but I really have no idea what you're talking about."

"No, I didn't think you would." He went back to reading the paper. After a moment, he said, "Now see here, this is what we're dealing with. This article reports that the symptoms are, and I quote, 'high fever, clogged airways, and delirium. At times, blood pours from noses, ears, and eye sockets. Victims lay in agony. Many have been known to drown in their own lungs. There have been cases of cyanosis reported in which the victim's body turns almost black, for which some are labeling this another Black Plague—'"

"Oh really, Cosmo!" Mother cried. "Must you—"

"'—and many die, delirious and incontinent, while struggling to clear their airways of a blood-tinged froth that also at times pours forth from their nose and mouth—'"

"Cosmo!"

"'—while others, once caretakers and now themselves stricken, must lie for days beside the corpses of their loved ones, too weak even to remove the dead from their homes—'"

"That's quite enough, Uncle!" Rex snapped. He tossed aside the paper, rose from the couch, and strode to the window, his hands clasped behind his back. "I don't believe we need all the ghastly details."

"Oh, but I think you do."

"Just because you enjoy the macabre doesn't mean we are all so inclined."

"And have you forgotten," Mother added, "that Anna's in the room? She's just a child."

I looked at Mother and then at Uncle Cosmo. He didn't appear apologetic. "I'm merely trying to get you to understand the severity of the thing," he said. "Perhaps we should speak with Stanley about Philadelphia."

Uncle Rex, who stood gazing out the window, said, "I'm sure Stanley is well aware of the situation and will make the right decision about the troupe's going on to Philly."

"But Rex," Mother said, "we *must* go on to Philly and from there to New York."

At that, Uncle Cosmo threw up his hands. "The only thing we *must* do, Bernadette dear, is protect ourselves and take every precaution against this appalling sickness."

For the first time, I spoke up. "But what can we do, Uncle Cosmo?" I was genuinely frightened by the thought of bleeding out of my eyes and drowning in my own lungs. It made me want to blockade myself in my corner bedroom of Mrs. Tuck's boarding house, a sort of self-imposed quarantine until the danger had passed.

"Well, Anna," Uncle Cosmo answered me pleasantly. "It just so happens the paper has printed a list of suggestions from the Surgeon General on how to avoid the flu. Now let me see … yes, here it is. First of all, he says you must stay away from crowds—"

"But how can we do that," I asked, "when every night there's a crowd at the theater?"

"Well, if you must be around people, he says to be sure to cover your coughs and sneezes," he went on, paraphrasing the news report. "Always wash your hands before eating … remember the three Cs, that is, clean mouth, clean skin, and clean clothes. Ah yes, this one is interesting. He suggests we don't let the waste products of digestion accumulate—"

"Good heavens!" Mother cried. "As though we would. Just who does the Surgeon General think we are?"

Ignoring Mother, Uncle Cosmo finished by saying, "And lastly, he recommends that when the air is pure, breathe all of it you can, and breathe deeply."

I took a deep breath, filling my lungs with the pure air of Mrs. Tuck's parlor. I held it for a moment, hoping it would somehow inoculate me against this dreadful disease that, on this otherwise quiet October morning, suddenly loomed large.

"Where's Gina?" Uncle Rex asked abruptly. He turned from the window and looked about the room as though she had somehow been hiding there the whole time.

"I don't know, Rex," Mother said.

"I know where she is," I offered, as I'd seen her from the kitchen window half an hour earlier when I went to get a glass of milk. "She's out back in the garden with her admirers."

"Her admirers?" Rex said. "What do you mean?"

"Remember those two fellows who saw her at the theater Sunday night and waited for her after the show? They've been here every day since, only now there's six of them, maybe seven."

"How did they know where she's staying?"

I shrugged. "I suppose she told them."

"Haven't they anything better to do on a weekday? Don't they go to school or have jobs? Well, anyway, Anna, go tell her to come in. It's fraternizing like that we don't need."

"Now you're thinking, Rex," Uncle Cosmo said. "Keep her from the crowds so she doesn't get the flu."

"Never mind that, Cosmo," Rex said. "We haven't heard of any deadly outbreaks here in Pittsburgh, have we? No, it's what she might do to them that's got me worried. The last thing we need is for one of those dandies to ask Gina to sing, and then heaven knows we'd all be in hot water." He looked at me again. "Well, what are you waiting for? Go tell her to come in."

I shrugged. "She won't listen to me, Uncle Rex."

"Tell her I said so. Tell her we'll be having lunch soon, then heading off to the theater for rehearsal."

Mother said, "And find our boys too and tell them our plans. Where are they, anyway?"

I shrugged again. "They're probably all upstairs crying because Gina's out back with the locals. Poor Ray thought he actually had a chance with her, but now he's finding out how fickle she is, the big flirt—"

"That's enough, Anna," Uncle Rex ordered. "Just go call her in. I'll tell Mrs. Tuck we're ready for lunch."

I wandered reluctantly through the house and out to the back porch. The day was sunny and the weather surprisingly mild, even warm for early October. From the porch, a wide expanse of lush green lawn rolled down to a large garden, tended to daily by a man in overalls and a dirty straw hat that Mrs. Tuck referred to as Dan the Flower Man. Though near the end of the growing season, the garden was still colored by late-blooming flowers. I recognized only goldenrod and mums, but Dan had told me his favorite fall perennials were snakeroot, tickweed, turtlehead, and sneezeweed. I thought he might be pulling my leg, but Mrs. Tuck assured me that her garden was filled with these every year.

Stepping off the porch, I noticed the pebbled clearing in the garden was crowded with young men who stood like a half-circle of sentinels around Gina, who herself sat regally on a stone bench clutching a handful of mums. One fellow had a foot on the bench and his arms on his knees. He leaned over Gina and whispered something in her ear that made her laugh.

Halfway across the lawn, I cupped my mouth with one hand and hollered, "Gina! Uncle Rex wants you to come in now! We're going to have lunch and then rehearsal."

Gina looked at me, laughed and called back in a sing-song voice, "I can't heeaarrr youuu!"

Drawing closer, I repeated, "Uncle Rex said for you to come in *now*."

Gina laughed again, and the young men joined her. The one with his foot on the bench said, "Ah, don't listen to her, Georgia. You don't need to rehearse. You already have the most beautiful voice in the world. Stay out here with us."

Gina lifted the flowers to her nose, then said demurely, "You know, don't you, that I'd stay out here with you forever, if I could."

A murmur of pleasure rippled through the crowd. Another of the admirers said, "And anyway, Georgia, you still haven't sung for us like you promised."

I stopped where I was, about ten feet from them. Uncle Rex was right to worry; Gina's singing for them could spell disaster for us. "If you don't come in now, Gina," I said, "you're going to be in big trouble."

"Ah, shove off," a third admirer said, looking at me. "Nobody's going to get in trouble."

I frowned at him before turning around and heading back to the house. Still, I was close enough to hear someone else mutter, "Say, who's the squirt, anyway? Your kid sister?"

"If she is," another said, "you got all the sweet and she got all the sour."

Everyone laughed at that, Gina the loudest of all. "No, she's not my sister," she said. "Of course not. She's ... well, never mind. She's nobody."

I drew up short and turned back slowly to glare at Gina and her passel of admirers. Through clenched teeth, I whispered what might have been the curse that changed everything: "I hate you, Gina. I hope you get the flu and bleed out of your eyes and die."

CHAPTER 11

They were all out there that night, all the young men from the garden, sitting right in the front row of the Gayety Theater where we were performing. I peeked from behind the curtain before the show started, and just the sight of them rekindled my fury. How dare they laugh at me? How dare Gina call me a nobody?

I'll show them, I thought. *I'll show them all exactly what their little snow angel is. A big fake. A big talentless fake.*

I had a plan. But could I carry it out?

"What are you doing, Anna?"

Startled, I turned. Gina stood behind me, hands on hips. She was in full costume, ready for our act, even though the evening's performance hadn't yet gotten underway.

"Nothing," I said defensively. "Just standing here."

"You were looking at the audience, and you know you're not supposed to do that. It makes you nervous. If you get the hiccups tonight, I'll kill you."

I knew then that I could do it. I'd had more than enough meanness dumped on me by Georgia Snow. Time to show her which one of us was driving the train and which was the hapless passenger. Tonight, I would take her for the ride of her life.

"Oh, don't worry, Gina," I said evenly. "I'm not going to get the hiccups."

She narrowed her eyes. "You sure?"

"Of course I'm sure." I tried to give her my best smile and even raised my right hand dramatically. "In fact, I promise I will not get the hiccups."

Her eyes said she wasn't convinced. She stepped to the break in the curtain, pulled it back an inch and peered through the crack. "Oh, heavens! All the fellows are here, right in the front row!" Letting the curtain drop, she swung back toward me and grabbed my arm. "One slip up from you, and I'll never speak to you again."

I almost laughed. She considered that a threat? To never have her speak to me again would be a welcome change in my life.

But I tried to look alarmed. "Have I ever messed up so far?" I asked. "Have I ever done anything at all other than make you look good?"

She dropped my arm and huffed. With one final glare, she stomped off toward the dressing room to await her curtain call.

Uncle Cosmo began to play promptly at seven o'clock. The evening's show was underway. I waited backstage as each act performed, ringing my hands and feeding my fury with thoughts of Gina and her young men in the audience. I paced the floor behind the curtain. Every time the audience applauded, or laughed, or sent up a sigh of satisfaction, I almost changed my mind. Did I have the nerve to do what I had determined to do?

Out on stage the Sokolov family finished their act, joined hands, and took a bow. They worked together, those cycling Russians. They supported—even encouraged—each other and, except for the times Mr. Sokolov head-smacked the boys for crashing their bikes during rehearsal, they seemed to get along. Why couldn't the Rycrofts?

Because Gina hated me, that's why.

But could I do this to my mother? To Uncle Rex? To Uncle Cosmo?

With a heavy sigh, I turned away from the stage and paced some more. Back and forth I walked, stewing over my plight, mulling over my intentions, until one more abrupt about-face slammed me right into Mr. Stanley.

"Watch out, Anna," he snapped. "You're always in the way. Why don't you go wait in your dressing room like you're supposed to, instead of being underfoot out here?" He waved a dismissive hand. "Go on, shoo."

He walked on, calling for Mr. Meriwether and Troubadour. I didn't shoo but stood frozen in place. My eyes narrowed, and I felt my jaw grow tight as I stared after Mr. Stanley. I was remembering the time, not so long ago, when he had laughed at me. *No one will ever clap for you*, he'd said.

That settled it. I didn't waver anymore. The course was set.

When our turn in the lineup came, I sang the first two songs beautifully. From atop the ladder I looked down over Gina as she went through the routine below, pretending to sing, then moving off toward the center of the stage to dance with the boys. From the stage she flirted with her admirers, waving her parasol and blowing the occasional kiss to the first row. Wild applause followed and catcalls from the local boys. I felt dizzy with the anticipation of what I was about to do.

Moments later, we began our signature song, "Little Snow Angel." The first three stanzas were a wonder; we had the audience in the palm of our hand, right where I wanted them. We were coming up on another grand finale, in which the lovely Georgia Snow would sing her final note and conclude the act with yet one more audience won over by her charm, her grace, her beauty, and, of course, her voice.

> They call me pretty snow angel,
> Halo for a hat.
> But when my lips touch yours, dear ...

Every other performance, I'd stayed the course, sticking to the lyrics as written by Uncle Rex. But not this time. This time I didn't sing, "You may question that." This time, I sang,

> ... when my lips touch yours, dear,
> You may smell a rat.

The audience tittered, as though they weren't quite sure they had heard what they heard. Surely, they were out there scratching their chins, whispering to their neighbors, "What was that she just sang?"

"It sounded like 'You may smell a rat,' but surely not!"

"Shhh. Listen!"

For I was on to the next stanza:

> They call me little snow devil,
> Ugly as can be.
> My breath like fish and sauerkraut,
> You'll want to run from me!

At that, the audience gasped, then roared with laughter. I watched with satisfaction as down on the stage, Gina stamped her foot, threw down her parasol and, turning to look up at me, screamed in fury. The four dancers, bless their showbiz spirits, tried to go on dancing but managed only to bump into Gina and each other. Luther haplessly tripped over the parasol and sprawled face down on stage. Commotion swirled around me as the curtain was quickly lowered.

Mr. Stanley reached me first. "Annalise! What the ... you know you aren't supposed to say devil! Just what do you think you're doing? You're going to ruin us—"

Then Uncle Rex was there, yelling at me with language far worse than the word devil. "What's the matter with you, Anna?" he hollered as he waved both arms in the air. "How dare you ruin the song, you little—"

Then Mother, ashen-faced, scurried toward me across the cluttered stage. She was fanning herself with a sheet of music, as though to keep herself from fainting. "What were you thinking, Anna? How could you do such a thing? Come down from there at once and explain yourself—"

And most amusing of all, Gina. "Let me at her! I'm going to strangle her with my bare hands—"

I sat on the top of the ladder with my chin resting on my palms, looking down at them with an expression that I hoped was appropriately smug. *That,* I thought, *is what Georgina Slump gets for calling me a nobody, and what the rest of you get for letting her believe it.*

CHAPTER 12

I was in big trouble and I knew it. Uncle Rex promised that punishment would be doled out as soon as he could think of a penalty severe enough to fit the crime.

I didn't care. I went to bed that night laughing and woke up the next morning feeling nothing but relief. Yet only thirteen years old, I'd shown them all who had the power in this family. I was the one who would make or break the act, and it was about time they recognized that fact and treated me with respect.

A little after dawn, I dressed and went downstairs for breakfast, fully expecting to receive my sentence. Whatever it was, it couldn't be worse than having to sing for Gina. I entered the dining room with my head held high. Mother, my uncles, Gina, and the boys were already there. I was received with cold stares, but before anyone could say anything, the phone rang somewhere in the house, and in the next moment, Mrs. Tuck bustled into the room, saying, "Mr. Rex, it's your manager. I told him you were having your breakfast, but he says it's important. He needs to speak to you right away."

A little shiver ran up my spine as Uncle Rex rose from the table and left the room. Maybe Mr. Stanley had been consulted concerning my punishment, and he was calling with his verdict. I lifted my chin a little higher and sat down at the last open seat at the table. "Would someone please pass me the eggs?" I asked casually.

Everyone looked at me as though I had no right to ask for anything at all, but finally Uncle Cosmo, at the far end of the table, lifted the platter, rose from his seat, and carried it down to me. "There you go, Anna," he said quietly. "And would you like some toast?"

I nodded. "Yes, please."

He handed me that platter too.

Before I could take a bite, Uncle Rex blew back into the room like an angry wind. "Philly shut down yesterday," he announced irately. "Schools, churches, theaters, everything. All closed. Not only Philly, but this morning all places of amusement have been closed across the entire state of Pennsylvania. That includes the Gayety right here in Pittsburgh."

Uncle Cosmo, seated again, settled his coffee cup loudly in his saucer. "I told you this thing was serious—"

"Stanley's disbanding the troupe till the epidemic's passed," Uncle Rex interrupted. "He says he has no choice since theaters everywhere are closed or closing. He wants everyone to go home in the meantime."

"Home?" Mother cried. "And where exactly is home for us?"

Edith Tuck stood in the doorway, hands clasped at the waist of her white apron. "Well, you can't stay here," she said firmly. "I'll have to close the boarding house. I can't have folks bringing in the flu."

"But Rex," Mother said, "where will we go?"

"I'm putting the boys on a train back to Chicago."

A chorus of protest rose up from the young men. They didn't want to go. They wanted to stay with us. Wherever we went to ride out the flu, that's where they wanted to be as well.

Uncle Rex rapped on the table with his fork. "Now see here," he said, once the room had quieted. "I'm responsible for your welfare and I'll decide what to do with you. You're going back to Chicago today and that's that."

His comment was met with a few half-hearted moans, but the boys knew there'd be no use arguing.

"Then I guess we'd better go pack," said Ray.

Uncle Rex nodded. "You do that."

Ray pushed away from the table reluctantly and stood. "Come on, fellas. Let's do as Mr. Rycroft says." He gave a sorrowful glance at Gina before saying, "But listen, Mr. Rycroft, sir, as soon as this whole thing's over, we want to go back on the road with you. We want to keep the act together. So you'll call for us, won't you, once the theaters are open again?"

The four hoofers seemed not to so much as breathe as they waited for Rex Rycroft to answer. Finally, my uncle sighed heavily and said, "Yes, Ray, I'll call for you as soon as I can. We'll keep the act going."

"Oh thank you, sir!" He waved an arm. "Come on, guys, let's pack and get ready to go to the station."

After they left, Mother pushed her plate away and asked again, "Rex, what about us? Where will we go?"

Mrs. Tuck, arms crossed, looked on silently. Gina, Uncle Cosmo, I ... we all waited to hear our fate.

Uncle Rex, still clutching his fork, tapped it on the table. It thudded dully on the white linen cloth. "Let me think, Bernie. There must be someone who owes me a favor, who'll take us in."

"Well, you can't stay here," Mrs. Tuck repeated.

Uncle Rex's lips formed a tight line, as though he were trying to hold back some words he knew shouldn't spill out. Finally he said, "Of course, Edith. I do understand—"

"And besides," Mother said, picking up the train of her earlier thought, "even if we had somewhere to go, how will we get there? I don't mind sending the boys home on a train but, well, think about it—trains are filled with people, and anyone could have the flu and—"

"I have a thought," Mrs. Tuck interrupted. "I have my late brother's Ford sedan in the garage that I'll sell you for cheap. Big enough to hold the lot of you. I inherited it last year, and I don't drive myself, so I've really got no use for it."

Uncle Rex brightened. "A sedan? That's the top of the line."

Edith Tuck nodded. "Ernie would never settle for anything less."

"Does it run?"

"Of course it runs."

"What year is it?"

"It's a 'sixteen. He only had it five months before he dropped with a heart attack."

"May I see it?"

"I'll get the keys."

Mother, Uncle Cosmo, Gina, and I watched them leave in silence. It seemed we had nowhere to go, but at least we now had a way to get there.

***

While Uncle Rex and Edith Tuck took the car out for a test drive, I sat on the back steps of the boarding house, thanking my lucky stars that the flu had broken up our act and at least temporarily postponed my punishment. I didn't care if the boys never came back, and I could only hope our present circumstances silenced the voice of Georgia Snow for good. If the dice kept rolling in my favor, we'd get to New York in time for Mother and Uncle Rex's audition at the Palace, the outcome of which could take us all dancing in a whole new direction.

While I congratulated myself on my good fortune, Uncle Cosmo opened the squeaky screen door and stepped out onto the porch, a sweater draped across his arm. "There's a bit of a chill in the air, Anna," he said.

"Is there?" I said. "I hadn't noticed."

"I thought you might need your sweater." He draped the sweater around my shoulders. "May I join you?" he asked, nodding toward the steps.

"Sure." I patted the wooden boards beside me and scooted over a few inches.

He eased himself down and settled in with a grunt. We sat in silence for a few moments. Finally, he said quietly, "You were very wrong to do what you did, you know."

I hung my head, pretending to be sorry. "I suppose you mean, changing the words to the song."

"That's exactly what I mean. But ..." He paused and patted my knee with one of his beefy hands. "I understand why you did it."

"You do?"

He nodded. "Of course. Gina has treated you with nothing but contempt since she joined the troupe. She's been very mean to you. No one has called her out on it, not even me, I'm sorry to say. I kept hoping Rex would put her in her place, but since he didn't, you had to."

I looked at my uncle, thankful that he did understand. "She hates me for no reason, Uncle Cosmo."

"Oh no. She has a reason, a very good one," he said.

"What? I never did anything to her."

"It's not because of anything you did. It's because she envies you."

"Envies me?" I shook my head. "She's the star. She's the one everyone adores and thinks is so wonderful."

"She's not really a star and you know it. And she knows it too, somewhere deep inside. It's all pretend, with nothing real about it. The only thing she knows for sure is that you have a future and she doesn't. Think about it, Anna. How far can you go on a borrowed voice?"

I thought a moment and realized my uncle was right. A person can't travel her whole life on someone else's talent. It was all an illusion, and illusions are fragile things. Gina was riding a passing wave, and that wave was bound to hit the shore and eventually recede. She had no future. But did I? "Do you think so, Uncle?" I asked eagerly. "I mean, do you think I have a future?"

"Without question, Anna. You have a rare talent. It will take you far."

"But … well, look at me, Uncle Cosmo." I lifted my skinny arms from beneath the sweater, the better for him to view my angular frame. "Whoever's going to think of me as Georgia Snow?"

My uncle laughed kindly. "First of all, you will never be Georgia Snow. You will be Annalise Rycroft, and that is far better. Second, you are a late bloomer, but don't worry, my dear, you will bloom in due time, and you will become all you were meant to be."

No one had ever told me what Uncle Cosmo was telling me now, not even my mother. I moved closer to him, tucked my arm in his and leaned my head on his shoulder. "I'm glad I have you, Uncle Cosmo," I said.

He patted my arm. "I'm glad I have you too, my dear."

"What do you think Uncle Rex and Mother will do to punish me?"

"I don't know. They haven't told me."

"Do you suppose, after the theaters open again, I'll have to go on doing Georgia Snow?"

"I suppose you will. It's where the money is for now— though hopefully not for long. But you'll be a good girl and go along with it while it lasts, won't you?"

I thought a moment. "I guess so, if you think I should."

"I think you should. We do have to eat, after all, and keep some kind of roof over our heads. Just in the past weeks there has been more money in the coffers than ever before, and not because of Georgia Snow, but because of you. There's a lot riding on those skinny little shoulders of yours, but you're a strong one, strong enough to carry the load."

His words made me feel important, and I liked the thought of helping to take care of him. "I'll do my best, Uncle Cosmo."

"I know you will, Anna," he said. "And don't forget, it's only for a time. Someday you will be the one standing in the spotlight. Mark my words."

I closed my eyes and smiled, dreaming of that spotlight. "Uncle Cosmo?"

"Yes, dear?"

"Do you suppose someday people will clap for me?"

"But of course. That's all part of the territory, isn't it? We perform, and the audience applauds, and that's the entire give and take of our lives as theater folks."

Uncle Cosmo sounded a little sad, though I couldn't imagine why. The future at last looked promising, and I finally sensed something in my heart that felt oddly like hope.

CHAPTER 13

After making some phone calls and sending out any number of telegrams, Uncle Rex was able to track down someone who owed him a favor, a man named Walt Spinner who lived with his wife, Anita, in the little town of Hockessin, Delaware. Unlike Albert Littleworth, who was indebted to Rex for saving his life, Walt was indebted to my uncle for reasons I wasn't supposed to understand and so wasn't told outright. I did overhear Mother mention a Mitzi LaRue the Tassel Twirler in the same sentence with Walt Spinner and something about a scandal, and Uncle Rex confirmed that yes, old Mitzi was our ticket out of Pittsburgh, and Walt was still plenty glad for Rex's intervention.

We tied our luggage to the roof and running boards of the late Ernie Tuck's Ford and, with one loud backfire of protest from the newly awakened engine, we started our journey east through the vast expanse of the entire state of Pennsylvania. Uncle Cosmo and his violin sat between Gina and me in the back seat. He spent much of the journey reading a variety of newspapers picked up along the way, often aloud. We grew tired of hearing about the flu, the sick and the dying, the overcrowded morgues, the numbers that we couldn't fathom. The day we skirted Philadelphia, three hundred people were dying in that city alone, although we had no way of knowing. Nor did we know that by the end of the epidemic, Philly would claim the greatest number of flu deaths of any city in the nation, 13,000 in all. Nor could we have imagined as we bumped along those Pennsylvania roads that this month of October 1918 would be the deadliest month in the history of the United States, with 195,000 people dying of flu.

We just wanted to get to where we were going. We wanted to get out of this miserable Ford Sedan and into a house where there were beds to sleep in and bathrooms to wash in and food on the kitchen table. At least we were headed in the right direction, as far as our future was concerned. New York City was just a hop away from Delaware, and Mother and Uncle Rex still had every hope and expectation that November 7 was going to be their lucky day at the Palace.

"Hey, listen to this," Uncle Cosmo said as he snapped and folded the Harrisburg *Patriot-News*. With one plump index finger, he pointed to his place. He cleared his throat and started to read.

"It seems that a little ditty has arisen from the ashes of our current national—nay, even international—epidemic, and it goes like this:

> I had a little bird,
> Its name was Enza.
> I opened the window,
> and in flew Enza.

"The now popular ditty originated in our grand state of Washington, in the Hotel Colville, to be precise. As the story goes, a little feathered visitor flew in through an open window of the hotel where it made itself at home among the potted plants in the lobby. Thus far, no one has had the heart to shoo the little fellow outdoors again, and in fact, the hotel staff have put out birdseed and are calling their winged guest by the name of Enza. When asked why they chose that name, the night clerk explained that he opened the window and 'in-flew-Enza.'

"Whether or not this story is apocryphal, it demonstrates the American spirit of cheerfulness and perseverance in the midst of national hardship. It is this very perseverance, the refusal to give up, that will get us through this epidemic and back on our feet as a nation."

Uncle Cosmo settled the newspaper on his lap and sighed. "Now isn't that lovely?" he said.

On the other side of him, Gina moaned and turned her face to the window.

From the front passenger seat, Mother hollered, "If I hear one more thing about the flu, Uncle Cosmo, I have half a mind to put you out, and you can just walk the rest of the way!"

"That goes double for me," Uncle Rex added.

I patted Uncle Cosmo's hand. "Don't listen to them," I said. "I thought it was very clever." The old man rewarded me with what might have been a smile.

Finally, three hundred miles, twenty-two hours, and three flat tires from where we started, we crossed the Pennsylvania state line and entered Delaware, which was officially closed. Uncle Cosmo had read the announcement aloud to us from one of his newspapers: "Whereas a very serious epidemic of influenza is now raging in the state of Delaware, all schools, theaters, motion picture houses, dance halls, carnivals, fairs and bazaars, billiard rooms, pool rooms, and bowling alleys in the State of Delaware shall be closed and kept closed until further notice."

"What a bore," Gina said with a sigh. "What will we do to pass the time?"

No one answered. We reached the town of Hockessin in the late afternoon. Autumn had settled in, and fingers of sunlight played with the leaves of the many trees that lined the streets, illuminating the reds, oranges, and yellows like an artist working delightedly with paint. Driving through the town, we passed few cars, saw few pedestrians on the sidewalks. The place was eerily quiet and yet so beautiful. How could anything so dreadful as illness and death be happening here in this place of color and light and beauty?

I was staring out the window in wonder when I heard Mother say, "We must be almost there, aren't we, Rex? Do you know where you're going?"

Uncle Rex drove with one hand while holding a crumbled sheet of paper in the other. His gaze turned from the road to the paper and back again. "Well, according to the directions on the telegram from Walt, we should be there in just another mile, maybe less," he said. "At the top of this incline, I'm to turn right off Lancaster Pike ... yes, I think I see the turn now."

We turned and found ourselves winding down a dirt lane through fields of apple trees, their leaves autumnal, their branches hanging heavy with fruit. Those apples that the trees had cast off congregated like throw rugs tossed over the ground. I cracked the window and breathed deeply; a faint scent of cider mixed with wood smoke hung in the air.

Up ahead, at the tip of a circular drive, appeared a two-story clapboard farmhouse, white with black shutters, a wispy gray cloud drifting up from one of the two chimneys. A man I assumed to be Walt Spinner sat in a straight-back chair on the porch, wearing a plaid jacket and smoking a cigar. He stood when we were still a short distance away, and I could see he was a very tall, very thin man, almost skeletal in appearance. His eyes were sunken and his cheekbones prominent, and atop his head was a scraggly bush of unkempt white hair. He didn't look like anyone who would get mixed up with a tassel-twirler named Mitzi, but I was thankful for the indiscretion—whatever it might have been—that brought us to this place.

At last, Uncle Rex eased the car to a stop and cut the engine. Walt Spinner crushed out his cigar on the porch railing and moved down the steps toward us.

"Well," Mother said quietly, "they sure live out in the middle of nowhere. And a good thing too. Maybe we'll be isolated enough that the flu won't find us."

Uncle Rex nodded in satisfaction. "We'll be safe here," he said confidently.

Walt Spinner had an open palm extended before Uncle Rex even got out of the car. The two men shook hands and my uncle introduced us all around. We were a ragamuffin group, tired, dirty, hungry, our luggage tied to the car every which way, but Mr. Spinner seemed genuinely pleased to see us. And that made us feel as though we had found the sanctuary we sought, a safe haven in which to hunker down while we waited out the storm.

We stepped up to the Spinner's porch with a sigh of relief. Footsteps echoed somewhere inside, and in another moment Anita Spinner was at the door, wiping her hands on her bibbed apron and smiling broadly. She was as squat and plump as her husband was tall and lean; they brought to mind the image of Jack Sprat and his wife of the nursery rhyme. I could almost see them sitting at dinner, licking the platter clean.

"Welcome, everyone," Mrs. Spinner said. "Excuse the way I look; I'm just making supper. Well, come on in and make yourselves at home."

It was as though we had known this friendly couple all our lives. What we didn't know was that the minute Anita Spinner stepped aside to usher us in, the winged bird of the popular ditty accepted the invitation as well, and "in-flew-Enza."

CHAPTER 14

For the first few days, since we were thrown together in this place of quarantine anyway, Gina and I called a truce. We passed the time wandering the acres around the farmhouse, collecting colorful leaves and plucking and eating apples from the trees. We even ventured to make an apple pie together, under Mrs. Spinner's supervision. She was an excellent cook, and three times a day we all gathered around the kitchen table and sated ourselves on her home-cooked meals. Mother, who couldn't cook at all, made herself useful by cleaning up and washing dishes and trading stories with Anita Spinner. I couldn't imagine two more different women: one a simple housewife, white-haired, plump, rosy-cheeked, her blue eyes flitting here and there behind wire-framed glasses; the other a sensual Vaudeville singer with her sights on the Palace in New York. But I don't think I ever heard Mother laugh quite so much, nor so genuinely, as she did in the hours she spent with Mrs. Spinner. For their part, Uncle Rex and Walt Spinner smoked cigars on the porch, ran errands into town, and chopped firewood for the fire that burned in the hearth every evening. Uncle Cosmo was content to be alone, settling himself in a wing chair by the fireplace where he listened to music on a hand-cranked Victrola, the same music over and over, as the Spinners had only five or six shellac records. More than once a scratching sound drew one of us to the front room where we found Uncle Cosmo asleep, the needle stalled in the final groove of the still-turning disk.

They were wonderful days, those first few days at the Spinners, and I thought that if we had to stay there forever, I would be happy. I loved the soft bed with the warm quilt and the feather pillows, the way the floor squeaked in the upstairs hallway when I walked, the scent of baked goods wafting from the kitchen at all hours, how the world outside looked like a painting framed by the lace-curtained windows. *This must be what it's like to have a home*, I thought. This ... being in a place where all the little things became familiar and beautiful at the same time, and where the people wanted you to be there, which had never been the case at the Littleworths. You can never be at home where the people don't want you, but for whatever reason, the Spinners wanted us, enjoyed our company, made us feel ... yes, at home. As I learned about their four children, all of whom had "escaped Delaware and scattered themselves to the wind," as Mrs. Spinner put it, I realized that the old couple was lonely for family too, and I was glad we could be there with them for a time.

On the evening of our fourth day there, I sank down onto the throw rug in front of the crackling fire, intending simply to be among the grown-ups and to listen to their conversation. I tried to keep my eyes open, to watch the flames shimmer and jump, the sparks flying upward and disappearing into the dark chimney. But I was tired, so tired. Everyone was gathered there in the front room, chatting quietly, sipping cups of after-supper coffee. I heard them, but their words were muted, like bees buzzing around rose bushes. The fire's heat touched me from the hearth, and yet I felt oddly chilled. Light and shadows danced beyond my lids. The rug felt rough beneath my cheek, and yet I couldn't lift my head to change positions, nor ask anyone to toss me a pillow from the couch.

As I lay there in half-dreams, I saw leaves falling from the apple trees, twirling earthward in slow motion. Round and round until, soundlessly, they settled on the grass. I heard Uncle Cosmo playing his violin, playing so slowly that each note stretched out like a banshee's wail. I felt myself floating weightlessly, as though the rug were suddenly a flying carpet, carrying me to distant places. And yet, my limbs were heavy, so heavy, a thousand pounds, solid stone. I couldn't move.

Then Mother's voice: "Anna, are you all right?"

And Uncle Rex: "She's just tired."

Mother: "Anna, dear, go on up to bed."

Muffled voices. Falling leaves. Long sorrowful notes.

Uncle Rex: "I'll carry her upstairs. She'll be fine in the morning. Too much fresh air. She's not used to it."

I felt myself lifted into Uncle's arms. He grunted slightly, staggered, steadied himself. I tried to open my eyes but couldn't. My head fell against his shoulder.

Then Anita Spinner: "Do you think she has a fever?"

Uncle Rex: "Hard to say. She's warm, but then, she's been lying by the fire."

A hand on my forehead, a clucking sound. Anita Spinner tsk-tsking. "I hope it's not …"

"She'll be fine in the morning," Uncle Rex said again. We moved across the room and up the stairs. Mother followed.

"Let me turn down the covers," she said.

Then, gently, Uncle Rex lowered me onto the bed. My head was a rock on the feather pillow. Someone slipped off my shoes, lifted the covers to my chin. I felt lips on my forehead, heard Mother's voice, "Good night, dear."

Leaves stopped twirling, the music went silent, the flying carpet landed, and everything went black.

***

In the morning, I was conscious enough to know that Gina was in the double bed beside me. The heat of her body reached me beneath the covers. She was on fire. I wanted to cry out and ask someone to put out the flames, but no words came.

A man was there, a stranger, with a black bag and a stethoscope in his ears. He was listening to the sounds in my chest. It was then that I became aware of how hard it was to breathe, to draw air into my lungs.

Through drowsy eyes, I saw the doctor rise from the side of the bed and toss the stethoscope around his neck. "It's flu all right," he said.

Someone gasped. Mother. "What can we do?"

From somewhere in the room, Walt Spinner's voice: "They can't stay here. I'm sorry, Rex."

I wanted to laugh. Not even Mitzi LaRue the Tassel Twirler could save us now. But my lungs ached and my head pounded and no laughter came.

"Of course," Uncle Rex said. "They need to be in the hospital. The best one, whatever it is. I want them to get the best medical care possible."

The doctor's voice: "The hospitals are all full."

"Full?" Anita Spinner. "How can that be?"

"There are just too many sick—"

"Even Wilmington General?"

"Yes. Wilmington General, Memorial, Delaware Hospital— all full. People are being turned away at the doors."

Walt Spinner: "What about the hospitals in Philly? Can we take them there?"

The doctor: "It's no better in Philly. In fact, it's worse. Much worse."

The room fell silent.

From some distant place, I heard Mother say, "Dear God in heaven, what shall we do?"

She wasn't one to pray, but maybe it was a prayer because after a moment, the doctor said, "I need to make a call. I'm going into town to use the phone at Bart's store. I'll be back as soon as I can."

Footsteps going down the stairs. I drifted into semi-consciousness and out again. Gina coughed and moaned in the bed beside me. I was afraid that if she got too close, the fire would burn me. I tried to turn away from her but couldn't. Instead, I began to sink again into strange fever-dreams. My body was heavy and inert, but my mind was a restless wanderer, flitting from one nonsense thought to another, from one roiling image to dozens more.

I watched the horror show play across my mind until the doctor's voice broke in: "It's all arranged. They've just opened a temporary infirmary down at the university where they're bedding the sick in Alumni Hall. An ambulance will be here within the hour to fetch the girls. I'll accompany them myself and will make sure they're settled and comfortable. They can have no visitors while they're there, of course."

In another moment, I felt a strong hand take my own. Uncle Cosmo. He had been a silent presence in the room, but I knew he was there. I wanted him to go with me. I wanted at least to say good-bye. To him, to Mother, to Uncle Rex, to the Spinners. I was afraid I'd never see any of them again.

***

Gina and I were placed side by side on cots in Alumni Hall. The Hall was a very old building, and the room where we landed was spacious, with a ceiling that seemed to stretch all the way to the sky. But the whole space was filled with the sick and the dying, with moans and coughs and murmured voices and quiet weeping that seeped into all the cracks and crevices, making it hard to breathe for lack of air. Nurses hovered over us wearing white masks that hid most of their faces. They were eyes only—tired, troubled eyes that came and went.

Despite everything, I felt myself gaining strength. Gina, too, seemed to rally. When we had been there for a time—a day, maybe two—we were able to reach out to each other across the narrow space that separated our cots. Her hand felt hot but comforting. Her eyes, wide and eerily bright, flitted about the room, as though she wondered where we were. Finally, her gaze settled on me.

"Oh Anna," she said, "I'm afraid."

She didn't look anything like Georgia Snow. She didn't even look very much like Georgina Slump. Her hair was darkened with sweat and plastered against her head. Her face was drawn and pale, with one bright scarlet dot on each cheek. Her lips, oddly enough, appeared almost blue. I squinted at her to see if her lips might look red through narrowed eyes. They didn't.

"You're going to be all right, Gina," I assured her. "I know you will. See, already we're better, aren't we? We can talk with each other, at least."

She wetted her blue lips with her tongue. Then she coughed, winced, and coughed again. "We were only getting started … Georgia Snow … the whole act … it could have been something great."

"It still can be. I messed it up, but when we get back on the road, I'll make it right. I promise."

"Anna, I was awful …"

"No, you weren't. You were wonderful. Really you were."

"No, I mean, to you. I was awful to you. I'm sorry."

Silence. Then, "It's all right. Try not to think about it. Get some rest if you can. We'll both be better soon."

"We'll be friends then, won't we—when we get better?"

"Of course, we will."

"Promise?"

"I promise."

We lay there for a time, holding hands between the cots. I don't know whether it was minutes later, or hours later, or days later, but at length I felt her hand go limp and slip from mine. A nurse appeared and, bending over Gina, lifted her hand into the bed and tucked it under the covers. Then, maybe minutes or hours or days later, that same nurse came back with another nurse and together they wrapped Gina up in the sheets, lifted her in that linen cocoon, placed her on a gurney, and rolled her away. I knew she wasn't coming back, but I couldn't cry out because I was myself sinking once again into the deep end of the disease, where I knew I too might drown in my own soggy, flu-riddled lungs. I wondered briefly, before I went under, whether the shroud of Georgia Snow was the last thing I would ever see.

CHAPTER 15

"Annalise. Anna, wake up."

Slowly, I became aware that someone had a hand on my shoulder, gently shaking once, twice, three times. I felt my brows tighten, my face frown.

"Anna, you must get up, lass. I have something to show you."

I think I moaned. Someone did, because I heard it. I didn't want to get up. I wanted this person, whoever he was, to go away.

"Hilli-ho, Anna dear. Open those eyes. That's a girl!"

I opened my eyes. Hovering over me was an old man in a Welch wig, a capacious black waistcoat, and a burgundy cravat. He seemed vaguely familiar, but I couldn't place him.

He straightened and clapped his hands. "Yo ho, there you are! Come along then. We haven't any time to waste."

"But I don't understand," I said. "What do you want?"

"I have something to show you."

"But who are you?"

"Ah!" He lifted his chin. "I beg your pardon. I haven't introduced myself. I'm Fezziwig."

"Fezziwig?"

"That's right."

My eyes narrowed. "Do you mean, Old Fezziwig in the story about Scrooge?"

"That's the one."

"The one what?"

"I am he. Old Fezziwig, to whom Ebenezer Scrooge was apprenticed."

We stared at each other a long moment. Finally, I said, "I don't believe you."

He shrugged slightly. "Very well, but I've been charged with taking you somewhere, so you'd best come at once."

"But I'm sick!"

"Are you?" He bent toward me, pulled out a monocle from the pocket of his coat and studied my face. His eye behind the glass moved up and down. "You look perfectly well to me."

I looked down at myself. I lay on the cot in Alumni Hall, but I was on top of the covers, fully dressed. Sitting up, I looked around. The room was just as it had been when I arrived, quietly busy with the activity of the dying. Every cot was occupied, the one beside me holding someone I didn't know, someone who wasn't Gina.

I stood, and discovered I was strong. "But I don't understand," I said to this man who claimed to be Fezziwig. "I was sick with flu. It was a terrible sickness. I might have died."

"But you didn't, did you?"

I looked down at myself once more and had to agree. "No, I didn't die."

"Then you obviously got better," he said. "Come along, then." And he held out his hand to me. I took it.

"Where are we going?"

"You'll see."

We started walking, and with the first step we weren't in the Hall anymore. We were in a town, and it was night. We walked by lamplight through the quiet residential streets. A few carriages clip-clopped by. And a couple of cars, Model Ts.

"I know," I said. "I'm dreaming, aren't I? I *am* sick and this is a fever dream. Something my brain has cooked up, the way an undigested bit of beef made Scrooge dream about Marley, right?"

He didn't answer.

I went on. "You look just like that illustration of Fezziwig in my book. And you know I've read that old book so many times, your face is as familiar to me as my own mother's face. Of course I'd dream of you."

We turned a corner, and Old Fezziwig nodded toward a house. "Almost there," he said. "That's the one."

I stopped, cocked my head. "I know that house," I said.

"You ought to," Fezziwig said, tugging at my hand and pulling me along. "You lived there for a time when you were a very small child."

"I don't remember much."

"It was your grandfather's house. Your father's father. You stayed here a few months when you were three years old."

"We're in Connecticut, then."

He nodded. We turned up the front walk and headed toward the porch. "Come along inside. We don't have much time."

"But we can't just walk right in."

But we were already in, standing in the front room, a dimly lighted parlor where a little girl sat in a rocking chair by the empty fireplace. I let go of Fezziwig's hand and tiptoed toward the child. Suddenly weak, I dropped to my knees beside the chair and stared. "It's me," I whispered. "It's me, Mr. Fezziwig, and I'm holding … he's real, isn't he? The baby is real."

For in my arms was the baby of my dreams, wrapped in a quilt with pink and blue lambs embroidered on it. Tucked into the quilt with the baby was the small velveteen bear with the black button eyes and the sewed-on smile.

Fezziwig's hand touched my shoulder. "Yes, Anna, he's real."

"But I don't understand. Who is this baby, Mr. Fezziwig?"

"He is your brother Henry."

"My brother?"

"Yes. You think you only dreamed him up, but I assure you, he's quite real."

"My brother Henry," I repeated, marveling at the thought. I knew that he was real because all my life I had been missing him. "But ... what on earth happened to him?"

"We will have to watch and see."

In another moment, as though on cue, a man entered the room. I recognized him. He was the piano player from the Chaplin movie I had seen with Mother. He was my father. He brushed past me and Mr. Fezziwig as though he didn't see us. He *didn't* see us, I decided—didn't see the me that I was now, only the me that I was then.

He held out his hands. "Say good-night to him now, Anna, and let me have him. It's getting late." He pointed to a clock ticking on the mantle. "Eight o'clock already. Bedtime."

"But I want to stay here with him all night, Daddy," I said.

My father chuckled. "Well, you can't. Come on now, give him here."

He wiggled his fingers, and I heard my small self sigh and saw myself hand over the baby. Mother came into the room then, a younger version of herself, wearing a floor-length robe, her long hair in a single braid down her back. "Come on, Anna, I'll tuck you in."

Fezziwig and I watched Mother take me from the room, heard our footsteps on the stairs. Father sat in the chair I had just abandoned. A few moments later, Mother returned, sat in the chair opposite Father.

Her face was ashen and pinched. "Are you sure we're doing the right thing, Charles?"

Sometime between my father's coming into the room and my leaving, my father's countenance had turned to stone. He looked at Mother with vacant eyes. "We've been all through this, Bernadette."

"Yes, but Charles—"

"We can't keep him. You know that. Think of what it would do to us, to our future."

"But maybe there's another way ..."

"There is no other way."

"And Anna? She'll ask questions. She's old enough to know."

"We'll tell her he has gone to a place where he will be taken care of, and that will be the truth. I suspect she will soon forget about him, she's so young. Now, I suggest you go on upstairs. Get some rest. Early rehearsal down at the theater tomorrow."

My mother stood, and in the dim light I saw that her face, too, had turned to stone. She took two steps, stopped by Father's chair, tentatively reached out a hand as though to touch the baby. Father's voice interrupted her. "Better if you didn't, Bernadette."

She paused, her hand hanging in the air like a trembling leaf. She let it fall to her side. And then she left the room.

In an instant, the clock on the mantle moved ahead two hours. Out in the street, we heard the clopping of a horse's hooves. Father untucked the baby from the quilt, laying it and the stuffed bear aside. From beside the chair he picked up a small blanket and wrapped the baby in that instead. All the while, the baby slept silently.

There was a quiet rap at the door. Father went to answer it, carrying Henry in his arms. He opened the door and nodded to the man outside. They spoke; I couldn't hear their words.

Tears slid down my face; I let them fall. "Father gave Henry away," I whispered.

Fezziwig nodded. "Yes, so it appears."

"But why? And where was he taken?"

"I can't tell you that, my dear. My task was only to bring you this far. Someone else will have to show you where he went."

"But who?"

"Here he comes now."

I turned to see a boy about my own age—twelve, maybe thirteen—enter the parlor. He wore a rather tattered coat and a cloth cap on top of his blond head. He was obviously not as well off as Fezziwig.

"I'll take it from here, Fezziwig," he said confidently. But he didn't say here, he said 'ere, a sure sign he came from the working class of London.

I turned back to say good-bye to Old Fezziwig, but he was gone.

***

He had to be another character from *A Christmas Carol*, though I wasn't sure which one. He reminded me of Tiny Tim, but he didn't have a crutch.

"Come on, then, Anna," he said, holding out his hand. "Let's go."

But I didn't want to go until I knew who I was going with. "I don't suppose you're Tiny Tim?" I ventured. Maybe Scrooge had given the Cratchits enough money for Tim's medical care. Maybe he had grown strong after the story ended and had thrown away the crutch.

But the boy shook his head. "I am Tiny Tim's brother. His younger brother."

"Then you should be only five or six. You don't look five or six to me."

"I can be any age I want."

Frowning, I said, "I don't understand."

"I don't expect you to understand," he replied. "How could you?"

He had dropped his hand. We stared at each other expectantly. "Well," I said finally, "you know my name. What's yours?"

"I'm afraid I can't tell you."

"But why not? You have a name, don't you?"

"Sure I have But Mr. Dickens chose not to tell it in the story. That's all right. Mr. Dickens knows my name, and that's right good enough for me."

"Do you mean to tell me you don't know yourself what your name is?"

He laughed then, a hearty laugh. "Of course I do, silly."

"But what should I call you?"

"You may call me Boy Cratchit."

"But that's not a name at all!"

He shrugged. "It'll have to do, I'm sure."

"But why didn't Mr. Dickens tell your name? He gave everyone else a name."

"Oh no, he didn't, actually. My sister closest to me in age also isn't named. Now, my two older sisters are Martha and Belinda, and my older brother is Peter, and everyone knows Tiny Tim, but my sister and I are simply called boy and girl. That's it. To everyone who knows the story, we're Boy and Girl Cratchit."

"That doesn't seem fair at all."

He shrugged again. "As I said, Mr. Dickens gave me a name, but he didn't think you needed to know what it is. He had his reasons, sure. Now, enough about names. I've someplace to take you. Come along then."

He held out his hand again. This time I took it. His skin was rough and callous, but at the same time warm and comfortable.

"Are you going to show me where they took my brother?"

"Yes. Where they took him and where he is now."

"Has he been in the same place all this time?"

"That's right. All this time."

We were outdoors again, and it was day. We moved through woods, past streams, valleys, a town, more woods, another town. We were walking but not walking. Flying, but not really flying, as we weren't above the ground. In a way we were floating, or flowing, maybe—yes, that's it, flowing the way water flows within the banks of a river. Moving forward effortlessly, without the need to walk.

"Do we have far to go?" I asked.

"Yes, somewhat, I suppose. And we can't dally."

"But are we still in Connecticut? Is my brother in Connecticut?"

"Yes. We're almost there."

Just as he said those words, we reached a long, tree-lined drive with tall pines reaching toward the sky on both sides. We slowed then and began to take real steps. In another moment, our destination came into view. I gasped as I took it in.

"Do you mean to tell me that Henry lives here? In this mansion?"

For what rose up before us was a magnificent three-story, redbrick structure with a wide columned porch, a mansard roof, and a cupola on top like a crown. And the windows! So many windows. I could only imagine the light that played in the rooms inside.

"Yes," Boy Cratchit said with a nod. "This place is where he lives."

For a moment, my heart was filled with hope. Henry must have been given to a rich family. I couldn't imagine why, but maybe the reason didn't matter. Maybe the only thing that mattered was that he had been offered a home. He hadn't been shuffled from hotel to cheap hotel all his life as I had. Imagine living in so beautiful a dwelling and never having to leave!

"So this is where he has been these past—how long has it been now? Ten years? Why, he must be ten years old by now," I whispered. "He must be so happy here."

My companion stopped. He looked at me and squeezed my hand. I tried to smile, but the look on his face held me back. His eyes glistened, as though he were going to cry. "Anna," he said, "I wish I weren't the one to bring to you here. I told him we shouldn't do it, told him we should leave well enough alone, but he wouldn't listen. He said you needed to know. He said it was important."

"Who are you talking about? Who's he?"

"Marley, that's who. He's always the one who decides such things."

"Decides what things?"

"Who needs to be told. He's the messenger, you know. Always has been. Always going here and there to tell people, that Marley."

"Do you mean, Scrooge's business partner? Jacob Marley?"

"The one and the same. Old dead Marley."

I shook my head. I was near tears myself now. "I don't understand. I don't understand any of this."

"You will." He tugged at my hand. "Come along. We can't put it off no longer."

I was suddenly afraid, and my stomach turned as we stepped up to the porch and entered the mansion. And then we were inside. And there was little light, despite the many windows. We entered a dim, shadowy place that smelled of mold and rancid food and human waste. Women dressed like nurses moved about the long front hall and down the halls that stretched out on either side. They pushed carts and wheelchairs, moving past scantily clad bodies curled up on benches, on chairs, on the floor. A chorus of mumbling permeated the place, and moaning, and occasional screams.

This was no mansion and never had been. This was some kind of asylum. I had heard of such places, but never had I seen one.

I squeezed Boy Cratchit's hand. "I can't go any farther," I said. "I don't want to see him. Don't make me see him."

"I'm sorry, Anna," he said. "But you must."

"But why?"

"Because you need to know."

"No! I don't. I know enough already."

"Come along. I'll shut your eyes to the worst of it, but you must see Henry."

I began to cry. My legs were so weak I could scarcely walk, but somehow we were climbing an impressive staircase up to the second floor. Here the halls were empty, save the occasional cart or unused wheelchair pushed to the side. The doors to the rooms were closed, and each one had a window without glass in the center. Here and there an arm protruded from those windows, hands sagging at the wrists like dead flowers. At other doors, the windows framed faces, gaunt, colorless faces with wild eyes that seemed to see even greater horrors than I was seeing in that place. Here, too, as on the ground floor, the mumbling and moaning continued, haunting wails that chilled me to the bone.

At last, we stopped before an open door. I willed myself to look into the room. The place was sparsely furnished—a bed, a small table, a straight-back chair. The only light came from one small, grimy window on the far wall. A small figure lay on the bed, directly on the mattress, as there were no linens. Nor was there a pillowcase for the pillow that cradled his head. Both mattress and pillow were thin and ragged, sorrier than any I had seen in even the worst hotel. The boy wore something like a hospital gown; it might have been white once but now was a dirty shade of gray. It was much too large for him, as small as he was—he was scarcely more than skin and bones. His legs were covered with small, open sores and, to my horror, I saw that his left ankle was shackled; he was chained to the metal railing at the foot of the bed. And yet he slept peacefully, one lanky arm thrown above his head, the other at his side. Stepping closer, I peered at his young face. I saw now what I couldn't see when he was a baby—the creaseless eyes, the flat nose, the tip of the too-large tongue that poked out between his colorless lips. His neck was short and thick, his ears protruding.

"Henry," I whispered. "Oh, Henry." My hands clenched into fists; I lifted them to my heart. Tears flowed down my cheeks. "He's … he's …"

"He's what they call an idiot," my companion finished for me, saying what I could not say.

An idiot. A lunatic. A moron. I knew all the words to describe one such as he. And now I knew why Mother and Father had given him away. He was a burden. He would have held them back, interfered with their dreams.

A nurse swept into the room, carrying a tray. She was young and pretty, and she stepped lightly, almost as though she were dancing. She placed the tray on the little metal table beside the bed. "Time to wake up, boy," she said, not unkindly. "I have your supper."

She shook Henry awake, then hoisted him up so he was sitting with his back against the wall. The chain on his ankle rattled when he moved. The nurse settled the pillow behind Henry's back, then stood as though to survey her handiwork. "There we go. Are you comfortable like that?"

Henry opened his eyes, blinked, looked dazed. He lifted his gaze to the young woman's face but showed no recognition.

"Well, then," she said. "Let's see what we can do with this supper, shall we?"

She pulled the straight-back chair to the bed, pulled a large linen napkin from the tray, and spread it across Henry's chest. Then, settling the tray on her lap, she lifted a spoonful of whatever was in the bowl to Henry's lips.

"What's that she's feeding him?" I asked.

My companion shrugged. "It looks like the gruel that Charles Dickens fed to Oliver Twist when he was in the orphanage. Do you know the story?"

"Yes, I know it. He asked for more and was thrown out in the street."

"That's right. But old Oliver, he got his happy ending, didn't he?"

I didn't respond. I was thinking of Henry, watching him eat, watching the lumps of oatmeal dribble down his chin. The nurse dabbed at his mouth with the napkin. "That's a good try, boy, but you're getting more on your face than in your mouth. Shall I sing to you again like I did yesterday? That seemed to help now, didn't it?"

She began to sing. I didn't recognize the song, but it seemed a lullaby, something about shiny stars and a glowing moon and sweet dreams. Her voice was untrained but pretty.

"At least," I said, "this woman is nice to him."

"For now. She hasn't been here long."

"What does that mean?"

"She'll turn hard. They all do eventually."

For a while, I don't know how long, we listened to her sing to Henry and feed him as though he were a baby. I tried to connect the child in the bed with the baby in my dreams, but I couldn't see them as one. Didn't want to see them as one, nor even to believe what I was seeing. At one point, he paused in his chewing and smiled at the nurse. Tears rose to my eyes again. How could he be here like this—chained to a bed, eating a tasteless and surely insufficient meal—and yet still smile?

"There now, boy," the nurse said. "I'm glad to see you like your supper."

But it wasn't that he liked that miserable gruel, I was sure of that. He was smiling because ... that was his heart. That was my brother's heart.

"I wish she would stop calling him boy and call him by his name."

"He has no name," my companion informed me.

"He does too!" I turned to him and actually stomped my foot. "His name is Henry."

"Not here, it isn't. That chap who dropped him off didn't give a name. And so he was assigned a number, and he's never had a name since. But that's how it is with so many of them who are left here."

"So everyone just calls him boy?"

Young Cratchit hesitated a moment. Then he said, "That. Or worse."

I turned my gaze from him back to Henry. "What kind of a place is this?" I asked quietly.

"A place where they put the surplus population," young Cratchit said.

"But I thought Scrooge was talking about the poor."

"He was. The poor. And the sick, the feeble-minded, cripples, criminals, those who are mad. To Scrooge, most of the world was surplus population."

My jaw clenched, and my hands became fists again. "That's a lie," I said.

Cratchit nodded. "That's what Scrooge came to understand. But you see, Anna, there are hundreds, maybe thousands, out there who bear the name of Ebenezer Scrooge. That's why Marley still walks the earth, looking for people to warn. He never rests, you know, because there is always one more person who needs to be told."

"And I am one of them?"

"Yes."

The nurse wiped Henry's face one last time, put the napkin beside the bowl, and set the tray back on the table. "Get some sleep now, boy," she said quietly. She rose and moved the chair back against the wall.

"Cratchit?" I asked.

"Yes, Anna?"

"What will become of him?"

"Someone else will tell you that."

"But who?"

The nurse helped Henry settle into the bed, the chain on his ankle rattling again as he moved. But even as he lay still, the rattling continued, and only grew louder. The nurse lifted the tray, and I watched her leave the room, and even as she walked through the door, someone else came in.

That someone was a man in a waistcoat, tights and boots, his disheveled hair tied back into a pigtail. His body was transparent, so that I could see right through him, all the way to the two buttons on the back of his coat. He was wrapped all around with chains that flowed from him like metal appendages, long lengths of chains made up of cashboxes, keys, padlocks, ledgers, deeds, and heavy purses wrought in steel.

I gazed at him, trembling. The man who was to show me Henry's future was old dead Marley himself.

***

The chains rattled dreadfully as he extended his hand to me. "Come, child," he said. His hollow voice reached me as though from the end of a long tunnel. I slumped to the floor in fear and buried my face in my hands.

"Wherever it is you're taking me, I don't want to go," I wailed. "I've changed my mind. I don't want to know what becomes of Henry."

"Give me your hand, Anna."

I peered through my fingers. His translucent hand hovered in the air inches from my face. "But you're not real," I said. "I can't take hold of you."

"Oh, I am real, Anna. Very real. And I'm here for your own good."

"No, I don't believe it. I don't believe any of this." I wrapped my arms around myself then, as though suddenly cold. I tried to look at Marley but couldn't. With my eyes to the floor, I said, "You're probably what Scrooge said you were—an undigested bit of beef, or a blot of mustard, or a crumb of cheese—"

"But you haven't eaten for days, except for sips of broth. You've been sick, remember?"

"That's it, then. Fever gives a person strange dreams. You're nothing but a dream, an awful nightmare."

"Think what you will. But what if Ebenezer Scrooge hadn't listened? He would be in chains today, as I am."

I didn't respond. I was trembling; even my teeth began to chatter.

"Anna," he went on, though his voice took on a certain tenderness. "I am here so that you might not end up in chains—as you might, if you refuse to heed my warning."

"But I'm afraid of what you're going to show me. Henry can't have a happy ending, not like in a storybook. I don't want to know his future."

"But the future isn't fixed as yet, just as it wasn't for Scrooge. I'm only here to show you what might be."

"And I suppose you expect me to set things right, the way Scrooge did."

"I don't expect you to do anything. I'm only giving you a chance. Now come; I have much to show you."

I relented then and, taking a deep breath, I reached for his hand. Though translucent, it had an unpleasant solidity to it. Against my own skin, his hand felt scaly and cold, like a dead fish. The moment we touched, we were outside on the grounds behind the asylum. Looking over my shoulder, I glanced up at the imposing brick structure, at the window I thought might be Henry's room. I wished I had been able to speak to him, to let him know somehow that I was there, that I had seen him, that I knew he was alive.

"Come along, Anna," Marley urged. "It's over this hill."

We climbed the slope, and at the top, Marley paused. I stood beside him and looked out over an ordinary field of grass and clover that stretched out ahead of us and finally ended at the edge of a woods.

"Well," I said, "I don't see anything."

"Yes," Marley said, "that's the point."

"What's the point?"

"That there's nothing here. Nothing you can see, anyway."

"You're talking in riddles. Why don't you just tell me what you mean?"

His chains rattled, as though he were suddenly angry. But when he spoke, his voice was calm. "This is where they buried them."

"Buried who?"

"The patients from the asylum, of course."

"But where are the stones? Don't the graves have markers?"

"No," Marley said. "Nothing marks the place where those people lie."

I shivered. I didn't want to ask, but after a moment, I did. "I suppose my brother is here."

The ghost nodded. His chains clattered. "His body is laid to rest here. Somewhere in this potter's field."

"But couldn't they have used something to mark the place?"

"And what would it say? Here he had no name. No birth date."

"What about his death date? Did they note the day he died?"

"Probably. But there was a small, contained fire in the basement where all the records were stored. Small, but large enough to destroy the records of the people who reside within those walls now. It's as though they had never been."

I let that sink in. Finally, I said, "But Henry was. I held him when he was a baby. I just now saw him, up there in that room." I pointed in the direction of the asylum.

"Yes," Marley agreed, but that was all he said.

"How did he die?"

"He died of cold, starvation, deprivation."

"What about the nurse? The one young Cratchit and I saw feeding him. Did she stop taking care of him? Did she grow hard the way Cratchit said she would?"

Marley's ghostly head moved from side to side. "She was fired for complaining about the care of the patients. She wasn't there for long."

"She was fired for being kind?"

"Are you surprised?"

"Yes. I mean, no. I mean … I suppose Cratchit showed me one of the few moments Henry was treated with kindness. Why?"

"To show you that Henry was human. That there was something in him that responded to goodness."

"And yet he was allowed to die. And to be buried here in a pauper's grave."

Old Marley didn't respond. He just kept looking out over that field.

"If what you're showing me is the future, can Henry be saved?" I asked.

"With proper care, yes. He could live reasonably well into adulthood, if someone cared for him."

"Mother knows he's here, doesn't she?"

"Of course. She put him here, along with your father."

"How could they be so cruel?"

"Cruelty is a common trait of humankind."

"If I ask her to save him, will she?"

"No."

"Then what am I to do? I'm only a child myself."

He gave me no answer. Instead, we were moving again. "We must go," he said. "I still have more to show you."

"But what else is there?" I said. "What else do I need to know? My brother is dead. I wish I had never known he was once alive."

"But you see—"

"Wait!" I stopped abruptly, tugged at his hand. "Did you hear that?"

The chains about him rattled and clanked as he turned first one way and then another, listening. "What is it, Anna?"

"Stand still and stop making such a racket with your chains. Listen! Someone's calling me. Don't you hear it?"

We both stood perfectly still. I hardly dared to breathe, and if Old Marley needed to draw in breath—which perhaps he didn't since he was dead—he, too, ceased to inhale.

And then it came, like the smallest whisper of wind at first, then gathering strength enough to form a word. *"Annalise!"*

I turned expectantly toward Marley. "There! Did you hear it?"

"I'm not sure. I—"

"Shh! There it is!"

"Anna, darling, wake up."

"It's Mother. She's calling me. I have to find her."

"But you can't. I haven't finished showing you all that I need to show you."

"Anna, dear, be a good girl and listen to your mother."

"That's Uncle Cosmo!"

Old Marley's chains churned up a terrible ruckus as he lifted his arms. "Don't go, Anna. We only need a little more time—"

"Look, Uncle, she's opening her eyes!"

Jacob Marley gave off a most fearful moan. Then he seemed to be joined by other moaning spirits, but I couldn't be sure. He began to grow more and more translucent until he disappeared altogether, his leave-taking punctuated by one last rattle of his chains.

***

I felt a hand on my cheek. Mother's hand. I willed my eyes to open, and a blurry form appeared above me, slowly settling into the shape of Mother's face. She was crying and laughing at the same time. "Oh, Anna," she said, "you're all right! You're going to be all right!"

Someone else appeared beside the bed. Uncle Cosmo. "Thank God," he said quietly. "You've come back to us. We couldn't bear to lose you too."

I tried to speak, but my mouth was too dry to form the words.

"Uncle," Mother said, "hand me the water glass."

With Mother's help, I sipped a little water. It felt soothing on my tongue.

"Don't try to talk, darling," Mother said.

"Just get some more rest," Uncle Cosmo said.

I shook my head. "Gina?" I whispered.

Mother glanced at Uncle Cosmo, then looked back at me. "Don't think about anything right now except getting better." She tried to smile, but her lips trembled. "We were allowed to bring you back to the Spinner's farm, once your fever broke and your lungs began to clear. The doctor said he thought you would make it, so we were allowed to bring you home."

Home. I had no home. We had no home because we were always on the road, always traveling here and there ... and then I remembered.

"Henry," I whispered.

Mother touched my face again, brushed the hair back from my forehead. "What is it, darling?"

"My brother," I said, more urgently now. "Henry. You have to save him. You—"

Mother's eyes widened and she drew back. "You have no brother, Anna. What are you talking about?"

"I saw him. In the asylum. He was starving, and they're going to let him die!"

I was crying now, but Mother brushed away my tears with the palm of her hand. "Darling, you've been dreaming. It was the fever. It must have given you terrible dreams."

"But I saw him! He was chained to the bed by his ankle. He was so skinny. He was nothing but bones."

"You mustn't let yourself get upset or you won't get better." She lifted her anxious gaze to Uncle Cosmo. "Tell her, Cosmo. Tell her that she has no brother, that she has been having a terrible dream."

I turned toward Uncle Cosmo. His mouth hung open, as though he wanted to speak but didn't know what to say. Finally, he shook his head slowly and patted my shoulder. "Go back to sleep, Anna. That's a girl."

As to what happened in the next moment, I don't clearly remember. I might have called them both liars, or I might have simply slipped back into sleep. Either way, it doesn't matter. It wasn't long after my illness that my star began to rise, just as Uncle Cosmo had predicted, and as I settled into the spotlight on the stage of my own life, Henry moved farther and farther back into those dark and silent places in the wings.

PART 2

1932–1933

CHAPTER 16

A knock came at the dressing room door. "Ten minutes, Miss Rycroft."

"Thank you, Mr. Sedgwick."

I gazed at myself in the mirror. Tonight, unlike most nights, I studied myself with a critical rather than an admiring eye. I was no longer the skinny little girl who suffered hiccups because of stage fright. No longer did I have to perform atop a ladder, lending my voice to someone else, someone prettier and more appealing. The years had grown me up and filled me out to just the right shape, and common consensus claimed that I was beautiful.

But for how much longer, I wondered. Today was May 21, 1932, and it was my birthday. I was now twenty-seven years old, not exactly in the first bloom of youth by anyone's standards, much less those of the theater. No doubt I could pass for younger; there were as yet no telltale wrinkles, no gray hairs, no sagging skin around my jaw or neck. But still … I understood now why Mother had cried on every birthday. Surely, she had felt as I did today, wanting to freeze time, wanting to preserve both youth and beauty so as to go on living the dream indefinitely.

Because that was what I was living—my dream—and I was far more successful than Mother had ever been. She never auditioned at the Palace—but I did. I was only just recovered from the flu in January 1919 when Mother took me by train to New York and coaxed me into the spotlight on that grand and intimidating stage. She didn't audition herself because the driving force behind her act was gone. Not only Gina had succumbed to the flu, but Uncle Rex had as well. The epidemic that annihilated nearly twenty-two million people worldwide had also lowered the final curtain on the acts of both Georgia Snow and the Singing Sweethearts.

But I … I was the current sweetheart of the stage, a star of musical comedy, someone the public flocked to see. This had been my life for more than a dozen years. I thought often of Mr. Stanley, and always with great satisfaction. I hoped he was enjoying the taste of crow.

Rising from the dressing table, I ran my hands down the front of my rose-colored silk dress. "Wish me luck, Charlotte," I said. Charlotte Tennant was my companion; she had been hired by my agent Saul Blasberg two years before when Mother died suddenly of a stroke.

"May you break a leg, Miss Rycroft," Charlotte said primly, hands clasped properly at her waist. "You look lovely, as always."

I nodded my thanks, as always. It was our pre-performance routine, reminiscent of the routine Mother and I followed whenever she performed. I neither liked nor disliked this middle-aged spinster who'd been chosen for me at Mother's passing; she was simply there to do my bidding, to help me dress and undress, and to act as chaperone to me, as I was still unmarried.

"Oh, and Miss Rycroft?"

"Yes, Charlotte?"

"Happy birthday, once again."

"Thank you."

I opened the dressing room door and stepped out into the back-stage hallway. Music from the Palace's orchestra pit reached me from a distance. Yes, tonight I was again performing at the Palace, where it had all begun. Stagehands and chorus girls flittered here and there but stepped aside to let me pass as I made my way to the wings. There I found Mr. Sedgwick, the stage manager, conferring with Frederick Mansfield, my leading man.

When he saw me, Frederick smiled and held out both hands to me. I offered him one of mine, which he raised to his lips and kissed. "Anna, darling, it's always a pleasure to feast my eyes upon such beauty."

I laughed demurely. "You flatter me, Frederick."

"Of course. How can I do less? Best wishes for great success tonight."

"And to you, too, I'm sure."

The act was for the sake of Mr. Sedgwick who, when asked by reporters and the merely curious if we were an item, could say no. We were much too formal and unfamiliar for that, as far as he could see. No, Miss Rycroft was quite unattached. One day, some lucky man would win her heart.

Part of my mystique was that I was available. It kept the men in cities everywhere buying tickets.

The truth was, though, that I was in love with Frederick Mansfield and he with me. We would marry one day, just not yet.

"One minute before curtain," Mr. Sedgwick said. "Take your places, please."

Before we parted, I discreetly sniffed the air around us. No overwhelming odor of alcohol, thank goodness. We could lose ourselves in the performance without my worrying about that. The backdrop might fall, a chorus girl might stumble, or a minor character forget his line, but for tonight, at least, Frederick Mansfield was sober, a welcome omen, for his performance was key to our success.

Frederick winked at me and left to take his place on stage. He was, as always, the first performer in the spotlight when the curtain rose.

Waiting offstage, readying myself, I took a deep breath. Always, I felt that small knot of fear, the tremor of stage fright. I had faced an audience hundreds of times, and yet, a

performer always wonders, *Will this be the night my luck runs out?*
No, I told myself. Not tonight. Everything will be fine. I am
ready. We are all ready. Freddy is in top form.

The orchestra played and the curtain rose. Frederick
Mansfield appeared in the spotlight, looking grand and flashy
and every bit the desirable ladies' man that he was. I would
make my entrance in a moment, to join Freddy in the opening
song.

Just before stepping on stage, I said aloud what I always
said at the outset of a performance: "This is for you, Henry."
It made no difference to Henry, of course, but it was a kind of
talisman to me, a good luck charm. More than that, it helped
assuage my guilt and made me feel as though I were doing
something for him by simply acknowledging his existence.

Because I knew for certain that Henry had once lived, and
that by now he was most likely dead. My shame lay in the fact
that I had done nothing to find him.

***

In the spring of 1925, Uncle Cosmo caught a cold and thought
he was dying, and that was how I learned that I really did have
a brother named Henry.

It was the evening of May 16, and Mother and I were to set
sail in the morning for my first European tour. We were staying
at the Grand Hotel in New York, and I was getting ready for
bed when the telephone rang.

"It's Uncle Cosmo," Mother called from the sitting room.
"He says he wants to wish you a *bon voyage*."

Then back to the phone: "How lovely of you to call,
Cosmo. Yes, we're both terribly excited … you sound awful.
Have you tried hot tea with honey? Maybe gargle with some
hot salt water then … all right. Well, here she is. Yes, we'll come
visit as soon as we return to the States."

She handed me the phone. "Hello, Uncle Cosmo," I said. I held my satin robe together at my chest; I was tired and wanted to sleep. "So nice of you to call. We have to be up early to be at the dock—"

"Darling, I want to offer you all my best wishes—"

"Thank you, Uncle. Can you believe it's really happening? We're off to Europe in the morning! Sometimes I have to pinch myself—"

"Yes, yes, you see, I'm not well and—"

"You do sound wretched. Another cold? Spring colds are really the worst, so be sure to get plenty of rest."

Uncle Cosmo succumbed to a coughing fit. I waited for him to collect his breath. Finally, he said, "I really must ... well, you see, if I'm not here when you return—"

"Not here? Where else would you be?"

"I mean, my lungs are rather weak, and I'm no longer a young man." He managed a small chuckle. "I haven't been a young man for a very long time, have I?"

"Never mind that, Uncle. The important thing is, have you called the doctor?"

"Oh yes, yes, he was here just this afternoon."

"Then I suggest you follow whatever advice he gave you, and we'll be sure to see you when we get back."

"But you see, Anna, I must tell you something before you go."

He paused. I waited. Another coughing fit reached me from the other end of the line, but this time it seemed contrived, as though Uncle Cosmo were merely hesitating.

I was suddenly afraid that he would tell me that he really was dying. That the doctor had discovered emphysema or cancer or something equally as dreadful, something from which my uncle could not and would not recover. I had to force myself to say, "What is it, Uncle Cosmo?"

He sighed. Heavily. "Anna," he said. "Anna ..."

The sniffling coming from the other end of the line was not just a symptom of my uncle's head cold. It dawned on me, however slowly, that my uncle was crying.

I looked out the window, over the twinkling lights of the New York City skyline. My legs weakened with fear, and I gripped the telephone receiver more tightly so it wouldn't slip from my hand. "Uncle?"

"Anna, we should never have lied to you."

"Lied? About what?"

"Your brother. Anna, when you awoke from the flu … It's true. You have a brother and his name is Henry."

"Henry?"

I hadn't thought of him in years, had dismissed the fevered journey just as Scrooge had tried to do, as an undigested bit of beef, a blot of mustard, a crumb of cheese. My visit with the storybook characters, my visiting Henry in the asylum—it had only been a dream! A vision that had risen up from my fevered brain and out of my love for the story that both my unknown father and I had read as children. That was all it was; nothing more. Even the recurring dream of my childhood had stopped haunting me at night, my dream of holding the baby, the dream that had held me captive for years. Somehow the flu had burned it out of my mind and heart, releasing me from it. But now …

I turned from the window and looked at Mother. She stood ashen-faced, unmoving, solid as stone. Then she leapt at me and tried to grab the phone from my hand.

"What are you telling her, Cosmo?" she said angrily.

The telephone receiver hung in the air between her ear and mine as we both vied for it. From the earpiece Uncle Cosmo's tiny voice reached us. "I had to tell her before I die. I can't go to my grave carrying this secret. Anna, he was real. They put him in an asylum. He may yet be alive. I can tell you where and maybe you can find him—"

I let go of the receiver and fell back into a chair, my legs no longer able to support me. I could only stare helplessly at Mother as she berated Uncle Cosmo. "You foolish old man! What are you doing? Have you completely lost your mind?"

She ranted on, but I was no longer listening. Bound and numbed by my uncle's confession, I was trying hard to believe what I had always known to be true. The baby was real. I had a brother named Henry.

Mother slammed the handset onto the telephone's cradle, and the room fell silent. We stared at each other—Mother and I—as though we were strangers seeing each other for the first time. And in a way, she was a stranger to me. She was a mother I didn't know.

"You lied to me," I finally said.

Instead of arguing, she came and kneeled in front of me. "Anna," she said quietly. "You must believe me when I say we could do nothing for him. It was beyond us. We had to put him in a safe place."

"A safe place? It was an asylum, Mother. It was awful. I saw it."

She shook her head and took both my hands in hers. "Darling, you never saw it. You must believe me. You never saw the place."

Hadn't I? Hadn't I been there with Marley? But oh, how foolish it seemed to say that I had been there with a ghost, a storybook phantom. That couldn't be true.

"How did I know his name was Henry?"

Mother frowned in thought for a moment. Finally, she said, "You dreamed of him for years, you know. I always told you it wasn't true, though it was. You were just old enough to remember him—you must have heard us call him Henry, and the name stayed with you."

My brain was whirling, trying to sort fact from fiction. How did I know what I knew? How did I know what I wasn't supposed to know? "He was ..." I hesitated, looked Mother in the eye. "He was an idiot child?"

Mother nodded. "He could never have lived a normal life. There was nothing we could do to change that."

"But how could you give him away?"

"Anna, darling, please try to understand. How could we have kept him?"

"Didn't you love him?"

Mother hesitated. As I gazed at her, waiting for an answer, something shifted in her eyes, and a familiar cast fell across her brow. "It was love that convinced me to give him away," she said quietly.

The moment she said the words, I knew they weren't true. This was my actress mother speaking. She wanted me to believe that giving Henry away was a noble act, something that had broken her heart, something she had done as a sacrifice for love's sake.

My eyes narrowed and my jaw tightened. I pulled my hands from hers. "Love for your own self, for your own dreams. Not love for Henry."

She shook her head, still in her role. "You have to believe me, Anna. I did love him. He was my son. But we couldn't keep him."

"You couldn't keep him and still fulfill your dreams for yourself, you mean."

"That isn't true!"

"It is true! Your own success was all that ever mattered to you. It mattered to you even more than your own children. And now you're still trying to find success through me."

She drew back, as though I had slapped her. I rose from the chair and walked back to the window. It had started to rain, and the lights of Manhattan glimmered like jewels in a shallow pond.

"We have to find him," I said.

"It's too late, Anna." She sank from her knees to the floor and leaned against the chair.

"What do you mean, it's too late? Is he dead?"

I turned to face her. She looked pale and small and defeated. She was my mother again. "I don't know. I don't know whether he's dead or alive. I've heard nothing since the night he was taken away."

"Where was he taken? Do you know?"

"Yes, I know."

"Then we have to go there."

"And do what, Anna?"

"Find him, and—"

"What? Bring him home?"

What, indeed? We were about to embark for Europe for two months. Even if we found Henry alive, what then?

"There must be something—"

"Anna, listen to me." Mother rose and took a step toward me. "It's you who matter. You. You have the whole world at your feet. You must simply go on and live your life. All of Europe is waiting for you."

With those few words from Mother, the image Uncle Cosmo had called up—the image of Henry in his bed at the asylum—started to recede while Europe slid back into view. I saw myself standing on the deck of the steamship *Mauretania,* the "Grand Old Lady of the Atlantic." This luxury liner was to carry me across the waters, to the most important cities in Europe, to the greatest theaters on that old continent where the stage lights would shine on me. I was the star, and Mother was right: Europe was waiting for me.

When I spoke, it was barely a whisper. "If we don't find him, he will end up in an unmarked grave, you know."

"What, Anna?" Mother frowned. "What did you say?"

I tried to repeat myself, but couldn't. The words died on my tongue. "Nothing, Mother. I'm tired. I'm going to bed."

"Yes. Yes, that's right. Get some sleep. You'll feel better in the morning."

"Good night, Mother."

"Good night, darling. Sweet dreams."

The next day, I stood on the deck of the *Mauretania*, watching as America, New York City, Pier 54, and Henry grew smaller. Mother and I never spoke of Henry again.

CHAPTER 17

S ome performances were magical, in which everything and everyone came together perfectly. When this happened it was as though, rather than putting on an act, we were in fact living out our lives right there on the stage. No—it was better than that because no life could be as good as the thing we created. When Frederick Mansfield and I joined our voices, when we danced, when we performed together, something enchanting rose up from us and filled the entire theater, capturing the audience in its grip. I could feel it, could feel the good thing rolling out of me, out of us, and creating something beautiful. That's how it was that night, the night of my birthday.

After our final bow, Frederick followed me off the stage. "That was marvelous, darling. Truly stunning. Your best performance ever."

I gazed up at his handsome face, so perfect in it shape and symmetry—the fine strong features, piercing dark eyes, narrow Greek nose, slightly pouting lips over even white teeth. I loved everything about that face, especially the lines that formed parentheses on either side of his mouth when he smiled.

"Do you really think so, Freddy?"

"Of course. You were superb."

I stood on tiptoe and kissed one of the beloved lines. "We were superb together, darling. It really was an exquisite night, wasn't it?"

"Indeed," he said, taking my hand and tucking it in the crook of his arm. We strolled toward our dressing rooms while all around us extraneous actors and members of the stage crew scurried about, calling out their congratulations to us as we passed. Frederick acknowledged their words with nods and nearly imperceptible bows as walked. "And the night is far from over," he went on. "We have the party at Olivia's, of course. With you as guest of honor."

Olivia de Silva was a society matron, a patron of the arts, who often entertained actors and writers and artists in her penthouse on Park Avenue. I laughed lightly. "I suppose there will be a clown jumping out of a cake for me."

"I don't know about a clown, darling, but there will be cake, I'm sure, and plenty of champagne." We had come to the door of my dressing room. "Shall I pick you up in twenty minutes?"

"Yes. I'll be ready."

Charlotte was waiting for me inside, ready to help me out of my costume and to dress for the party. In the two hours I was gone, the room had turned into a veritable florist shop, with bouquets on every flat service, including the windowsills, and the seat of the straight-back chair beside the cot.

"Oh, Charlotte!" I cried in delight. "Have you ever seen so many blossoms all in one place?"

She shook her head. "I've done nothing all night other than deal with delivery boys. There are telegrams too, dozens of them."

I sat down at the dressing table, though before I could see in the mirror, I had to move one of the bouquets to the floor. Pulling the pins from my hair, I said, "Well, I don't have time to deal with them now. There's the party at Olivia's—"

"There's one from Mr. Blasberg. It's only just arrived."

Saul Blasberg, my agent. "Read it aloud then, will you?"

Charlotte picked up the top telegram from a pile on a small table beside the door. She slit it open and began to read. "Happy birthday, Anna dear. I trust it shall enhance your celebration to hear that I have very nearly secured you a screen test with MGM. Details to follow. As ever, Saul." She folded the telegram and replaced it on the table. "I suppose that is good news?"

"Yes," I said, "it might be."

"Might be?" Charlotte stepped behind me, picked up my hairbrush from the table, and started to work through the knots in my long blonde hair.

"Saul is so sure my future is in pictures. He calls it the logical next step, especially now that the Depression is on and people are more inclined toward radio and film. But ... it's all so different from the stage, you know? Working on a set, filming scenes all out of order, and ... well, no audience there to cheer you on. It's the audience that gives me my vitality. How can I perform without them?"

"You will perform for the other actors on the set. The director. The lighting crew. The cameramen. There will be plenty of people there to appreciate your performance while you're giving it, though your fans will have to wait to see you on the screen."

"Oh, Charlotte." I sighed. "I think you're in cahoots with Saul, aren't you? You sound just like him."

"I should think you would be thrilled to conquer Hollywood, Miss Rycroft."

"Yes, but—"

A knock came at the door. Charlotte muttered something I couldn't hear and stepped away from the dressing table to answer it. In a moment she returned with yet another bouquet in her arms, one that was familiar: red roses and white calla lilies, the same arrangement Uncle Rex had sent to Mother every year on her birthday. I had received such an arrangement numerous times in the past couple of years—not from Uncle Rex, of course, as he was long dead, but from someone who by happenstance had stumbled upon the same stunning collusion of blossoms.

"I suppose it's from that so-called secret admirer," I said.

Charlotte removed the card and read it aloud. "Happy birthday from your secret admirer, CC."

I sniffed and turned back to the mirror. "It's annoying to think he knows it's my birthday when I don't even know who he is."

Charlotte laughed lightly. "You seem to forget you're rather well known, Miss Rycroft. Plenty of people who are strangers to you know it's your birthday." As she spoke, she stood with the flowers in her arms, turning one way and then another. "I don't even know where to put them."

"You may toss them out the window, for all I care."

"Really, Miss Rycroft, they must have cost a precious bundle. I hate to simply be rid of them."

"Then you may keep them for yourself. I don't know who this CC is, but I'm beginning to wish he would stop bothering me with his nonsense."

"I'm afraid that's the price of fame, Miss Rycroft. Men will love you even when they don't know you."

"I'm well aware of that, Charlotte. Now, I must get dressed for the party. What should I do with my hair?"

"I—" She was interrupted by another knock on the door. "My heavens! I haven't the arms for one more." Another rap, sharper this time. "Yes, I'm coming." Charlotte shifted the flowers into one arm and opened the door with her free hand. "Can I help you?"

The doorway framed a tall, older gentleman, well-dressed and well-groomed, a brown fedora in one hand. "I see you received my flowers," he said.

"You sent these?" Charlotte asked.

"Indeed I did."

In the next moment, Mr. Sedgwick's voice came from somewhere in the hall. "I tried to stop him, but he insisted."

"It's all right, Mr. Sedgwick," I called, rising from the dressing table. "Let him in, will you, Charlotte?"

Sighing audibly, Charlotte stepped aside and allowed both men to enter the room.

Mr. Sedgwick wiped his brow with a handkerchief. "I'm sorry, Miss Rycroft—"

I waved away his apology. "It's all right, Mr. Sedgwick," I said again. "You may go. This won't take but a minute."

"But—"

"And Mr. Mansfield is on his way to escort me to the party. He'll be here any moment."

Mr. Sedgwick looked from me to Charlotte and back again. Tucking his handkerchief back into his breast pocket, he said, "Very well, Miss Rycroft." Before leaving, he gave the visitor one stern look, as though in warning. The visitor smiled warmly in return.

When Mr. Sedgwick had gone, I turned my gaze to the visitor. He seemed to me slightly familiar, though I couldn't place him. He smiled at me and gave a small nod of his head, as though to say the ball was in my court. "So you are the mysterious CC, my secret admirer," I said, trying to sound braver than I felt. "Well, sir, who exactly are you and what do you want from me?"

Smiling still, he said, "I don't want anything at all from you, other than to see you again at long last."

"Again?" I echoed. "Have we met before?"

"Yes, though I don't expect you to remember. Allow me then to re-introduce myself. My name is Charles Cullen." He hesitated only a moment before adding, "Anna, I'm your father."

***

The room tilted, and I stumbled back into the chair at the dressing table. My chest heaved, and I felt as though I couldn't breathe. Charlotte put the flowers aside and rushed to pour me a glass of water. "I don't know who you are," she said angrily to the stranger, "but I suggest you leave at once. What do you mean, coming in here and claiming to be her father?"

"I'm sorry. I didn't think—"

"You didn't think what? You didn't think you would upset her, coming in here and making such ludicrous claims? Leave, or I shall call for help and have you tossed out on the street. Imagine, coming in here and doing such a thing!"

"I assure you—"

"Better yet, I'll have Mr. Sedgwick call the police. They'll not hesitate to deal with the likes of you."

I had never before seen this protective mother bear in Charlotte Tennant, and even in my distress, I was rather touched. I sipped the water and tried to gather my wits. Settling the glass on the dressing table, I said, "It's all right, Charlotte. Just give me a minute."

I waited for my breath to settle, and when it did, I studied the man's face. He seemed to study me in return, though a look of concern, or perhaps remorse, had settled over his brow. I inhaled deeply one more time and said, "If you're my father, what was my mother's name?"

"Bernadette," he said without hesitation.

"Where was she born?"

"Joliet, Illinois."

"What year?"

"Eighteen eighty-three."

Silence. Then, "Come closer."

"What?"

"Come closer so I can look at you."

He came closer, actually knelt at my feet. His eyes grew moist as I studied him. His dark hair was streaked with gray and lines fanned out from the corner of his eyes but ... my mind traveled back to a long-ago day in a darkened theater in Maysville, Illinois. After a moment, I said, "You're the piano player."

"Piano player?"

"In the movie."

"Ah." He nodded. *"Tillie's Punctured Romance."*

"Yes. Mother took me to see it. To see you. She said you left us for Hollywood."

The eyes grew shinier. "To my great regret."

My eyes narrowed. I wasn't sure I believed him.

"So you know today is my birthday because you are my father."

"I know that you are twenty-seven years old today. I first held you when you were only minutes old."

"Why have you been sending me flowers? Why did you come? Why now?"

"Anna, I have always wanted to be in touch with you, but your mother wouldn't allow it."

"Mother? She said you abandoned us, that there was never any word."

"I left, but I still wanted to be in touch with you, to send you letters, flowers on your birthday ..."

Then I remembered. "On her birthday every year, Mother received roses and calla lilies, just like the flowers you've sent me. I always thought they were from Uncle Rex."

"You were understandably mistaken."

"They were from you."

"Yes."

"You knew where we were all along."

"Yes. Bernadette was willing to stay in touch with me. She wrote, she gave me news about you but, as I say, she wouldn't let me contact you directly. I abided by her wishes. Then, when she died, I thought perhaps ..."

Two years ago. That was when the flowers from the secret admirer had begun to arrive.

I stood and began to pace the room. He rose too, slowly, as though it pained his knees. "I don't know what to think," I said. I came up to the window, turned, and walked back to the cot. "I don't know whether to be happy or angry."

"Don't be anything at all, Anna," the man said. "Just give us a chance to get to know each other."

I looked at Charlotte. All this time, she had been standing quietly by the still-open door of my dressing room. She looked tense, but other than that, I couldn't read her thoughts. She offered no clue as to what I should do, how I should respond to this unexpected twist in my life.

He continued, "I have a home in Connecticut, in the countryside, just outside of Stamford."

"Connecticut? Uncle Cosmo is living in New Haven."

"Cosmo? Really? The old man's still alive?"

"Oh yes, very much alive. I bought the house for him there a few years back. He's really the only family I have ..." My words trailed off. The stranger and I looked at each other.

"Not anymore, Anna," he said. "Won't you come? Have dinner with us? I'd like you to meet my wife, my children."

"You're married? You have other children?"

He nodded. "Six."

"Six!"

"Well, five adopted. One is ..."

"One is my sibling."

"Yes. A girl."

"I have a sister." I lifted a hand to my head. It was too much.

Charlotte at last intervened. "Miss Rycroft, perhaps Mr. Cullen should come back another time. Surely you need time to adjust—"

But she was interrupted by the swift entrance of Frederick Mansfield, who flew through the open door without knocking. "Anna, darling," he said, "you haven't even changed out of your costume. We're expected promptly at—" And then he noticed the visitor. "Who's this?" he asked, his tone wary.

"Freddy, this is ... this is Charles Cullen," I muttered.

"But what is he doing here in your dressing room?" He turned to Charlotte, as though to find the answer there.

"Mr. Cullen was just leaving," Charlotte said.

"Oh? And what was his business here with Miss Rycroft?" He was looking at the stranger when he said it.

"Freddy," I said, "Mr. Cullen is ... he's my father."

"Your father?" He drew back, as though he had touched a flame. "You can't be serious, Anna."

"I am, Freddy. Quite serious."

For a brief moment, Freddy eyed the man who stood in my dressing room, still clutching his fedora. Finally, he said, "He's playing you, Anna. This man is no more your father than I am."

"No, Freddy, I know it seems odd, but it's true. I recognize him."

"But I don't understand."

"Perhaps I can explain," Charles Cullen began, but before he could continue, Charlotte interrupted.

"You can explain everything another time, Mr. Cullen. I think it's best you go now."

"But I'd like—"

Freddy jumped in. "Can't you see Miss Rycroft is upset? You've done her no favors by coming here. I suggest you leave, just as Miss Tennant said." He put a comforting arm around my waist and drew me close.

The room fell quiet. Charles Cullen looked at me and I at him. I offered him no encouragement to stay. At length he said, "Very well. But Anna, won't you consider my invitation to dinner?"

I had no chance to reply before Charlotte said, "Good night, Mr. Cullen. I'm sure you can see your way out."

The man looked at me one last moment, then drew himself up, settled his hat on his head, and walked out the door. Charlotte closed it behind him.

Freddy turned me around then and held me at arm's length, both hands on my shoulders. "Anna, what's this about? Are you sure you should believe him?"

I shook my head. Tears were close. "I don't know what it's about. But I do believe him."

"You must be careful, darling. That man could be anyone. An imposter. Someone who wants to impose himself in your life simply because you're Annalise Rycroft."

"But Freddy, he knows things. And I know his face. I remember now."

Charlotte took a step closer. "Really, Miss Rycroft, even if he is your father ... well, all these years away, and now he wants to come back into your life? You may very well be better off without him."

"But you heard what he said, Charlotte. My mother wouldn't allow him to contact me."

"And she's not here to tell you whether she did or she didn't. So how can you know if he's telling you the truth?"

Freddy nodded his agreement, adding, "I say, good riddance to him, darling. And you must hurry. We're due at Olivia's. Everyone will be waiting for us."

"But Freddy!"

"What, Anna? Dry your eyes. That's a girl. Charlotte, help her get ready, won't you? We really mustn't be late."

"Of course, Mr. Mansfield, it will just take a moment ..."

By now, I had stopped listening. Pulling myself away from Freddy, I moved toward the door. I had to reach Charles Cullen before he stepped out into the night.

I opened the door and was ready to rush into the hall but was stopped short by the imposing figure just beyond the threshold. As ours eyes met, he nodded as though we had reached an unspoken understanding.

"What day can you come?" he asked.

"Wednesday," I answered quietly. "I can come Wednesday."

"I'll send my driver to fetch you at three o'clock." He tipped his hat and smiled once more, then turned and disappeared.

Chapter 18

Olivia de Silva's Park Avenue penthouse was all gilded mirrors and chandeliers and fountains of champagne, in spite of Prohibition. Drinking was not illegal; it was the "manufacture, sale and transportation of intoxicating liquors" that brought out the feds in swarms, ready to round up the bootleggers, moonshiners, and rum runners. Drinking we could do to our heart's content, and that is what we did.

Some of us more than others.

I watched as Freddy stumbled off in search of yet one more glass of bubbly. He had a full flask of bathtub gin in the breast pocket of his jacket, but that was for later, for the ride home. We had played out that scene together many times, in many cities, and it always ended the same way: Freddy upending the flask in the back seat of the limousine. Freddy staggering through the hotel lobby and into the elevator. Freddy passed out on the floor of his hotel room. He could never seem to make it so far as the bed. I managed always to guide him through the door, and then down he'd go. That was his final bow before the closing curtain of the night. I'd throw a blanket over him and go off to my own hotel room.

The hour was late now, nearly four in the morning, and the party at Olivia's was winding down. I had done well, I thought, at being the guest of honor—cutting the enormous cake, receiving toast after toast, mingling with the biggest of the Broadway crowd, accepting their adoration and good wishes with a never-ceasing smile. Now the crowd was thinning, and

I was tired, but Freddy wanted one more drink. "One for the road," he slurred, though the one for the road was in his pocket, unopened.

"You would leave him if you knew what's good for you."

Startled, I turned to see Helen Highfield standing at my elbow, the long stem of a champagne glass clutched in one delicate hand. The blue sequins on her sleeveless Coco Chanel evening gown sparkled as she raised the glass to her lips and took a polite sip. Though she had addressed her words to me, her eyes were on Freddy as he shadowed a server and his silver tray about the room.

I should have been offended by her words, but I wasn't. Helen and I were long-time friends, ever since we had appeared together in a production of *Ringlets and Riches* on Broadway in 1924. She was a well-regarded actress in her own right, and a couple of years before, upon marrying producer Maxfield Kerr, she had made the transition to Hollywood. She was in New York for the premier of her latest movie. We had greeted each other earlier in the evening but hadn't had time to talk until now.

I sighed loudly. "I would," I said, "but I have a problem."

"And what's that?"

"I love him."

"Ah." She nodded knowingly. "More's the pity."

My hand went to the heart-shaped pendant that hung on a chain about my neck. "He gave me this," I said. "On the ride over. For my birthday."

Helen leaned in closer. "Twenty-four carat gold, I'm sure. Three embedded diamonds. It must have cost a pretty penny."

"I'm sure it did."

"What does the engraving say?"

"'Always in my Heart.'"

"Ah. Trite, but sweet. Not what you wanted, I assume."

"I had hoped for a diamond on my finger. Don't you think it's about time?"

Helen laughed lightly. "I'm afraid that's not up to me, my dear."

"No, it's up to Freddy, and he's not budging. I don't understand why."

"Fear of commitment, I suppose. Plenty of men feel that way. Marriage puts an end to all the fun, so why bother?"

"But he says he loves me."

"And he very well might. But a man like Frederick Mansfield will always love himself more than he can ever love a woman."

I sighed again. I didn't want to believe that. "Someday, Helen," I said, "Freddy is going to end up married to someone. It might as well be me. Besides, I harbor the audacious belief that I can change him. That once we're married, I can convince him to stop drinking for my sake and the sake of our children."

Helen was quiet a moment. "I suppose it could happen." Then she added, "More often, it doesn't."

She should know. She had been married to—and was now divorced from—two alcoholics herself. Her third husband had no such vice; she had made sure of that before she married him. Max's only downfall was gambling.

I looked around the room. "By the way, where is Max? I saw him earlier."

"Oh, he was here," she said, "but he left about an hour ago. I suppose he has found himself a blackjack table for the remainder of the night."

"At least he doesn't come home drunk."

"No, never drunk, though sometimes tipsy. And generally with his pockets a lot lighter than when he left. Poor Max rarely wins. That doesn't deter him, though. He's persistent if nothing else."

"Oh Helen, I'm sorry."

She shrugged. "As long as he doesn't bet the house, we should be all right. Otherwise he's mostly a dear, most of the time."

I said, "Why do we hold so tenaciously to our dreams, Helen?"

"Because," she said, pausing to take another sip of champagne, "we have so little without them."

Across the room, Freddy grabbed another glass from the traveling silver tray and downed it in one gulp.

"By the way, Anna dear, happy birthday," Helen went on. "I should have begun with that rather than with words of unsolicited advice."

I smiled. "Thank you, and it's all right. You wished me a happy birthday hours ago, even before the cake was brought out."

"Did I? Perhaps I've had a bit too much to drink myself." She raised the glass of champagne as though in a toast, then drank again.

"Tell me truthfully, Helen"—I turned my face to her fully—"do I look old to you?"

She looked at me and laughed, one piercing soprano yelp. "Darling, you can't be serious. You're the picture of youth and loveliness."

"I'm twenty-seven today."

"And?" She shrugged. "And I am thirty. No one has to know. All we have to do is pretend to be twenty for as long as we can. I think you will get away with it for quite some time."

"Maybe. But I can't get away with it forever."

"Cheer up, darling. You have miles to go before you are … forgotten."

Her words did little to cheer me up. I decided to change the subject. "You know, you look stunning, Helen. That dress suits you. I'm sure you're excited for the premier."

"Oh yes. You'll be there, won't you?"

"Wouldn't miss it for the world. You know, Saul is trying to get me a screen test with MGM."

"Oh, that's wonderful! If you come to Hollywood, we could have such fun. You'll come, won't you?"

"I don't know. It depends on whether MGM wants me."

"Of course they will. They'd be fools not to. In fact, I'll put in a good word for you myself."

I smiled, but didn't respond. Freddy was speaking with one of the chorus girls from our production, his arm resting casually around her shoulder. I saw her face light up with laughter. My heart grew one shade dimmer as I watched from a distance.

Helen guffawed. "Not only a lush but a ladies' man," she said.

"I'm beginning to think you don't care for Freddy."

"Freddy? He's all right for a chorus girl, but he's not nearly good enough for you."

For a long time, I didn't respond. Finally, I said, "I don't think I have the strength to give him up."

She laid a hand on my arm. "Come to Hollywood, Anna. You can begin a whole new life there, I promise. You'll forget him soon enough."

"I can't just leave the production. I'm under contract."

"Silly girl!" she said with another laugh. Downing the last of her drink, she added, "You're Annalise Rycroft. You can do whatever you want."

CHAPTER 19

As the chauffer-driven Chrysler Sedan carried me through the Connecticut countryside, I began to second-guess my decision. Why had I agreed to visit Charles Cullen? What would I say to this man who had disappeared from my life so many years before?

I rolled down the window a notch and breathed deeply, trying to steady myself. The driver glanced at my reflection in the rearview mirror.

"You all right, Miss Rycroft?"

"Yes, I'm fine, thank you, Jensen."

"We're almost there. Just a few more miles."

I nodded, then pulled a pendant watch out of my handbag. Almost 4:30. A few minutes later, the car slowed as we turned down a long, pine tree-lined lane. Up ahead about a quarter of a mile was a sprawling two-story white clapboard house with black shutters and a wrap-around porch. As we drew closer, I felt as though conveyed into a bucolic painting. The lawn was a fertile green, and along one side ran a fieldstone fence that started at the edge of the circular drive and disappeared into the woods behind the house. Tulips and daffodils bloomed in profusion along the path that led to the front porch.

I wondered what Charles Cullen had done that had brought him to this place. What did he do now to earn his living, as he was obviously well off, even in the midst of the Depression. What kind of journey had taken him from Vaudeville to

Hollywood to … *this*? I realized I knew almost nothing at all about this man who was my father.

Once we reached the circular drive, the driver parked the car at the foot of the porch steps. The sudden stillness was almost jarring. I rolled the window all the way down and breathed deeply. Birds sang somewhere off in the trees. Such an idyllic setting, and yet I was filled with anxiety. What would the next few hours bring? Maybe I should have listened to Freddy and Charlotte and declined the man's invitation. But it was too late now.

The driver had moved around the car and was opening the door to the back seat. He offered me a hand. I took it and moved as gracefully as I could through the always awkward motions of exiting a car. Once upright, I smoothed the wrinkles from my skirt. For the occasion, I had chosen to wear a tailored suit, pale brown, and a matching brim slouch hat. I was aiming for simplicity—and perhaps conformity.

I smiled at the driver. "Thank you, Jensen."

He bowed slightly. "Certainly, Miss Rycroft."

Straightening my hat nervously, I looked up at the porch. In that moment, the front door swung open and Charles Cullen himself appeared, looking casual in tan slacks, a white shirt, and a navy blue single-breasted vest.

"Welcome, Anna," he called, but he got no further in his greeting before a swarm of children buzzed out from behind him. Immediately, the air was filled with questions and exclamations.

"Is it really Annalise Rycroft?"

"Oh, she's beautiful, isn't she?"

"Just like her photograph, only better!"

"I can't believe she's really here!"

At length a woman appeared in the doorway; I assumed her to be my father's wife. She was younger than he by about ten years, which put her around forty, and while she wasn't a classic beauty, the kind that surrounded me on the stage, she had her own kind of loveliness, an open-faced sweetness about her that I was drawn to at once. Her eyes were blue and clear and honest, her narrow face bore only a hint of makeup, and her bobbed brown hair hung close to her head in marcelled waves. She wore a pale yellow cotton dress with a lace-trimmed V-neck, and, on her feet, white heels with straps. Seeing her and Charles Cullen both, I felt justified in my decision to wear the tailored suit.

"All right, everyone," Charles hollered above the fray. "Let's settle down and greet our guest properly, shall we?"

The children squirmed but quieted, six eager faces trained on me. I guessed their ages to be somewhere around fifteen all the way down to three or four.

"Children, this is Annalise Rycroft," he said by way of introduction.

"We know that, Papa!" one of the children cried. "Tell her who *we* are."

I couldn't help but laugh in delight.

"I'm getting to that if you'll just be patient. All right, Anna, oldest to youngest we have"—here he pointed with an open hand—"Margaret, Alan, Peter, Sylvia, Teddy, and Julia."

"How do you do," I said politely, shaking hands with each, one at a time.

"Tell us about Broadway!"

"What's it like to be famous?"

"Will you sing for us?"

"Children! Children! We're not even in the house yet. All of this can wait. Now, Anna, I'd like to introduce you to my lovely wife, Elinor."

She held out a slender hand. "Please, call me Ellie. I'm so delighted to meet you, Miss Rycroft."

"Anna," I said, taking her hand. "You must call me Anna. I'm happy to meet you too."

"As you can see, the children are quite excited. It isn't every day we have a Broadway star at our house."

I smiled while trying to decide how to respond, though Charles saved me the trouble. "Let's all go inside, shall we? It's beginning to be a bit chilly out here, and I'm sure our guest would like to sit down and maybe enjoy a cup of tea before dinner."

"Yes, do come in," Ellie said. "Let me take your hat. Betty has the teapot on and—come on, children, everyone inside. Upstairs with you for now. No complaining. You know what we said. We'll allow Papa and Miss Rycroft to enjoy some time together before dinner, and then you can ask her all the questions you want."

"But what are we having for dinner?" one of the children asked.

"Betty is making a nice roast of lamb and mashed potatoes," Ellie said. "Won't that be nice?"

"But what's for dessert?" the same voice inquired.

"Well, I saw her cutting up apples earlier, so I believe we're having an apple cobbler."

"With vanilla ice cream?"

Ellie laughed. "Of course."

She herded the cheering children up the stairs while Charles Cullen took my elbow and guided me across the hall into a large front room. Furnished tastefully with a number of chairs, couches, and tables, I found the room warm and inviting. Of particular beauty was the fieldstone hearth, which seemed the heart of the room. Enormous built-in bookcases hugged the fireplace on either side, with each shelf filled to capacity with books, some laid sideways on top of others to fit them all in. The Cullens' personal library must have harbored hundreds of volumes. Two wing chairs, each with its own footstool and side table, were situated in front of the hearth. I could well imagine sitting there by a crackling fire in mid-winter, enjoying one of those books.

"Do you like to read, Charles?" I asked mildly. He waved me into a wing chair, so I sat.

"Oh yes, it's my favorite pastime … well, I shouldn't say pastime, really, as I don't read simply to pass the time." He smiled and settled in the chair across from me. "One's whole life can be changed by a good story, can't it?"

"I suppose it could," I agreed. I crossed my legs and dropped my handbag on the side table. "Do you have a favorite?"

We were interrupted then when Ellie entered the room pushing a rolling teacart. "Here we are," she said cheerily. "Tea and a few of Betty's finger cakes, fresh from the oven."

"Sounds delicious," I said, though at the same time Charles was saying, "Darling, you could have sent Betty in with it."

Ellie smiled. "But I wanted to bring it myself, to make sure everyone is comfortable."

"Thank you, Ellie," I said. "We're quite comfortable. Such a lovely room."

Ellie began pouring the tea. "Cream and sugar, Anna?"

"None for me, thanks."

She smiled again, this time directly at Charles. "I don't have to ask you, dear. I've already put the four lumps of sugar in your cup."

"He has something of a sweet tooth, does he?" I reached for the cup and saucer that Ellie proffered.

"Oh my yes," she said. "And yet he never gains a single pound. Now I, on the other hand …" Her words trailed off to a quiet laugh.

I raised a hand. "Say no more. I understand completely."

She nodded and handed Charles his cup of tea. Then she turned back to me. "It was kind of you to come today, Anna. We know it might be—" She paused a moment before going on, "Well, we want you to feel welcome and at home. Charles has been hoping for this opportunity for—" Again, she stopped herself. "Well, I'll leave you two alone for now so you can get reacquainted. I'll leave the tray here with the cakes, in case you want any."

"Thank you, Ellie," I said, not knowing what else to say.

"Call us when dinner's ready," Charles called after her.

"Of course, dear."

I followed her retreating figure as she stepped from the room, then said, "She's lovely, Charles."

"Yes." He nodded. "I'm a lucky man."

"She's very gracious to be so welcoming. I am, after all, the child of another wife."

"A former wife," he corrected gently.

"Yes, but still ... I suppose she has always known about me."

"Of course."

"And she really doesn't mind my being here?"

"Not at all. Quite the contrary. She encouraged me to invite you. She knows how much it means ..." His voice trailed off. He took a sip of tea. When he spoke again, it was on another subject. "I hope you don't mind the children," he said. "They can be a rather rowdy bunch."

"Not at all," I countered. "They're delightful."

"They're pretty good kids, just a bit unruly at times. And right now, understandably keyed up by meeting someone ... well, such as yourself."

"I understand." As soon as the words left my mouth, I wondered whether they might sound arrogant. I tried to soften it. "I suppose they've heard of me."

Charles smiled indulgently. "Hasn't everyone?"

I tried in my mind to look over the blur of faces that had greeted me on the porch. "Which one," I began, then stopped. "Which one is not adopted?"

"Which one is your sister, you mean?"

I nodded.

"Julia."

"The youngest?"

"Yes. She's only just turned three. Ellie and I didn't think we could have children and then, after adopting five—well, then came Julia. It was a bit of a shock, but a happy surprise."

"I suppose it was. She's a beautiful girl." I was trying to fathom that such a little girl could be my sister; I was old enough to be her mother. Charles Cullen at—what was he now? Fifty? Fifty-one?—was old enough to be her grandfather.

"Why, may I ask, did you adopt so many?"

"Ah, you see ..." He took another sip of tea, reached for one of the cloth napkins on the tray and dabbed at his mouth. "There's an orphanage in Stamford. Ellie's father has been a long-time benefactor. He's rather wealthy, a railroad man. I've worked for him in a managerial position since marrying Ellie eleven years ago."

"I see. So you left show business altogether."

"Oh my yes, ages ago."

"I'm afraid I never followed your career as closely as you've followed mine."

"What career? I was a miserable failure in the theater."

"Were you? Mother always implied you were immensely talented. What happened?"

"Long story, not worth telling. I left Hollywood, came back here, met Ellie, and married her."

I thought about how Saul Blasberg was working to get me that screen test. "So you aren't sorry you didn't stay in Hollywood?"

"Not for a moment. Sometimes failure can be a godsend, you know. If I hadn't come back, I wouldn't have this"—he swept the air with both hands—"a home, Ellie, the children. This is what I really want."

And you couldn't have had it with us? I wondered. *With me and Mother? And Henry?*

Before I could say anything, Charles went on, "When Ellie and I realized—or at least thought—we couldn't have children, we decided to adopt. So many children need homes, you know."

"Yes, I'm sure they do." I knew only too well, I thought, never having had a home myself as a child.

I studied Charles Cullen a moment. My mind harbored so few memories of the man. Just a few spotty images of him dancing on stage, sitting beside me on a train, reading to me as I lay in bed at night. The most distinct image came to me from the fever dream of 1918, when Old Fezziwig took me back to the night of Henry's abandonment. I saw Charles at the door, handing his son over to a stranger. It was a dream fragment, not a memory at all—and yet, I felt myself growing angry.

My heart pounded and my palms grew moist. My cheeks felt warm even as the room itself seemed to turn cold. I wanted suddenly to run from the room and far away from this house and Charles Cullen. But more than that, I wanted to lunge toward the man sitting so contentedly in his wing chair and beat my fists against his breast.

"Anna?" he said, leaning slightly forward in his chair.

Stay calm, I told myself. I would have to perform, to put on the act of my life. "I suppose," I said evenly, "that this act of kindness to these orphans is your way of trying to make up for what you did to your first family."

He paled. His eyes grew wide. "Anna, I—"

"That's it, isn't it? By taking in the children of strangers, you don't have to feel guilty for what you did to Mother and to me. And to Henry."

The cup and saucer rattled loudly in his trembling hand as he lowered them to the side table. The sword I had thrust had hit its mark and sunk deeply. I knew it was cruel, but I felt avenged by hurting him as acutely as he had once hurt me.

Small beads of sweat broke out along his hairline. His pale lips parted as though he wanted to speak, but he remained silent. He stared at me beseechingly, a gaze that begged me to stop, to rewind our conversation to a place of civility. But I wouldn't let it go.

"Yes," I went on, "I know about Henry. I know you gave him away because he was an idiot child."

His lips touched, parted, trembled. Finally, he managed to say, "Your mother said you had no memory of him."

"She was wrong. She denied Henry's existence, but Uncle Cosmo told me the truth."

"Cosmo?"

"Yes, he told me everything. Some years ago, just before I sailed for my first tour of Europe, he called and told me all about Henry. Poor Uncle Cosmo thought he was dying, so it was something of a deathbed confession, you see. Still, I knew long before that. There was this recurring dream—it used to torment me when I was a young girl. I dreamed I was holding a baby, a little child wrapped up in a quilt. I was rocking it to sleep, but then, suddenly, I would look down and it was gone. I used to wake up crying. Mother told me it was only a bad dream. But then, as I said, Uncle Cosmo told me the truth."

Charles Cullen leaned back in the chair, tugged on the front tails of his vest, then clasped his hands together in his lap. "I see," he said at length. "So that's why you came today, then. To confront me for my wrongdoing." He managed a small sad smile. "And rightly so. If I were you, I'd have done the same. What is it that you want now? A confession of guilt? An apology? A promise to suffer a lifetime of shame for what I've done? I can offer you any of these—all of them, if you wish."

I gazed at him and found myself beginning to feel something like pity. What did I want from him? My jaw clenched and unclenched. I breathed deeply to calm myself as well as to gather my thoughts.

Finally, I said, "Did you ever love us? Mother and me?"

"Desperately, Anna, I swear."

"Why did you leave us?"

"I was a fool."

"How could you give my brother away, have him put in an asylum?"

"You must believe me when I say that since then, not a day has gone by when I haven't thought of him, regretted—so deeply—all that happened, all that I did. I don't even recognize the person I was then. I abhor that person. And you're right. I've been trying to make amends. That's why I wanted to find you … to know you … to tell you that I'm sorry, truly sorry."

"Are you?"

"I don't expect you to believe me. But I know it now, so well, what I was meant to know, that 'no space of regret can make amends for one life's opportunity misused.'"

I shook my head. The words … they were familiar. A snatch of poetry? "I don't understand," I said. I rose from the chair. "Perhaps I should go."

He rose too, quickly. "Wait! Please. Let me show you something. May I?"

I hesitated, then said. "All right."

"I'll be right back." He disappeared into the hall, and in a moment returned with a tin box, the kind used for storing cherished letters or family keepsakes. When he stepped into the room, he turned and closed the door behind him. Then he moved to a couch by the far window and motioned for me to join him. "Please, come sit. It will just take a moment."

I stepped across the room and tentatively eased myself down on the couch beside him. When he undid the latch and lifted the lid of the box, I couldn't help but gasp. I recognized at once the pattern of the quilt, a white background with pink and blue embroidered lambs. It was Henry's quilt, the one wrapped around him in my dream, the one he was tucked into the last time I saw him, on the night he was taken away.

"It's Henry's," I whispered.

"Yes." Charles Cullen lifted it gently from the box. He unfolded the quilt to reveal within it a small velveteen bear with black button eyes and a sewed-on smile.

The room and everything around me receded as I reached for that small bear and held it in my hands. This had been Henry's bear. His baby hands had touched it. Its soft velveteen cheek had nuzzled his. This was the bear I had seen in my dreams, and yet it seemed as though this moment itself were a dream, because it was so odd to hold this evidence of Henry's life.

"You still have them—his quilt, his bear." My eyes burned with tears. I couldn't hold them back.

"I kept them all these years."

"Why?"

"I was going to get rid of them ... that night. But I found I simply couldn't part with them."

"Did Mother know?"

"No." He shook his head. "I never told her."

"Was it you who wanted to give Henry away, or was it Mother?"

"Both," he said quietly. "And neither. I know it's hard—impossible—to understand. We wanted to keep him, yet we believed we couldn't."

"You couldn't," I said, "and still pursue your dreams? Henry would have held you back?"

He touched the quilt, rubbing one corner between thumb and forefinger. "You have to understand, Anna, things were different back then. Many families with children like Henry didn't keep them. The vast majority ended up in asylums. But it was not done without consequences to fathers and mothers. Few people could be so heartless as to feel no sense of loss. Certainly, I felt the loss deeply."

"You never forgot him, then?"

"I hoped I would. I hoped that a new life and a measure of success would make me forget, but it didn't happen that way. There was no success, and there was no forgetting."

"I'm sorry, Charles." When I said the words, I knew that they were true. For the first time, I was sorry for how this man had been affected by the episode of loss in our lives.

"When I came back from California," he went on, "it was to try to find Henry, but it was too late. I went to the asylum, but he had died a year or two before. I asked when he had died, and they couldn't tell me exactly."

"There was a fire," I said. "All the records were destroyed."

Charles frowned as he looked at me. "Yes. How did you know?"

I tried to think. I wiped the tears from my eyes with the tips of my fingers. "I don't know. It was just a guess. Or maybe Cosmo told me."

"Well, you're right. That's exactly what happened. I don't know when Henry died. Nor do I know where he's buried. And so it was too late to make any kind of amends with Henry. I grieved for weeks after that. Until I realized that, though Henry was gone, I myself was still alive, I still had time. I could do *something*. You see"—and here his voice became animated, hopeful—"I knew I could still interfere, for good, in human matters, even though it seemed I had lost the power forever."

Then it came to me. For all the times I had read the story, I knew those words. Charles Dickens. Marley's Ghost. Charles Cullen was repeating the words of Old Marley.

I was about to say something when there was a brief knock at the library door. When Charles said, "Come in," the door opened, and Ellie leaned in, holding on to the knob. "I'm sorry to interrupt, but dinner's ready. I've asked the children to wash up. Betty will be serving in about two minutes."

"Thank you, darling," Charles said. "We'll be right along."

Ellie smiled, took a step back, and gently shut the door.

Charles turned to me. "You'll stay for dinner, won't you, Anna?"

I fingered Henry's quilt, ran my hand along the crown of the black-eyed bear. "Yes," I said. I nodded and smiled. "Of course I'll stay."

184

CHAPTER 20

"So how did it go with that Cullen fellow?" Freddy asked.

"Very well," I said curtly. Charles Cullen was not the topic I wished to discuss with Freddy Mansfield. I had something else on my mind.

But he wouldn't let it go. "Is he really your father?"

"Of course he is, Freddy. How can you even ask such a question?"

"Well, you haven't seen him for years and suddenly there he is, claiming paternity and fidelity and all that. Seems a bit strange, doesn't it?"

"I don't know what's so strange about it. Mother wouldn't let him have contact with me. You knew Mother. You knew how she was."

"Yes." He nodded. "Yes, I did." Freddy had never cared for Mother, and the feeling, I'm afraid, had been mutual. Once Mother died, I thought Freddy might feel free to marry me, but so far it hadn't happened.

We were in my apartment on Central Park West, the place I called home in New York. It wasn't terribly fancy, as far as Manhattan penthouses go, but it was adequate for the time I spent there, and it had a charming view of the park. Freddy was at the bar, fixing himself a drink. I watched as he shook the tumbler, then poured the martini into a glass.

"You sure you don't want something, darling?" he asked.

"Yes, I'm sure. It isn't even noon."

He shrugged. "Suit yourself." He speared an olive and dropped it into the glass.

I fingered the pendant around my neck while waiting for Freddy to join me on the couch. As he walked toward me, he said, "I know what you're thinking."

"Do you?"

He sat beside me and lifted the martini. "You're thinking I drink too much."

I let go of the pendant and dropped both hands to my lap. "That's not what I was thinking at this moment, but since you brought it up—"

"Well, you can put that thought right out of your pretty head," he interrupted. "My drinking is under control."

"Is it, Freddy?"

"Of course. I drink no more than any other lush in the theater." He laughed at that and took a long swallow of the martini. "Besides," he went on, "this is the stuff that brings out my creativity, that greases the wheels of—of—well, of whatever it is that makes me a star. This is the stuff that makes the magic."

"In other words, you'd be absolutely nothing on stage without it."

"On no, darling, I'm not saying that—"

"But I believe you're saying exactly that."

"Now, sweetheart ..." He leaned toward me and gently caressed my cheek with the backs of his fingers. "I am a star because of my talent. There you go. Yes, that's what I was trying to say. The alcohol is merely the sweetest of oil, the thing that greases the wheel of my talent, helps things along, you know."

"But Freddy—"

"But *Anna*," he chided, mocking me light-heartedly. "You worry too much. And besides, you don't want to be a prude, or worse, a nag. That's such a bore."

"I'm certainly not trying to be either one."

"Hmmm …" he purred as he downed the rest of his drink.

"I'm simply afraid that someday it's going to catch up with you, maybe even ruin you."

"Nonsense," he said confidently as he rose from the couch. "I think I'll have another."

He had been drinking the first time I met him, some four years earlier. But then, so had everyone else, as it had been at a New Year's Eve party hosted by Broadway producer Nils Granlund at the Waldorf-Astoria. I gave no thought at all to the drinking. I knew only that I wanted to become acquainted— well acquainted—with this man I'd seen perform on Broadway, this man of uncommon talent and undeniable charm. In those days, he hadn't yet reached his peak of success. His star was only beginning to rise, and he was far less sure of himself, far less confident of his place in the theater and in the world.

He was still a bit of a small-town boy, a product of Midwestern living, the son of an insurance salesman and his wife who'd spent their whole lives in Mason, Ohio. That he, little Freddy Mansfield, had somehow broken free of the provincial life and journeyed to the heights of Broadway— well, that was to live out the impossible dream to the starry-eyed folks back in Mason. At the dawn of 1928, Freddy was still trying to get used to being a hero in his own hometown, let alone an icon of the stage, known across the country and around the world.

That was when I fell in love with him.

As his success increased, so too, in seemingly perfect measure, did his alcoholic consumption. But I believed—I *knew*—that if he and I could somehow settle into domestic life, things would change.

"What else is on your mind, darling?"

I sighed. I was suddenly hesitant to talk about it. "Oh, I don't know, Freddy."

"Come on. I can always tell when you're mulling over something. You might as well tell me."

I took his free hand, the one without the second martini, and squeezed it. "All right then, here it is. I need to know whether or not you love me."

His jaw dropped even as he smiled, as though he were amused. "Dearest, you have to ask? You know I'm mad about you." He let go my hand and lifted the pendant from my chest. "What do you think this is all about?"

I touched the pendant lightly, nodded. "Yes, I know. But ..."

He leaned toward me and kissed my brow, my cheek, my lips. "Come now, Anna, what's this all about?"

My gaze dropped to the floor, then back to him. I blurted, "Don't you want children, Freddy?"

He looked at me a long moment and finally laughed, one brief guffaw. "Of course I want children. Don't be silly."

"But don't you see? The time is now. We should be having children now, not in some unforeseeable future."

He shook his head. "Darling, you're merely panicking because you had a birthday. We have plenty of time for all that."

I unclasped my hand from his and rose from the couch. Suddenly, I had to pace. I moved to the window, looked out over the green expanse of Central Park, turned back to Freddy. "You don't intend to marry me," I blurted.

He, too, stood, ran a hand through his hair, and downed the last of his drink. "Do we really need to discuss this, Anna?"

"Yes, I think we do."

"You know I have every intention of marrying you—"

"But when, Freddy?"

"Oh, Anna." He moved back to the bar. I thought he might fix himself yet another drink, but he merely settled the glass on the counter. "We will marry when the time is right. I really don't care to argue about it, darling."

"I'm not trying to argue, I just ..."

"Just what, Anna?" He sounded impatient.

"Need some assurance, I guess."

"But I've already told you. Must I tell you again that I intend to marry you?"

My hands met and became a tight knot at my waist. I felt myself floundering. "But Freddy, I'm always wondering how devoted you really are. If it weren't for the flirting—"

"Flirting? What are you talking about?"

"Oh, don't play dumb with me. I saw you at Olivia's party—"

"At Olivia's party? Doing what?"

"You were with that chorus girl. You were throwing yourself at a chorus girl!"

He had been pacing, but he stopped suddenly. He frowned. "Was I? A chorus girl, you say. I don't remember."

"You don't remember?"

"No. You're probably imagining things."

"I didn't imagine it. Helen Highfield saw it too. As did everyone else, I'm sure."

He shook his head. "If I was talking with one of the girls, it was probably about nothing at all—the weather, or the wine, or the food at the party. I have no memory of her. So you see, she—whoever she was—was completely forgettable."

"You had your arms around her, Freddy. I doubt you were discussing the weather. And your not remembering is no excuse. You don't remember because you were drunk. I have a feeling you would have flirted with her even if you'd been sober."

"Nonsense. I don't waste my time with chorus girls. You know that, Anna."

"Do I, Freddy?"

"Well, if you don't, you should. I would never set my sights on a mere line dancer. You and I, Anna—we're not ordinary people. We will never live ordinary lives. We are far above all that. You should be thankful."

CHAPTER 21

The late afternoon sun settled over the grass like a contented sigh. The air itself felt weightless and happy, a breeze somersaulting through the trees while the leaves quietly clapped their hands. All was immeasurably peaceful, as though some long-forgotten part of Eden had found its way to this place and settled in. I listened intently, half expecting to hear angel wings, or maybe even the voice of God whispering through heaven's portals, but there was only the festive leaves, the distant birdsong, and the occasional rustle of paper as Margaret, beside me, turned the pages of the newest edition of *Harper's Bazaar*.

We sat reading in white wicker chairs on the Cullens's front porch, a table with two glasses of iced tea between us. It was mid-July, and I was enjoying one of my now frequent visits to the Cullen home. Each time I arrived, I was welcomed warmly, and in fact my visits were greeted with great excitement among the children. Very soon each of the children and I had our special routine: fifteen-year-old Margaret and I styled her hair and experimented with makeup and read fashion magazines like *Harper's Bazaar* and *Vogue* and *Miss Modern*. Thirteen-year-old Alan and I played a running tournament of checkers. Peter and I talked trains because I had traveled on so many of them and he wanted to become an engineer and drive the big locomotives. Sylvia and I performed plays with her dolls, and Teddy and I painted pictures using little pots of watercolors. Three-year-old Julia was always eager to sit on my lap and listen to a story. Often, I brought the children little gifts, and I reveled in seeing their eyes light up at the latest offering: baked goods from the city, chocolates from my favorite confectionary on Fifth Avenue, and small toys I picked up here and there.

The children were, in fact, what primarily drew me to the Cullens's home. They made me feel loved and wanted and … part of something. Perhaps the best thing about being with the family was those times when, after dinner, we all gathered around the piano to sing, accompanied by Charles. The pleasure these hours brought me was genuine, and something other than the joy I knew while performing on stage. Not better, but more solid somehow.

The second reason I came was for the peacefulness of the place. The bucolic setting offered a vast difference to the frenetic life of New York. I found renewal in the restfulness it offered. It was also a place to escape the one thing that plagued me most—Freddy and his unwillingness to commit to me. I never invited him to accompany me there; I wanted to keep my two worlds separate, at least for now.

Spending time with Charles, I'm afraid, was rather far down my list of reasons for journeying to Connecticut. I remained wary of him, wrestling still with the question of abandonment—why, after all, had he left Mother and me all those years ago? I had yet to get a satisfying answer to that nagging question, although I don't think he could have said anything that would have made his leaving us seem right.

From the corner of my eye, I saw Margaret drop the magazine to her lap. "I wonder what's keeping Mother," she said. "She should have been home by now."

I looked out over the long barren drive—no sign of Ellie's Ford heading toward the house. "I'm sure everything's fine," I offered. "After all, she didn't go alone, did she?"

Margaret shook her head. "She never goes alone. She always has somebody with her. Maybe I should have gone this time too."

"I wouldn't worry yet, dear. She said she'd be back at five, and it's now only a few minutes after. You said yourself you always feel perfectly safe whenever you're there."

"I do." She nodded. "But there are always people coming and going, and you never know who might show up."

Just before I met her, Elinor Cullen had started volunteering at a soup kitchen in New Haven where she became acquainted with the residents of a nearby Hooverville, so named after President Hoover, who seemed incapable of pulling the country out of its current severe economic depression. The number of men out of work was enormous, with families left homeless and destitute. Camps sprang up around the country where they settled themselves and tried to survive. It was at such a place that Ellie was now. She and a few of the other kitchen volunteers—another woman and two young men from a seminary school—had formed a group to visit the shantytown weekly to see what the residents needed. They held drives to collect goods for the folks: blankets, clothing, soap, canned food.

Ellie had her own Ford sedan, a four-door, into which she'd pile the goods, and she, along with the other volunteers, would head off to Hooverville to distribute whatever had been collected that week. I had no idea whether Charles worried about her mingling with the down-and-outers, but apparently he didn't stand in her way. Nor did he accompany her, as she went while he was at work and the younger children were with their nanny.

Margaret appeared thoughtful as she gazed out over the yard. After a moment, she said, "The people we've met there seem like good people. Just down on their luck, is all. But oh Anna, it's a miserable place. Terrible, really. You can't imagine. Try to picture rows of shacks made of tin and cardboard and bits of wood, all thrown together this way and that. That's what those people call home. The streets are dirt—or mud when it rains. That's where the children play." She paused and shook her head. "Those poor children. I feel sorriest for them. Their clothes are practically rags. And they're so thin, all of them, just skin and bone. Even the children in the orphanage are better fed than they!"

She paused then, long enough for me to say, "But of course, that's why your mother and the others are there, to give them food and clothing—the things they need."

"Yes." She looked at me and smiled. "Still, I wish Mother would get home."

"I'm sure she'll be here any minute."

"Maybe someone was sick or something. It seems someone always has a fever or has been burned by one of the cooking fires. Mother's trying to find a doctor who will volunteer to care for them, but until she finds one, she and the others are managing as best they can."

I shivered at that. Who knew what kinds of diseases might be festering in the shantytown. It was certainly good of Ellie and the others to go, but was it wise?

"Last time I was there," Margaret said, "there was a baby sick with impetigo. It had open sores all over its poor little face."

"Impetigo!" I repeated. "That's highly infectious."

Margaret nodded. "Mother wouldn't let me touch the child, of course. One of the young men from the seminary prayed over it—that was all we could do. That's why Mother is trying to get a doctor to help. I know a doctor could have made that baby better in no time."

I stopped listening. I looked down at the magazine in my lap and started quietly turning the pages. I didn't want to think of that baby—of anyone living in the shantytown, not then, not ever—certainly not on that lovely summer afternoon on that wraparound porch overlooking the Connecticut countryside. I had never slept in a cardboard house, though I'd had my share of cheap hotels, of roaches and bed bugs and ants, broken windows and frigid rooms, dirty sheets and smelly blankets.

Those days were long ago, and I didn't want to return to them, not even in my mind.

But Margaret called me back to her with a laugh. "You know, Anna," she said, "I actually asked Mother whether we might invite you along sometime."

"To the shantytown?"

"Yes. Can you imagine? What was I thinking?"

I shuddered slightly. "What did your mother say?"

"She said a shantytown is no place for a Broadway star, and of course she's right." She smiled at me, and I smiled in return, hoping she hadn't heard my sigh of relief. She went on, "I can't imagine you walking through the mud handing out blankets. And besides, she said people might recognize you and it would cause all kinds of an uproar. Folks would swarm you looking for an autograph, and it all might leak out to the press and then they'd do a story saying you were handing out clothing at the Hooverville, and then, Mother said, the people who might want to do you harm would say you were only doing it for publicity. But really, Anna, who would want to do you any harm? You're so nice and kind to everyone. Why, it's just like you're a regular person and not a famous actress at all. That's why I thought you might like to come. Would anyone really want to hurt you?"

I thought about that a moment, thought of the back-stabbing in the theater, the unkind remarks of other performers, especially the women who envied me, thought of the searing comments of the critics as they pounded out their reviews on typewriter keys worn smooth by years of caustic remarks. I had been lauded, but I had been hated too, and there were always those who were waiting for you to fall.

"There are always people who want to hurt you, no matter who you are," I said at length.

"Even if you're beautiful and talented, like you are, Anna?"

"Oh yes."

She shook her head. "People are something."

At last we heard the engine-roar of Ellie's car approaching, and in another moment, she hopped out and handed the car off to Jensen to park it in the garage.

"You're finally home, Mother!" Margaret said as she stood to greet Ellie on the porch. "I was beginning to worry."

"I'm sorry to be late, dear," Ellie said. "There's just so much to do ... ah, don't hold me too close, darling, I'm afraid I'm hot and sweaty."

Margaret squeezed her mother in a hug anyway. I went on sitting haplessly in the wicker chair, unsure of how to greet this wealthy woman who looked as though she had just battled all of nature and lost. Her clothes and shoes were dirty, her short bobbed hair in disarray, her face pale from the heat. Finally I settled on, "Can I get you a glass of iced tea, Ellie? Or maybe some cold water?"

"Thanks, but don't bother, Anna," she said cheerfully. "I'm headed straight for the bath. I can hardly show up for dinner like this."

"Mother," Margaret said, "I was just telling Anna how I thought she might want to join us at the shantytown. That was silly, wasn't it?" She finished with a laugh.

"Yes," Ellie agreed, "that was rather silly, I'm afraid. I hardly think a famous actress would want to end up looking like this." And at that, she laughed too.

I stood. "Well, really I ... I admire you, Ellie. I think it's awfully good of you—"

She cut me off with a wave of her hand. "I enjoy it. And it gives me something to do."

"But maybe I *should* go with you sometime ..."

"Nonsense. You'd be recognized, and that could lead to all kinds of trouble. Better if you didn't go." She took a step toward the front door and stopped. She turned back to me. "I have an idea, though. If you'd really like to do something, you should come with us to the orphanage sometime to sing to the children. They don't know who you are ... but, oh, they would love to hear you sing, Anna, since you sing so beautifully. So much better than the rest of us. Except for Charles, of course." She smiled.

Before I could say anything, Margaret exclaimed, "Oh Mother, that's a great idea! Anna, you really should come with us! We have so much fun. The children are wonderful. We sing to them, and then we invite them to sing along with us, and afterwards we play games and have hot cocoa when the weather's cold or lemonade when it's hot. I know they'd all adore you if you came."

"Well"—I thought a moment. Why was I hesitating?— "maybe I will, then."

Margaret actually clapped her hands, just once, a gesture of triumph. "Oh, would you, Anna? It would mean so much to the children. Some of them ... well, an orphanage is no place to grow up, you know. I mean, this one is run by good people, so if you have to live in an orphanage, this is the place you want to be. But nothing can compare to having a home and family, really. All these children have lost their families or been abandoned. Some—oh, it's so sad. Some of them are sickly, like the girl who was left crippled by polio. And then there's the infant who was recently brought to the orphanage because he was born blind. I suppose his parents didn't want him if he couldn't see. Can you imagine?"

I took a deep breath, shaking my head no, while all the while thinking, *Yes, yes, I can imagine. I can imagine parents who would do that. Your father ... and mine ...*

Ellie laid a hand on Margaret's arm, as though to cut her off. "Well, listen you two," she said, "I'm off to clean up. Why don't you just relax and enjoy each other's company until Betty has dinner ready."

She left us then, and Margaret and I resumed our seats. I picked up my glass of iced tea, but the ice had melted, and the tea had grown warm. I set it down again. There was a distinctly unsettled feeling in my stomach, though I couldn't quite place its source.

"When I grow up," Margaret said, "I'm going to adopt a whole bunch of children, maybe twelve."

"Twelve!"

"Yes, if I can. Every time we go to the orphanage I want to gather all the children up in my arms and bring them home with me. I want to do for them what Mother and Daddy did for me. You know, give me a family and a home."

"How old were you when they adopted you, Margaret?"

"I was almost three."

"So you have no memories of your real parents?"

She shook her head. "None at all. I have memories of the orphanage, very vague memories, but nothing of my life before that. I'm told my parents were killed in an auto accident, both at the same time."

"Oh Margaret, how awful. I'm so sorry."

"It *is* sad, I know. And yet, it's hard to grieve for people you never knew. Don't be sorry for me, Anna. I consider myself lucky because I was adopted by the best parents in the world. And you ... think how lucky you are that Daddy is your real father! Oh Anna, aren't you glad we have the same father? He's really the best father imaginable."

The best father imaginable. I had to think about that. Those were not the words I would have used to describe Charles Cullen when I was Margaret's age. Just the opposite. He was no father at all, someone who had given his own son away and later discarded Mother and me when we no longer fit into his plans. *He ain't no good to neither of us.* So said Tillie to Mabel at the end of the movie. So Mother had implied to me. And so I had believed. Now Margaret made it sound as though Charles Cullen could do no wrong. Were we even talking of the same man?

"Yes," I said, "yes, I'm glad we have the same father." But that was as far as I could go. I couldn't say he was the best father. I was still trying simply to adjust to the fact that he was my father at all.

***

I didn't visit the orphanage with the Cullens in the following weeks, nor was anything more said about it, to my relief. I didn't want to change anything about my visits right now; everything was fine the way it was. Besides, we would be taking the show on the road at the end of August, starting with Chicago, and I would be away for several months. Maybe I could rethink the orphanage when I got back.

Our final performance at the Palace was set for August 27. A few days before, I visited the Cullens for a final time before embarking on the tour. It was heartbreaking to have to leave the children, and they were in tears when it was time for me to go. But Charles surprised us by announcing that they would all be coming to see me in my final performance on Saturday, including little Julia and the nanny. That eased the pain of separation, and I promised—with tears, hugs, and kisses—to see them all again as soon as I got back from tour.

Charles walked me to the drive where Jensen waited to take me back to the city. "May we visit you in your dressing room after the show?" he asked when we reached the car.

"Of course, Charles," I said. "Give me a few minutes to get out of costume and then come back."

"Wonderful, Anna. I think the children will get a huge kick out of that. It'll be something special for them."

I laughed lightly. "Well, I'm glad I can so easily amuse them. I'm afraid my dressing room isn't much to see."

"But it's you they want to see, of course." He smiled, and I returned it. "Now, when you get back from tour, you'll fall right back into visiting with us, of course."

"Yes, of course. As soon as I get back to New York, I'll make plans to come."

"You're always welcome here," he said, "I hope you know that, Anna."

I smiled again. "I appreciate that."

"But more than that," he went on, "I hope you will come to think of this as your home. That is, if you haven't already."

He looked at me expectantly, but something in my heart crumbled in that moment, and I could give him no satisfactory answer. "I have no home," I said at length. "I never have."

"I know," he said. He looked at the ground, then back at me. "I do know that, Anna, and it's my fault."

I shook my head. "It doesn't matter now."

"Oh, but it does. I want you to be happy, dear."

"Do you think I'm not happy?"

He hesitated a moment, then said, "I hope you are, Anna. You certainly have every reason to be. You managed to do what your mother and I were never able to do. All our dreams came true in you, and I'm proud of you for that. Still, I know what life is like in the theater. I know …"

His words trailed off. He wanted to hug me, I could tell, but I found such acts of affection awkward. Instead, I held out a hand. "I'm afraid I really must go." He took my hand in both of his. "I'll see you all after the show on Saturday night."

I was willing to give only so much leeway to Charles Cullen.

CHAPTER 22

Saturday night, the entire cast was feeling a great sense of joy and relief—just one more performance to get through and we could call it a stunningly successful run on Broadway. The exhilaration backstage was almost palpable. I myself felt lighthearted as I prepared for the performance in my dressing room. I smiled at the thought of the Cullens in the audience, cheering me on. I looked forward to having them visit me in my dressing room afterward, especially Margaret, to whom I felt a close attachment.

A knock came at the door. "Ten minutes, Miss Rycroft!"

"Thank you, Mr. Sedgwick!" I stood and fairly twirled in front of Charlotte Tennant. "How do I look, Charlotte?"

"More beautiful than ever, Miss Rycroft."

"Good. Wish me luck, then!"

"May you break that leg tonight, Miss Rycroft."

I didn't see Freddy in the wings, which should have been my first clue that something was wrong. Mr. Sedgwick was there, clipboard in hand, speaking with some of the chorus girls. I pulled him aside. "Where's Mr. Mansfield?" I asked.

I didn't like the look in Mr. Sedgwick's eyes when he turned them on me. He tried to smile as he said, "Mr. Mansfield arrived late, but he's getting dressed. He'll be ready momentarily." His last words were spoken as he wiped his brow with a crumpled handkerchief.

"Is everything all right, Mr. Sedgwick?" I asked.

"Oh yes. Yes. Everything's fine."

"But—"

"Excuse me, Miss Rycroft. Felix! Felix," he hollered at a stagehand somewhere beyond my shoulder. "I told you to take those dresses upstairs at once." With that, he was gone, just as the orchestra began warming up in the pit.

I was suddenly anxious, knowing something wasn't right. Despite my foreboding, I knew of course that the show must go on, that as professionals we would somehow right whatever might be wrong. Few shows were completely flawless, but we always got through, and managed to do so without the audience noticing anything amiss.

It was when the curtain rose that I knew what was plucking at the stage manager's nerves. Frederick Mansfield stood in the spotlight, drinking in the audience's adoring applause. That was how it always went and yet, tonight, even before he moved, or said his first line, or so much as uttered a sound, I knew he was hopelessly drunk. No one in the audience would have known, but I knew because I knew Frederick Mansfield. So that was the reason for the sweat on Mr. Sedgwick's brow. Freddy must have come to the theater reeking of liquor. I thought at once of Freddy's understudy, Marcus Blaylock, and wondered whether he shouldn't be the one out there tonight. Marcus was wonderfully talented, every bit as good as Freddy, and if it had been my call …

But Mr. Sedgwick allowed Freddy to go on because he knew, as I did, that this wouldn't be the first time the great Frederick Mansfield performed drunk. He had done it before, any number of times, and had managed to pull through. But tonight of all nights! Our final night at the Palace. The night Charles and his family had come to see me perform!

When the moment came for me to step on stage, I did so with no small amount of fear and misgiving. I breathed in the applause and tried to steady myself. Then I gave Freddy a steely-eyed stare of warning, and he offered me an almost imperceptible nod to let me know he wasn't going to make a mess of things. His ego was just large enough to think that nothing, not even inebriation, could keep him from giving a stellar performance. I prayed that the pride in his soul was stronger than the whiskey in his veins.

The first two acts played out reasonably well, with only a few small stumbles and slightly slurred words. My fear and anxiety began to lessen as Freddy and I moved through our routine of song and dance. Two or three of the other actors glanced at me from time to time—it was impossible to be near Freddy and not smell the liquor—but I tried to encourage them with my eyes to just go on as though nothing were amiss, that we would get through like the professionals we were.

Freddy and I held hands and bowed to the audience at the end of the second act. We smiled graciously and nodded to acknowledge their applause. But as soon as the curtain came down for intermission, I pulled my hand from Freddy's. "How could you do this?" I cried. "How could you come to the theater drunk on our last night at the Palace?"

Freddy went on smiling graciously. "Darling, I assure you I am not drunk. Only pleasantly oiled, shall we say? It keeps the creative wheels spinning, you know."

"Oh, Freddy, I'm so tired of your talk of oiling your wheels! What a lot of nonsense. You know how important tonight is to me. Charles and his entire family are out there in the audience. Not to mention the usual critics!"

"Come now, darling, the show is going beautifully, as always. I don't know why you're so angry. Now, if you'll excuse me,"—it sounded like *ekskooz me*—"I'd like to retire to my dressing room for a moment before the next act."

I watched him leave and then, with clenched fists, I went in search of Mr. Sedgwick. He was in the wings talking with a stagehand. "Why did you let him go on?" I asked, not caring that I was interrupting.

He knew exactly what I meant. He dismissed the stagehand with a nod, then said, "This afternoon Marcus Blaylock suffered an attack of pleurisy. He wasn't available."

So that was it. The understudy was sick.

When I didn't respond, Mr. Sedgwick looked at me beseechingly. "Of course I immediately spoke with Mr. Downing and Mr. Comstock," he explained, speaking of the director and the producer. "We realized we had no choice. The alternative would have been to cancel the performance."

Cancel the performance? Impossible. "I understand," I said with a nod. "Of course you couldn't cancel."

"We made the call based on Mr. Mansfield's history. This isn't the first time, you know ..."

I sniffed out a little laugh. "I of all people know very well this isn't the first time. Well, Mr. Sedgwick, we've made it this far. We'll just have to hope the second half of the show goes as well as the first."

But during intermission Frederick Mansfield must have gone to his dressing room and tipped the spout of his oil can once more, because we weren't very far into the third act when it happened. Freddy and I were alone in the spotlight, in the midst of another romantic song-and-dance routine. As we moved across the stage, I could feel his body wilting. I tried to take the lead, but he was a ragdoll in my arms. His rancid breath turned my stomach. I struggled to smile, to hold back tears, but I began to despair.

"Freddy, buck up!" I whispered in his ear. "Pull yourself together!"

"Whatsa matter, darling?" he slurred. "Everything's marvelous."

In that moment, I detested him and swore I would never forgive him for putting me through a performance like this. As soon as the show was over, I would give him a tongue-lashing he would never forget.

The song was winding down. We had reached the final chorus. "Come on, Freddy. We're almost there. Don't fail me now."

We unlocked ourselves from each other and took one step back. We were supposed to turn once and then come back together for the song's finale. But instead of turning once and returning to my arms, he turned once, twice, and yet again, around and around, like a top in slow motion, until his legs twisted up on each other and his knees buckled, his dead-weight falling in a heap at my feet.

The music stopped abruptly. I stopped too, my hands still hanging in mid-air, waiting in vain to be met by the clasp of my leading man. For one interminable moment, I gazed in horror at the drunken sod passed out facedown at my feet, and wondered whether I were in the midst of a terrible nightmare. Was I really on the stage of the Palace Theater, standing over the wreck of Frederick Mansfield? Were there really hundreds of eyes on me, witnessing this disgrace?

A great gasp went up from the audience, followed by murmurs, a few hesitant chuckles, and finally a roar of laughter. My gaze turned, almost in spite of myself, from the unconscious heap on the stage to the darkened cavern peopled by the elite theater-goers of New York, the showbiz columnists and newspaper critics, the Broadway producers and big-wigs—and worst of all, Charles Cullen and his family. My father was out there somewhere, and Ellie, and Margaret, and ... oh dear God! As my eyes swept the laughing audience, I did the unthinkable. I hiccupped. And then I hiccupped again. Loudly. And when I did, the laughter intensified.

Frederick Mansfield and I were two of our time's most revered stars of musical comedy; we wanted people to laugh at us. But not like this. Never like this.

I heard shouting in the wings, followed by two stagehands rushing on stage. They bent over Freddy, turned him face up, slapped his cheeks. He moaned and opened his eyes. They lifted him to his feet and, tossing his arms around their shoulders, they dragged him from center stage into the wings, the toes of his shoes leaving scuff marks across the polished wood.

The curtain sank slowly. As soon as it was down, I tumbled to my knees and burst into tears. I was Little Miss Honeycomb again, hurting, humiliated, a child weeping into her taffeta dress. A hand touched my shoulder. A voice broke through my wailing. But it wasn't Uncle Cosmo, come to comfort me, to lift me gently and take me back to the dressing room. It was Mr. Sedgwick. He was saying something to me, but his words made no sense. I didn't care. No one could ever live down what had just happened, not even Annalise Rycroft.

I would have my understudy take over for me in Chicago. My agent had long wanted me to go to Hollywood. Now was the time to go.

CHAPTER 23

I stared out the train window at the passing landscape. I didn't know where we were, nor did I care. Charlotte Tennant was traveling with me. We were in a Pullman and had connected drawing rooms, each with a bed, sofa, lounge chairs, table, wardrobes, and private toilet, though Charlotte spent much of her time sitting in mine, eyeing me cautiously. She said little. I spoke even less.

We were on our second day of traveling west toward Los Angeles. At LaSalle Street Station in Chicago the previous night, we had switched from the 20th Century Limited to the Santa Fe Chief, a long black eel of a train whose powerful engine was now pulling us through unidentifiable Midwest farmland. Chicago—where Freddy and I were to have taken the show, where we would be right now if I weren't on a train to Los Angeles and he hadn't taken himself off to a sanitarium in an effort to dry out.

I reclined on the sofa by the window, my body swaying with every turn of the wheels, every curve, every bump. I was a fallen leaf trembling and tossed by each breath of the moving train. I was numb, silent, dark …

"Miss Rycroft?"

Silence.

"Miss Rycroft?"

I turned from the window to see Charlotte Tennant standing at my side. "Oh. Yes, Charlotte?"

"It's nearly noon, and you haven't eaten all day. Can I bring you something?"

"No, thank you. I'm not hungry."

"Still not feeling well?"

I shook my head. Since the night of that terrible final show, five days ago now, I had felt sick, slightly nauseous, dull aches coming and going in my side and moving across my belly.

"I'll have the porter bring you some more sodium bicarbonate. Will you drink it?"

"All right."

Charlotte buzzed the porter and spoke to him in low tones at the door. I kept my gaze out the window, toward the wheat fields gold in the sunlight. How many times had I passed this way as a child? Coming and going, always coming and going. Now I was going again, heading toward Hollywood. I hoped this would be a fresh start, but I was anxious and afraid— afraid that I wouldn't be right for the movies, or they wouldn't be right for me. All I had ever known was the stage. What did all of this mean for my career?

Shortly, the porter returned with a tray that held a glass of water made murky with the dissolving powders of sodium bicarbonate. Beside the glass was an additional pitcher of water. The porter, stiff and erect in his starched white uniform, settled the tray on the table.

"Anything else, ma'am?" He directed the question at Charlotte.

"That will be all, thank you."

Charlotte tipped the man, who responded with a slight nod of his head. "Yes, ma'am. Thank you, ma'am."

When he was gone, she handed me the glass. "Try to drink it all," she said. "If it doesn't help, we'll try Milk of Magnesia."

I took the glass and sipped from it.

"You really should eat something," she went on. "To keep up your strength. Mr. Blasberg will be disappointed if you show up in LA sick. After all, he's worked hard to get you this screen test."

Saul Blasberg, my agent. He was in LA now and would meet our train when we arrived. He had taken the whole dreadful affair in stride. Western Union had carried his words to me from across the country:

DON'T WORRY ANNA. ALL PUBLICITY GOOD PUBLICITY. HOLLYWOOD WAITING. COME AT ONCE.

How, I wondered, could any of this be good publicity? Had he not read the headlines? I had read them all, the words stopping me cold. I couldn't bear to read the stories themselves, to see what the critics were saying of me.

The Morning Telegraph:
Drunken Frederick Mansfield Collapses Mid-Song
Leading Lady Annalise Rycroft Hiccups Her Disapproval

Variety:
Mansfield Sinks to New Low…Literally
His love of the bottle leaves him kissing the stage

And leaves Annalise Rycroft high and dry
And hiccupping …

The New York Times:
Famous Duo Done in by Drunken Debacle
For Mansfield, Rycroft, the Show Doesn't Go On

"Miss Rycroft, did you hear me?"

"I'm sorry, Charlotte. What did you say?"

"I said, Mr. Blasberg won't want you to show up sick."

"I won't." I shook my head slightly. "I'll be fine."

She sighed and clasped her hands together at her waist, squeezing until her knuckles turned white. It was what she always did when she was frustrated with me. "Can I bring you some broth?"

"No. Thank you, but no." I took another sip of the bicarbonate. "Maybe later."

Though my gaze had returned to the rush of scenery passing by, I felt the heat of Charlotte's stare on the top of my head. "I wish …" she said. "How I wish I could say something to make you feel better. I really think Mr. Cullen said it best, you know. People have short memories. In another week or two, this will all be forgotten. You will go on being loved and admired, just as you always have been, and just as though nothing ever happened."

She waited. I nodded mechanically. "He did say that, didn't he? He was very kind."

Charles had come to my dressing room that night without Ellie and the children. He was the only person I had allowed in. He put his arms around me and quietly spoke to me the words that Charlotte had just repeated. I listened but I didn't believe him. I cried until the lapels of his jacket were soaked with tears. Nothing he might say could touch the humiliation I felt. After a long time, he kissed my cheek and told me not to let anyone ever defeat me, not the critics, not the audience, not Freddy. He said his home would always have a room for me. And then he left.

Charlotte turned as though to go, then turned back. "Excuse me for saying so, Miss Rycroft, but if you don't feel better by the time we reach LA, I think we should consult a doctor."

I looked at her and nodded, understanding her concern. What she saw before her was someone who had barely eaten for days, who even now, at noon, moped about in her bathrobe, her hair disheveled, her face untouched by makeup. "I'm sure

I'll be better by the time we get there," I said. "But if not, you may call a doctor. Perhaps he can give me something stronger for my stomach."

Her hands at her waist relaxed. She almost smiled. "Very good, Miss Rycroft. I'll let you get some rest, but call me if you need anything."

"I will, Charlotte. Thank you. Here, let me finish this so you can take the glass." I finished the bicarbonate and handed her the glass. On a sudden impulse, I said, "Charlotte, sit for a moment, would you? Pull a chair over from the table. That's right."

She set the glass on the tray and pulled a chair to my side. "Yes, Miss Rycroft?"

"Do you remember Fatty Arbuckle?"

Her brows rose slightly. "Of course. Why do you ask?"

"I've been thinking about him."

"Oh, now really—" She waved a hand, but I cut her off.

"He was the highest paid actor in Hollywood, you know, back in '21. He was the beloved comedian, the big money-maker because everyone flocked to see his pictures. And then that starlet died at his party, and everyone said he killed her. Everyone was so sure. He was as good as convicted before he even went to trial."

"He was acquitted, of course."

"But that's the point. He insisted he was innocent, and a jury found him not guilty, but it was too late. His career was already in a shambles. He never made another picture. The public that so adored him turned on him completely before he could tell his side of the story."

"Miss Rycroft, it's senseless for you to think of what happened to Mr. Arbuckle. He was indicted on charges of manslaughter. All you did was hiccup. They are hardly comparable offenses."

"No, but don't you see? If people had really loved him, wouldn't they have stood by him? And if people really loved me, would they have printed all those awful things in the papers?"

"You expect too much of others. What does it matter what people think?"

"What does it matter? In this business, it's everything! The public will make you or they will destroy you. And the speed at which they'll turn on you is frightening."

She leaned forward and actually patted my hand. "Now, my dear," she said. "You don't even know how much support you've received. You refused to read the telegrams and letters that came pouring in—hundreds of them—from people all over the country."

"I couldn't, Charlotte. I couldn't bear to read them."

"In case one of them said something negative about you?"

I didn't respond.

She leaned back in the chair. "You should have gone right back on stage, you know—taken the show to Chicago as was planned rather than running off to LA. Even Mr. Cullen said as much. If your career is ruined, it's because of you, not because of a few people who laughed at you. You are far too sensitive, my dear."

"You don't understand, Charlotte."

"Oh yes, I understand. I've been with you long enough to know you. The public's adoration is the air you breathe. It's what gives you life. You are dead without it. Even if only the few turn against you, you're devastated. And that's a very dangerous way to live, Miss Rycroft." She spoke kindly, though her words were pointed. I wasn't used to her speaking her mind about me.

When I didn't respond, she lifted the drinking glass from the table and stood. She waited another moment, but I had nothing to say. Of course I was dead without the public's adoration. I had no other way to live.

Finally she said, "If you'll excuse me, I think I'll retire to my room for a time. I have some letters I'd like to finish and get posted."

"Of course, Charlotte."

"But the door will be open. Call if you need me."

"I will."

Her mention of letters reminded me of those that were tucked into the pocket of my robe. I slipped a hand into the pocket and withdrew them. One was a letter from Margaret, received the morning I left New York.

Dear Anna,

I just want to make sure you know I thought you were wonderful in the show, truly wonderful. What happened was not because of you but was entirely the fault of that dreadful man, Frederick Mansfield. It's no secret he's a drunk. Everyone has known that for a long time. That's what they say in all the magazines. It was only a matter of time before he did himself in. I'm just sorry you had to be on stage with him when he finally did it. He got his just desserts, but you did not deserve to be laughed at with him. It's all so unfair.

I didn't know until you were leaving how much I've come to love your visits and the time we've spent together. I will miss you terribly. But I do understand why you are going away, and I know you will be a big hit in Hollywood, and I will be so proud of you. Please tell me, though, that you will come back and visit us again soon. Nothing will be the same now without you.

Ever, your loving sister,
Margaret
P.S. I hope you don't mind me calling you my sister, but that is how I feel.

I had written to Margaret at once and posted it just before heading for the train. I thanked her for writing and told her I'd miss her as well, but that, yes, I would visit as soon as I could. Meanwhile, she could write to me in LA, and I gave her the address where I'd be staying. And I told her that, of course, I didn't mind her calling me sister for, after all, that was what we were.

Another letter was from Uncle Cosmo, written the morning after the show when word reached him at his home in Connecticut.

Darling Anna,

Do you remember the time I fell off the stage and into the orchestra pit, breaking my kneecap and sending the audience into gales of laughter? I suspect you feel rather like that now. But you see, it wasn't you who fell off the stage this time, it was Frederick. He merely pulled you with him. You are not to blame. I do hope you know that, dear.

I never did like Mansfield, but always found him to be something of an arrogant brute. Oh, his star soared high, but it was destined to burn out. You, on the other hand, still shine. For you, this episode is but a momentary flicker. Yours is a talent practically unparalleled on the stage today, and you have become what I always knew you would be. A great star, Anna. A great star. Frederick Mansfield will not put out that light.

Go forward and keep believing in yourself, my dear. All will come around right.

Ever loving,
Cosmo

Dear Uncle Cosmo. I held his letter to my heart, savoring the comfort it gave me. Cosmo had always been my encourager, my rock. I couldn't imagine life without him.

And one—one was from Charles. He had written it in haste when he learned I was leaving for LA.

Anna dear,

I know I cannot change your mind about LA, though I would give my right arm to do so. The memory of my own years there fills me with a sharp pain that lies somewhere between fear and desperation. Not to say your experience would be the same as mine—no, you are a better person than I ever was, thank God—more grounded in your career, more sure of yourself and of your art. But let me warn you, Anna, that what looks so brilliant and promising has a dark underside, something grievous that lies just below the surface of things. It takes a measure of superhuman strength not to be pulled into it. Most of us have no such strength. Once waist-deep in muck, it is nearly impossible to get out.

Would that I could keep you close by and watch over you. But that is my father-heart speaking, and I know you are your own person and will do what you deem to be right. If anyone can navigate the swamp that is Hollywood and still walk upright, surely it is you. Just be careful, please, dear. God go with you.

Your loving father,
Charles

The other letters, six of them, were from Freddy. I had answered none of them. They were all long, rambling letters of apology, declarations of undying love, promises of reform. Judging from the scrawled handwriting, he was drunk even when he wrote them, including the last one, penned just as he was leaving for Glen Springs Sanitarium in Watkins Glen, New York. It was there that he hoped the healing waters would dry him out. But I now knew what I didn't want to believe before. He was hopeless. I could never reform him, and I doubted he would ever truly want to reform himself. And for that reason, he and I would never marry.

That was a hard truth to face because I loved him. And it was terribly painful to let go of someone you loved, no matter how dreadful he was. But I would do it. I would make the break because it needed to be done. I had to forget about Frederick Mansfield.

And then there was the other loss to consider, the children I had longed to have with Freddy. They were gone as well. In losing the one, I had lost them all. By the time I started over—met someone else, fell in love, decided to marry—how old would I be? Would it ever happen?

The train rumbled forward. The miles went by. I had to allow the distance to untangle from my heart the ties that I had to New York. I had to let go of what I was leaving behind.

Stubborn knots. Stubborn, stubborn knots. I had loved Frederick Mansfield for years. It would take time to let him go.

Why, Helen, do we hold so tenaciously to our dreams?

Because we have so little without them.

I called for Charlotte. In a moment she was by my side. I held up Freddy's letters for her to take. "Dispose of these for me, will you?"

She took them, glanced at the writing on the envelopes, looked at me as though to ask, *Are you sure?*

"Burn them," I said, "or rip them up into little pieces and toss them from the train window. I never want to see them again."

She was silent for a moment. Finally she said, "Yes, Miss Rycroft."

I followed her with my eyes as she walked off with the letters. There would be more from Freddy, I knew. I would ask Charlotte to return them, unopened.

Outside the window, a flock of birds rose upward from the ground and, as though one great creature, soared toward the open sky. I watched in envy, wishing I, too, could so easily leave all matters of Earth behind.

CHAPTER 24

Our arrival at La Grande Station in Los Angeles comes back to me in wispy pieces, like a long-ago dream. I remember Saul Blasberg waiting for us on the platform—squat, corpulent, a tan derby atop his round head, his wire-frame glasses perched securely on his sizeable nose. He is all smiles and good-natured cheer. He directs Charlotte and me to a limousine that will shuttle us to Helen Highfield's home in North Hollywood. As soon as we settle in—I in the middle of the seat between the two of them—he lights up a Lucky Strike and inhales deeply. As we wind along unfamiliar streets, he chatters the entire way, words I can scarcely absorb through the fog that my mind has become. Screen test, producers, directors, the studio … "This will be your next big step, Anna! Your next big step!"

I sink more deeply into the seat. I am hot, my side hurts, and a wave of nausea rolls over me. Saul's voice becomes a hammer against my brain.

After what seems an interminable time, the limo slows. "Ah, here we are!" Saul announces triumphantly. I silently beg him to stop beating me with his words.

Helen's home is a newly built Spanish Colonial on a tree-lined street. The palm trees stand out to me because they are foreign. I should find them appealing, but I don't. They frighten me. The house itself is white stucco with a red tile roof. I shudder when we pull into the long circular drive. I don't know where I am, nor what will become of me.

I am relieved, though, to step out of the limo, to draw in a breath of air untainted by Saul's cigarette smoke. At once, Helen rushes from the house, her arms open dramatically to draw me to herself in a tight hug. I wince in pain, try to smile, to respond politely to her questions about the trip. Yes, yes, the trip was fine, lovely really, such beautiful countryside.

Max appears, wearing a smoking jacket, a cigar in one hand. "Glad to have you with us," he says. "Your rooms are all ready."

"We're so grateful, really," I say. At least, I think I'm speaking. "It's only until I find my own place, of course."

"Of course, of course. No trouble at all. Stay as long as you like."

We take a step toward the house when Saul stops me. "Afraid I can't stay. I've a meeting in an hour. But Friday, don't forget, I'll pick you up at nine a.m. sharp to take you to the studio."

"Yes, Saul, of course. I won't forget. I'll be ready."

Having seen me safely deposited at Helen's, he's off in a whirlwind of haste. The limousine rolls down the drive and turns onto the street. Helen takes my arm. "Oh Anna," she is saying, "we're going to have such fun!"

A male servant has appeared and is carrying our two suitcases to the house. Everything else—all my trunks, boxes, bags—will be brought by the porters from the station. We enter the house, but I'm hardly aware of my surroundings. Everything runs together with no defining edges, nothing to separate wall from furniture from window. I want only to find a bed and drop into it.

"I've made all sorts of plans," Helen goes on. "We must visit the Brown Derby, the Beverly Hills Hotel, and oh darling, my biggest surprise of all, we're going to weekend at Hearst Castle! It's all arranged for two weeks from now—Bill and Marion are expecting us. That's Marion Davies, the actress, of course—not Hearst's wife, oh no, his mistress, though of course, one never uses that word. But then, you know all about Bill and Marion, don't you? Of course you do. How silly of me! Anyway, Max and I were at the Castle just recently. It was really quite unbelievable. You can't imagine until you see it! It's a regular Mediterranean town up there in the mountains, with the fabulous main house, Casa Grande, right at the center of it all. And oh, the gardens, the pools, the antiques, paintings, tapestries, sculptures! All simply unbelievable! And a zoo, an entire zoo with lions, horses, bears. And the guests, darling! It's a veritable Who's Who—all the important people, not just of Hollywood but of the world! And yet, it's the most extraordinary thing—everyone is there to have fun. Why, when we were there, Marion Davies and Harpo Marx turned somersaults together around the library! Can you imagine?"

I put my hand to my head. Why, oh why were there so many voices? And what is the matter with me that I can scarcely keep my head up, barely walk?

Max's voice: "Can I get you something to drink, Anna dear? A martini or a glass of wine, perhaps?"

Helen's voice: "Anna, you look dreadfully tired. But of course, you've traveled clear across the country. Let's get you to your room so you can rest before dinner."

From somewhere, Charlotte's voice. "Are you quite all right, Miss Rycroft?"

Helen again: "She'll be all right with a little rest. Off to bed with you, young lady, for a nice long nap."

Charlotte: "I'm afraid she hasn't been feeling well. Maybe I should call a doctor."

Max, cheerfully: "Nonsense! Soon as she's awake, I'll fix her a good stiff drink. That and a meal of venison steak will have her right as rain in no time."

We ascend a staircase, enter a room. As we enter, a maid is leaving. She has unpacked my bag, laid my nightgown across the bed, placed upon the bedside table the books I always travel with, have traveled with since childhood. *A Christmas Carol* is on the top of the pile.

Helen again: "There, darling. We'll leave you to get comfortable and crawl into bed. I'll come for you myself when dinner is ready."

The last thing I see in this murky lake of remembrance is this: I am alone in the room, reaching for the book, my father's book. I pick it up, hold it in my hand. And that is all. That must have been when I lost consciousness because I remember nothing after that.

CHAPTER 25

I heard the rattling of chains before I saw the glassy figure floating across the room. In another moment he was beside me, though I couldn't say exactly where that was. I knew only that I was face to face with Jacob Marley, someone I thought I'd never see again—someone I wasn't truly sure I'd ever seen before.

"Is it you, Jacob Marley?" I asked.

He nodded slightly, solemnly. "It is."

"Why are you here? What's happening?"

"You're having your appendix removed, my dear."

"My appendix?"

Another nod. "You are dangerously ill, you know."

"Am I going to die?"

"That depends on you. Do you have the will to live?"

His words both frightened and angered me. "You're speaking nonsense," I said. "I thought I was rid of you years ago. Why are you bothering me now?"

"For love's sake."

"For love's sake? What on earth do you mean by that?"

"Henry ..." He lifted a ghostly hand. His chains rattled.

"It's too late, you know. Henry is dead. I can't go find him. I suppose you're here to chastise me for not listening to you in the first place."

His hand reached me, touched my forearm. Though his hand wasn't solid, still I felt it, sensed the coldness of it. "I'm here to complete our unfinished task. You left me too soon last time. I want to take you someplace."

"Where?"

"To the Valley of the Nameless. Come along."

"The Valley of the Nameless? What—"

"Come."

We moved forward, though I wasn't aware of walking, nor was I aware of what was around us. Everything was indistinct, like a chalk drawing melting in the rain. Time and distance passed. I don't know how long we traveled nor how far we went. It wasn't until we stopped and stood still that our surroundings began to appear and come into focus. Around us, mountains rose up as though they were being formed by a shifting of the earth at that very hour. A thick fog was lifting, carried off on the back of the wind, replaced by light. We stood on the edge of a fertile valley, green like emerald, nurtured by a stream running through it. The sight of it took my breath. I felt small at the expanse of it, and small beneath the towering peaks that formed it. The Valley of the Nameless. *Henry must be here*, I thought. I took a step forward, wanting to see him, wanting to hold him if I could, wanting to explain. But there was no one, not one person, for as far as I could see.

"Where is Henry?" I asked Marley.

"He isn't here."

My eyes swept the great green expanse once more. "There's no one here, is there?"

"No," Marley agreed. "No one."

We stood in silence for a long while. I heard not even the faintest rattling of his chains, nor the hum of my own breath. He seemed to want me to soak up the place, to understand it, to memorize its vastness and its emptiness, to carry it away with me.

"Are you beginning to see?" he asked.

"Yes," I said tentatively. "I think so."

"Good." He laid his hand on my arm again. "Then let's move on."

"Is there more?"

"Yes. One last place."

We began to climb, though again, not of our own effort. We were ascending the side of one of the mountains, and as we moved upward, the sun began to set. When we reached the peak, it was night. From this great height, I felt as though I could reach up and touch the great canopy of stars above us. For it was a clear night, and the whole universe was on display, unimpeded by clouds or trees, buildings or shadows. It was all there, galaxy upon galaxy of sparkling lights.

"This, Anna," Marley said, "is the Pinnacle of the Stars."

"The Pinnacle of the Stars," I repeated, awed. "I've never seen the night sky quite like this. Why did you bring me here?"

He met my question with a question of his own. "How many stars do you see?"

I shook my head. "An infinite number. Who can count them?"

"There is One who can not only count them, but who has named them, each one."

"Named them? Who?"

"The One who created them. Do you remember what the prophet Isaiah said about the stars?"

Again I shook my head. I didn't know who the prophet was, let alone what he had said.

When Marley next spoke, his lips didn't move. It was as though the words flowed from him, or through him—not from his mind and mouth, but out of his heart—from the Bible book of Isaiah.

> Lift up your eyes on high, and see who hath
> created these things:
> who bringeth out their host by number,
> and calleth them all by their names:

by the greatness of his might, and strength,
and power,
not one of them was missing.

For a long while, I couldn't speak, so overwhelmed was I by the sheer number of lights. There seemed no end to them, so far did they stretch out from east to west. Finally, I said, "You mean, God named every one of these stars?"

Marley nodded. "Every one. And if he names the stars, would he not also name his living creatures, those with minds and souls, those who can know him?"

I thought a moment. "So that's why there's no one in the valley."

At that, Marley's features relaxed, his brow unfurled, his shoulders seemed to loosen as though his chains were suddenly less weighty. I thought I heard him sigh, if in fact a ghost can exhale air from lifeless lungs. He seemed relieved. He had finished his task.

"Marley," I asked quietly. "What am I to do now?"

He didn't look at me but kept his eyes on the stars. He lifted his arms toward the heavens. When he spoke, it was slowly, as though he were reciting, which indeed he was, repeating to me the words he had said to Scrooge: "Why did I walk through crowds of fellow-beings with my eyes turned down, and never raise them to the blessed Star which led the Wise Men to a poor abode? Were there no poor homes to which its light would have conducted *me*!"

His chains rattled in resignation as he lowered his arms to his sides. He sighed again—yes, I was sure this time—sighed heavily, a soft cry of despair. His transparent body began to dissolve into indistinct pieces, as though he were actually dripping sorrow. I could see that he was leaving me.

"Marley!" I cried. I wanted to cling to him, to keep him with me, but my hands sliced through him like the air that he was. "Marley, don't leave! I don't know where to go from here."

At once, we were surrounded by other phantoms like Marley, translucent and yet heavy with chains both visible and invisible. They moaned and moved in haste, wandering here and there but finding no place to stop and rest. No, not rest. Help. They found no place to stop and help. Among them, I recognized the old ghost of a man Scrooge knew, the one in the white waistcoat with the iron safe attached to his ankle. He wanted to help the wretched woman with the baby who sat upon a doorstep, but he could not reach down and help her. His pitiful cries filled the air and mingled with the moans of the others.

I turned to Marley, but he was almost gone. As the last of him disappeared into the sky, I heard him say, "The misery with them all was, clearly, that they sought to interfere, for good, in human matters, and had lost the power for ever."

I reached again for Marley, but found myself alone on top of the mountain, beneath the stars. All of the phantoms were gone. The final echo of their cries drifted off.

The host of stars went on shining overhead, undimmed and undisturbed by the host of sorrows below.

CHAPTER 26

I felt heavy, so heavy, as though my body were tied with rope or bound with chains. I couldn't move. Moaning, sighing, I tried to open my eyes. Someone was calling my name.

"Anna. Anna, dear."

The voice was familiar, but I couldn't place it. I had to know who it was.

"Anna, I'm here, darling."

I summoned my strength, turned toward the voice, and opened my eyes. Charles Cullen smiled.

"Charles!" I exclaimed weakly. My eyes left his face and fluttered about the room.

"You're in the hospital," Charles said.

"I am?"

"Yes, you had your appendix removed. You've been a very sick young lady."

I'd had my appendix removed. Someone had told me that. Who? "How long have I been here?" My tongue was sandpaper, my voice little more than a croak.

"Here," Charles said. "Let me help you take some water." He lifted my head gently and held a glass to my lips. I sipped slowly. The water revived me some, gave me a bit of strength.

"How long?" I repeated.

"Four days," he said, settling the glass on the side table.

"Four days? How can that be?"

"You've been drifting in and out, burning up with fever." He leaned over the bed, took my hand. "The fever broke at last this morning, and now you are finally really awake." He smiled again.

"I'm in Los Angeles."

"Yes."

"But … how did you get here so fast?"

"I flew."

My eyes widened. "You flew? On an aeroplane?"

He laughed lightly at that. "Yes, darling. On an aeroplane."

"Weren't you afraid?"

"Terrified. But I had to get to you as quickly as I could. I had to be with you."

I squeezed his hand. "I'm so glad you came."

"Of course, Anna." He sat down on the edge of the bed then and covered my hand with both of his. We shared a smile.

The room was full of light, the windows aglow with what must have been the afternoon sun. The sheets that cocooned me were crisp, clean, and comforting. Charles Cullen and I were alone in the room. The second bed, neatly made, was empty. I felt thankful for the privacy.

"Is everyone all right at home? Ellie? The children?" I asked.

"Everyone's fine. It's you we've been worried about."

"I'm sorry."

"Sorry?"

"To cause you so much worry."

He shook his head. "It's all right now. You're going to be all right." But then his brow furrowed, and his eyes searched my face, as though he were studying me.

"What is it?" I asked.

"Darling," he started. Then he hesitated, took a breath. "Marley met you, didn't he?"

Only when he said the name did I remember. Marley! He had shown me the valley, the stars. But … "How did you know?"

"When they found you, *A Christmas Carol* was on the floor beside you, as though you'd been holding it. The book was mine, remember? I used to read it to you when you were a child." He looked at me intently. "And besides, you spoke Marley's name, just now before you woke up."

I didn't know how to respond. Finally, I said, "Marley came to you too?"

Charles raised my hand to his lips and kissed it. Then he nodded.

"And Old Fezziwig?" I asked.

"Him too."

"And Tiny Tim's brother?"

"No, not his brother, his father. Bob Cratchit. I guess it took a father to show me how to be a father."

"I—I can't believe it."

"Believe it, darling. It's true."

"They came and spoke to you? What did they tell you?"

"Probably very much the same thing they told you."

"I don't understand. When?"

"Well, the first time Marley showed up—"

"He showed up more than once?" I interrupted.

"Yes, twice."

I nodded. "Go on."

"The first time was in 1909. You were four—no, maybe you had just turned five. Either way, you probably don't remember when I was hit on the head at the theater by a piece of falling scenery. It gave me quite the goose egg, not to mention a concussion to the brain that left me unconscious for a couple of days."

"I don't remember it, no, though Mother told me it had happened. She said when you woke up—that's when you left us, went to Hollywood."

"Yes. You see, Marley came and took me to task for what I had done to Henry. He's quite the long-winded fellow, isn't he—a bit flowery but certainly devilishly wise, though that may not be the best choice of words. Anyway—"

"Did he take you to the asylum?"

"No. No, that was Fezziwig. Marley, he didn't take me anywhere. Just showed me those confounded ghosts of his. Made me stand there listening to their moans and groans and cries for what seemed like an everlasting eternity."

"You mean the phantoms? Like the one with the huge safe chained to his ankle?"

"That's them. They're still around, I see. Suppose they always will be, poor devils. Ah, there's that word again. Sorry, darling."

I laughed lightly. "It's all right. I saw them, all those phantoms, just now when I was waking up. Saw them, and felt them too, as though all the chains they bore were wrapped around me. I felt so heavy I could scarcely move. Until I heard your voice calling me to wake up."

We shared another smile. He offered me more water. I drank.

I said, "What happened with Marley?"

He settled the glass on the side table and took a breath. "After a time of standing there with him listening to those ghastly spirits, I asked him, 'What's the point of all this? What are you trying to show me?' And he said, 'These people, when they were alive—they wanted what they wanted and would have nothing else. This is where their desires led them.' So I said to him, 'I don't understand. What has this to do with me?' When I said that, Marley's chains rattled so violently, I felt my bones were rattling right along with them. And then—I'll never forget it—then he turned his dreadful gaze on me and said, 'Everything. It has everything to do with you.'" Charles looked about the room, then back to me. His eyes glistened as though with unshed tears. In a whisper, he added, "I still didn't understand."

I squeezed his hand. "What happened then?"

"Fezziwig came. He took me to the asylum. There was Henry. He was lying in the infant's ward, in one of the cribs. He was just a little thing, about two years old, I think. It was a dreadful place, but Henry was clothed in pajamas. He looked well-fed and warm, and he was sleeping peacefully. But he was alone, and that's what was so insufferable. I don't mean that he was physically alone. There were others about, attendants and what-not. But he was not with the people he should have been with."

Charles Cullen let go of my hand, leaned slightly to the left and dug around in his right pants pocket for his handkerchief. He blew his nose, dabbed at his eyes, and cleared his throat.

"What did Fezziwig tell you?" I asked, urging him to go on.

Charles shook his head while sliding the handkerchief back into his pocket. "Not much. He simply said, 'It's not too late.' He didn't have to say anything else because I understood. I reached down and touched the boy's head. His hair ... it hadn't been cut in a while. It was this halo of blond ringlets, so soft. For a moment, I was tempted to claim him, to take him home. But ..."

"But what?"

"But in the end, I didn't choose him. I chose myself, what I wanted. What your mother wanted. We were so driven, so ambitious in those days."

"I don't understand. Why did you leave Mother then? Why did you leave us both to go to Hollywood?"

His brow furrowed. I waited. "It's hard to explain, Anna. I felt so ashamed, guilty ... but at the same time ... you see, your mother and I had begun to grow apart. We fought a great deal, especially after Henry left. I thought she would do better to pursue a career with Rex as her partner. As for me, I didn't want to stay on the stage. I wanted to throw in my lot with this brand new world of moving pictures. Bernadette would have nothing to do with Hollywood. And so I left."

I shut my eyes. A weariness settled over me. "I see. And after that, Mother never let you be in touch with me again."

"Yes. I didn't like it, but I can't say I blamed her. In a way, I got what I deserved."

Opening my eyes, I said, "When I saw Henry, a nurse was feeding him oatmeal. She was kind to him. She sang to him. It made him smile. Can you imagine? Henry smiling, feeling anything remotely like joy in a place like that?"

Charles nodded. "I can imagine. He was probably a delightful boy at heart, in a way that some of us can never be."

"If you and Mother had kept him, I would have taken care of him. Really, I would have."

"Nonsense, Anna. You were a child yourself. You couldn't possibly have given him the care he needed, even had he been a normal child."

He was right, of course. I'd hardly have been capable of raising Henry. I nodded in agreement. "There was a second visit, you said. One from Bob Cratchit?"

"Cratchit, yes." He pursed his lips and frowned. "The first visit was cut short, you see, when I emerged from the coma. One moment I was with Fezziwig at Henry's crib, and the next a voice was calling me, a woman's voice, the nurse. She was encouraging me to wake up. Just before I became conscious, I saw the face of Bob Cratchit. He wanted to take me somewhere, but it was too late. He held out a hand and tried to reach for me, but ultimately it was the nurse's hand on my shoulder. Bob Cratchit disappeared, and I found myself staring into the face of this nurse. As soon as I was better, I escaped to Hollywood."

"And you were there for a long time."

"A decade." He nodded thoughtfully. "It was a time mostly of failure, and near despair. I got some small parts in the pictures, like the one you saw. But mostly I survived by doing day labor and playing the piano in clubs at night. The man I played in *Tillie's Punctured Romance*—that's who I really was.

Your old man was nothing but a piano player in hole-in-the-wall dives. It's probably best that you didn't know."

We both sighed at once, as though to rid ourselves of the dust of those years. "And Cratchit?" I asked.

"It was November 11, 1918. Armistice Day. I heard the bells and knew the war was over. People were celebrating everywhere, but I couldn't join them. I was too sick with the flu."

"You had the Spanish flu, like I did?"

"Yes. Very nearly died of it. Should be dead, by all rights, but here I am. I was allowed to live. I'll always be grateful."

"And that's when Bob Cratchit came?"

"Yes. Came back, actually. Took me to where he had wanted to take me all those years before."

"The Valley of the Nameless," I whispered.

His brows rose. "Yes."

"The Pinnacle of the Stars."

"You too?"

"Yes. I was just there, with Marley. What did Cratchit tell you?"

"Just this. He said, 'My son Tiny Tim was a cripple, but without him there would have been no story at all.'"

We were quiet then, as though we both needed a moment to think. It was true, really—without Tiny Tim, where would the story have been?

At length, I said, "So you left Hollywood to find Henry?"

Charles dropped his eyes. "No. I let another year go by, still determined to chase my own foolish dreams. But finally one night—or rather, very early in the morning, I was at the piano at closing time. The place was shutting down. The last drunken guests were stumbling out the door to go home. After another riotous night, it was quiet now. The lights were being turned off. I had no home to go home to, just the latest hotel where I happened to be stopping. I had no family. Not even very many friends. Not real friends, anyway. I knew in that moment that what I was living wasn't life, but a kind of living death. I had taken one too many drinks, one too many lines of dope."

My eyes widened. "Dope?"

"Oh yes. It was everywhere you turned. Few were immune in those days, from the top on down. I knew that if I didn't give it all up, it would end up killing me, just as it has so many others. I'd been running far too long, trying to ignore Marley and Fezziwig and Cratchit."

"I suppose you told yourself they were a blot of mustard or a bit of undigested beef or some such thing."

He laughed. "Yes, I called them all those things and worse. I hated them for trying to interfere with my life. But at long last, I knew they were right, even if they *were* only a blot of mustard or a bit of beef."

Still smiling, he squeezed my hand.

"I left LA and went back to Connecticut in 1919," he went on. "But it was too late. Too late by only a few months, as it turned out. Henry had died sometime in the previous year and …"

"And there was a fire. It destroyed the records. We don't know when he died."

"That's right. We know neither when he died nor where he is buried. It was as though he had never been born."

I shook my head. "But you and I both know he once lived."

"Yes. And we know, too, that without him, there would be no story at all."

He retrieved the handkerchief from his pocket and used one clean corner to dab at my tears. Then he wiped away his own.

"After that," I said, "you married Ellie."

He took a deep breath. "I was fortunate enough— blessed—to meet Ellie and make a family with her. I was truly given a second chance. A second chance that made me happy for the first time. Though I will always carry with me here"

—he tapped his chest with an open hand—"a sadness for Henry. I only wish I could speak to him, ask him to forgive me."

A moment passed in silence. Then I said, "I have a feeling he has already forgiven you for what you did, and me, for what I didn't do. Maybe he's somehow looking down from heaven and forgiving us right now. I may be wrong, but it just seems to me that's how Henry's story would unfold."

Charles appeared lost in thought. His gaze dropped to our still-clasped hands, then lifted to my face. "I'm sure you're right, Anna. We can hope for that."

I closed my eyes again. I was tired, so tired, and heavy, as though every muscle in my body was made of lead. I heard Charles say, "Why don't you rest now, darling. Get some sleep."

But I shook my head and opened my eyes. "I still feel the chains."

"The chains?"

"Yes. The phantoms. They were all tied up in the chains of their own misery, and they can never escape. They will never escape. What was it that Marley said to Scrooge just before he left him? They were standing at the window, listening to that 'mournful dirge.' Do you remember?"

"Ah yes, I think I know. He said, 'The misery with them all was, clearly, that they sought to interfere, for good, in human matters, and had lost the power forever.'"

I nodded slowly. "That's it. All those pitiful spirits, they had lost their chance forever. Forever! Do you think ... is it too late for me?"

He grabbed my hand more tightly. "Of course not, Anna. It's not too late at all."

"But the stage is all I know."

"The spirits aren't asking you to change your life so much as to change your heart. The rest will follow."

"People can change, can't they?"

He laughed lightly. "Oh yes. People can change. That's one of the wonderful things about us. We don't have to stay as we have always been."

I gazed at the face of Charles Cullen, knowing that he himself was the proof of his own words.

"Dad?"

His eyes widened slightly; he seemed momentarily to stop breathing. I had surprised even myself by uttering the word. But it had come on its own because it was right.

"Yes, darling?"

"I need to come home. For a little while."

He smiled then, with his mouth, his eyes, his whole face. "Come home then, Anna."

"But Saul. The studio. I haven't even taken the screen test! Or did I? I can't remember for certain."

"No, darling," he said. "You had only just arrived in LA when you collapsed."

I lifted a hand to my brow, rubbed slowly at my right temple. I remembered now: Saul meeting us at the station, Helen and Max and the Spanish Colonial in North Hollywood. I had made it only as far as my room where I saw *A Christmas Carol* on the bedside table.

"Saul has it all arranged," I said. "The studio is expecting me. How can I back out of all that now?"

"Leave all that to me," Dad said. "I'll take care of it."

"Promise me? You'll take care of it?"

"I promise, Anna. Now get some rest. Soon as you're able, I'll take you home."

CHAPTER 27

Wootnote booked drawing rooms on the Santa Fe Chief, and Charlotte and I retraced the route we had only recently taken, over mountains, through deserts, past miles of farmland, stopping briefly in small towns and large cities. This time, Dad was with us in a roomette of his own. Charlotte tried very hard to suppress a smile throughout the long journey. I tried very hard to pretend I didn't notice she was smiling. I knew she was glad we were leaving LA. I was glad too, but not ready to admit it.

Once we reached the East Coast, Charlotte headed off to Rhode Island to spend some time with her sister while Dad and I went on to Connecticut. Saul had put out a press release about my unexpected hospitalization and my need to recover from surgery. The story had been picked up by all the major news wires, but I refused to read the papers, so I didn't know what was written about me. Card, letters, and telegrams from well-wishers were sent to Saul's office in New York, but I wasn't there to receive them. Through Saul, I made a statement to the press to thank my friends and fans, to assure them I was recovering nicely, and to ask for privacy. I wanted nothing to do with my former life for a time.

Eventually, I would return to the stage, but not yet.

The surgery left me so weak that even walking across the room was a challenge. All my strength had apparently been removed right along with my appendix. For the better part of three months, I rested and reveled in the loving care of

Dad and Ellie. Margaret often sat quietly with me. Mostly we read or listened to music while sitting by the fire. The younger children were allowed to visit me for only short spells at a time, but just hearing their voices off in the distance heartened me.

Early on, Uncle Cosmo came by train from New Haven for a weekend visit and ended up staying through the fall and winter and into the spring. Dear Uncle Cosmo. I'd rarely seen him since I'd risen to stardom a decade before, and Dad hadn't seen him for more than twenty years, since leaving us for Hollywood. I feared that a reunion between Dad and Uncle Cosmo might be awkward, but I worried for nothing. The whole family embraced Uncle Cosmo like he was a long-lost relative, which indeed he was, and in finding what was once missing, there is always reason to rejoice.

Cosmo was truly an old man now, nearing eighty. But he was spry and his fingers were nimble, as he had never stopped playing his violin, even when his only audience was himself. He brought his violin to the Cullens, of course, and played for me, and with the first notes, I realized how much I'd missed him, and that I'd been wrong not to visit him more often. When he wasn't playing for me, he simply held my hand and spoke softly of bygone days. Sometimes, we sat together in silence while I closed my eyes in rest. His music, his voice, and even his silences served as a healing grace.

I didn't tell Uncle Cosmo about Jacob Marley and Old Fezziwig and the others, as Dad and I promised each other to tell no one. Who, after all, would understand? But I did speak to Cosmo once about Henry.

We were listening to music on the radio in the library. We had actually pulled the wing chairs side by side so we could be together, my hand in the crook of his arm. I don't know what prompted me to ask the question, but suddenly there it was: "Where were you, Uncle Cosmo, on the night they gave Henry away?"

Startled, he drew back and gazed at me, his eyes wide behind his glasses. "Good heavens, Anna, that was ages ago. Why do you ask?"

"I was just wondering. Do you remember that night?"

He gave a small nod and sighed heavily. "I was on the road, traveling for a time with another troupe. I didn't learn of it until I got back."

"And what did you do?"

"Do? I didn't do anything. It wasn't up to me. I was livid, of course, but the child wasn't mine."

"What if he had been, Uncle? Would you have given him away?"

He thought for a long time. Finally he said, "I'd like to tell you I'd have done the noble thing and kept the boy. But how can I know for sure what I'd have done? How can anyone know for sure until they're faced themselves with such an unthinkable decision?" He shook his head and sat silently a moment. "We're all only human. Terribly, regrettably human."

I waited, but he didn't go on. "Did you ever get over being angry with Mother and Dad?"

He nodded. "Eventually, I forgave them."

"I suppose they asked you never to tell me about Henry."

"Of course. They believed you were too young to remember him, and they didn't think you needed to know. They were trying to protect you."

"Me? Or themselves?"

"You, I think. Yes, I'm sure they were trying to protect you."

"Then why did you tell me?"

"Because a part of you already knew. You dreamed about the boy. I remember how you were tormented by those dreams. When you were old enough, I thought you ought to know the truth."

"I'm glad you told me, Uncle Cosmo. You did the right thing."

He looked satisfied at that. I shut my eyes a moment but opened them when another thought came to me. "There must have been others who knew about Henry ... family, friends."

"Of course."

"What were they told?"

Uncle Cosmo shrugged, a small lifting of his shoulders. "A very few were told the truth. Most were told that the child had died suddenly. So many children died in infancy then, no questions were asked."

"Of those who knew, did no one object?"

"No. The child was an imbecile. Such children were routinely institutionalized. Most believed it was for the best."

I leaned my head on Uncle Cosmo's shoulder. "I'm trying to understand, Uncle. I know Dad was sorry and that he suffered the loss, but Mother ..."

"Don't think she was unaffected, Anna. No, after Henry, there was a change in her. A sadness came over her that never lifted. She'd never admit to it, but I know it was there. She was never the same. One doesn't lose a child—any child—and remain the same."

I thought about that for a moment. Then I said, "I'm sorry for her, then. It must have been difficult—more than I've ever realized."

I couldn't see his face, but I could see his hands. They were clasped together in his lap. His thumbs began to caress each other, as though he were deep in thought. "Your mother was a woman of many regrets, I'm afraid. Hers was not an easy life. I hope you can forgive her."

"For what happened with Henry?"

"For Henry. For everything. Your childhood was ... well, not exactly what a childhood should be, I'm afraid."

I nodded, my cheek rubbing against the smooth cotton of Uncle's shirt. "I do forgive her, Uncle. And Dad too. As you say, we are all, after all, only human."

He patted my hand. "That's a good girl," he said quietly, sounding just as he had when I was a child. I gave his arm a little squeeze.

The music on the radio played on, something by Brahms, I think. After listening for a time, I said, "How little we know about people, Uncle Cosmo—even those closest to us."

"Yes," he agreed. "There are so few windows into the hearts and souls of men and women. We're mostly alone, except for what we choose to reveal. How can anyone ever know us as we really are?"

"And yet, that's what is so ironic, isn't it? Simply to be known—isn't that the one thing that we all *do* want? To be known and loved for who we are?"

"Of course, Anna. It's that very irony that makes our existence so miserable at times. We want to be known by people who can never really know us and loved by those who can never fully love us."

I sat up then, and drawing back, gazed at Uncle Cosmo. Something from Dickens' story was sounding in my head, and I had to stop and listen. Scrooge was pleading with Marley, trying to appease the old ghost, trying to cajole him by telling him he'd done some good in the world because he was always a good man of business. But Marley was not appeased. "Business!" Marley cried. "Mankind was my business ... charity, mercy, forbearance, and benevolence were all my business."

And yet, for all the years he was alive, he had offered none.

When was the last time I had told Uncle Cosmo I loved him? For too many years I had been so busy shining my star, I'd had no time. I'd taken no time. After buying him a house, I had left him there and had very nearly forgotten about him.

Now, I wanted to tell Uncle Cosmo that when I was child, he was my father, and my mother, my anchor, my rock, my comforter. He was the one who had picked up a weeping Miss Honeycomb and whispered soothing words to her while carrying her out of the wings. Without him, there would have been no wall between me and what would have been a bleak and lonely childhood. Thank God I had Uncle Cosmo!

But I couldn't find the words for all I wanted to say. Instead, to Uncle Cosmo's alarm, I began to weep.

"Anna, darling, are you all right?" he cried. "Are you feeling ill?"

I shook my head while wiping my cheeks with the palms of my hands. "No, Uncle, I'm fine. I just …"

"What, Anna?" His eyes were wide behind his glasses, his face ashen.

"I've been so wrong not to tell you …"

"Tell me what?"

"… that I love you, Uncle. I've always loved you more than anyone."

His face softened. His brow relaxed. He smiled. So seldom had I seen Uncle Cosmo smile, I wasn't sure he could. But he did. He patted my hand. "I have always loved you more than anyone too, my dear."

My eyes filled again. "It isn't much, after all these years, but it's something, isn't it?"

"No, my dear, it's not something. It's everything."

I laid my head on Uncle's shoulder again, feeling very much as Scrooge must have felt when he awoke from the long dark night and, looking out the window, he saw the golden sunlight that was Christmas Day.

Chapter 28

On a December afternoon, after my strength had returned, I stood alone by a window in the library and watched a fine scattering of snow falling silently beyond the glass. Each flake appeared as out of nowhere and settled soundlessly upon the white lawn. The children had earlier made snow angels in the yard, a whole host of them all around the perimeter of the house, and the imprints of their scissoring arms and legs remained.

I thought of Georgia Snow, and found myself humming the tune I had sung for Gina as she pranced about the stage, receiving all the admiration for a voice that wasn't hers.

> They call me little Snow Angel,
> Pretty as can be.
> Skin so white and smile so bright
> You'll want to be with me.

How I had hated that song. How I had hated Gina. And how she had tormented me by taking advantage of what I could do for her.

But we had made our peace, as she lay dying. I wondered what might have happened, had she lived. Would our feud have gone on indefinitely? I had no way of knowing. I knew only that the course of our lives hadn't been up to me, or to her, or to any of us, really. Our story was written by a hand other than our own.

The snow came more heavily now. The snow angels began to lose their contours and disappear. As I watched from the window, feeling the frigid air permeate the glass, I wondered where I might go now—or rather, where that hand might take me. I would go back to the stage, of course. It was all I knew and it was my living. But it didn't seem enough anymore. I needed something else, something in addition to my work.

I needed a second chance. Dad had been given one. He had told me so. Where was my second chance? Making amends with Uncle Cosmo was a start, but there had to be more.

Shivering, I moved away from the window and back to the hearth. The house was empty, save for Betty preparing dinner in the kitchen. Otherwise the entire family, including Uncle Cosmo, was at the orphanage singing and playing with the children, something they did nearly every week. I placed a few more logs on the fire, then settled beneath a blanket on the wing chair, my feet propped up on the footstool. Watching the snapping flames, I fell asleep.

And dreamed. For the first time in years, I dreamed the old familiar dream. I was a very young child again, and I was sitting in the rocking chair, holding the baby in my arms. He was wrapped in his little lamb quilt, and the velveteen bear was tucked in with him. This time, for the first time, I knew who the baby was.

I held him to me more tightly. "Oh Henry," I said. "I won't let you go this time, I promise! I won't even let myself wake up. I'm going to stay right here with you."

Time passed—maybe a few hours, maybe only moments—as I rocked Henry and hummed to him. I was determined to cement myself in this story, to make this scene my only existence, to never wake up into any other world. This was all I wanted.

***

But I did wake up, of course. I awoke to the sounds of the family returning home, the banging open of the front door, muffled footsteps, distant voices, laughter, Ellie's cries of "Take your boots off here in the hall! I don't want snow all over the house!"

I felt Henry fade away, as though he were melting in my arms. A sadness came over me. I opened my eyes to the dying flames in the fireplace. The logs glowed red, and a jumble of scattered sparks flew upward, but the fire was almost out. I pushed myself up in the chair and rubbed my eyes with my fingertips. When Margaret, Peter, and Julia tumbled into the library, I tried to smile.

"Oh, Anna," Margaret said, "we had such a grand time. Dad was playing the piano, and Uncle Cosmo was playing the violin, and we were all singing when suddenly Julia got up and started dancing, and then the next thing you know we all jumped up and everyone was dancing—all the children and even Mother and some of the orphanage workers—we were all doing the Lindy Hop and the Charleston and, oh it was just crazy! We haven't laughed so hard in a long time."

"Even I was dancing," Peter said, and he twirled around the room as though to show me.

Julia crawled into my lap. I wrapped her up in the blanket with me. "Well, young lady," I said, "it sounds like you started a real party."

She nodded, put her head on my shoulder, and closed her eyes.

Margaret flung herself down in the other wing chair. "You should have seen us, Anna. Anyone would have thought we'd been sipping the bathtub gin!" She laughed loudly, then added, "But of course we were doing no such thing. We were just being silly and having fun."

I looked at her and smiled. "When are you going back, Margaret?"

"You mean, all of us together?"

"Yes, the whole family. When are you going back?"

"Christmas Eve. We're going to sing carols."

"Good," I said. "I'll go with you."

Margaret's eyes widened. "Really, Anna?"

"Yes, really. Don't you think it's about time I got out of the house and did something?"

"But are you feeling up to it? You've been so weak since the surgery."

"I'm better now, much better. And besides, there's something I need to do."

"There is? What is it?"

"I don't know yet," I said. "But I'm going to find out."

***

The orphanage was a three-story brick building in the heart of town. When we pulled up in front of it on Christmas Eve, all six downstairs windows were crowded with children's faces. They had been waiting for us, and when we stepped from the car, they greeted us with smiles and wide-eyed wonder. For one brief moment, I stood on the snowy sidewalk looking up, marveling at the contrast between the joy on the children's faces and the dreariness of the place in which they lived. I thought of Henry smiling in the asylum while being fed his drab meal of oatmeal, and understood for the first time the marvelous resilience of the human spirit. We were created for joy, and it was entirely possible for us to find it, though probably not in the places we most expect.

As soon as we entered the front hall, we were surrounded by thirty or forty children, all wanting hugs. The matron of the orphanage, a kindly sixtyish woman named Mrs. Waylon, ushered everyone into a large room off the front hall, a parlor of sorts furnished neatly but sparingly: a few couches, a set of wing chairs, a rolltop desk, a couple of bookcases, and by the front windows, a Christmas tree decorated with popcorn strings and handmade decorations of colored paper and ribbons. Under the tree were gifts that, Ellie had told me earlier, were donated by local churches. At the back end of the room stood an upright piano with a swivel stool. Some of its keys were chipped, and Dad said it was in need of tuning, but I had no doubt he could coax some music out of it that night.

And he did. We gathered around that old piano, Uncle Cosmo pulled his violin from its case, and for an hour we sang hymns and Christmas carols—the Cullens, Uncle Cosmo, the children, the orphanage workers, and me. It was magical, joyful, and satisfying in a way that I had never known while performing on stage. The cheer on the children's faces was far and away grander than the sound of any applause.

At the end of the hour, Mrs. Waylon suggested, "Why don't we have Mr. Cullen and Miss Rycroft entertain us with one last carol before we serve cookies and cocoa?"

And so we did, singing "O Holy Night" while Cosmo's violin accompanied us. As we sang—"O holy night, the stars are brightly shining"—I knew that where I was at that moment would be my place of second chances.

And so it was. After we finished, and while the orphanage workers were serving cookies and hot cocoa, Margaret slipped out of the room. A moment later she returned with a bundle in her arms. She came directly to me and pulled back the blanket to reveal the face of a sleeping baby.

"Look, Anna," she said quietly. "He's the one I told you about. He was left here because he's blind."

I gazed at him, at his perfectly lovely little face. "What's his name?" I asked.

Mrs. Waylon, who was standing nearby, took a step closer. "We call him Jack," she said, "because he showed up just as we were reading *Jack the Giant Slayer* to the children."

I frowned at her. "He had no given name?"

She shook her head. "None that we know of. He was brought to us by a young lad who looked like he came from that shantytown down by the river. I suppose somebody paid the boy to bring Jack to us, but the boy wouldn't say. He handed over the baby and a note with a birth date written on it, but nothing else. No name, no information about the parents. And then he was gone."

I held out my hands to Margaret. "May I hold him?"

"Of course." She gently placed him in my waiting arms.

I carried the baby to one of the wing chairs and sat. As I held him, I marveled at how solid he was, how real. Not like the baby in my dreams. This one was flesh and bone and soft downy hair and velvety skin and had—I counted them—ten fingers and ten toes. His tiny body was warm and smelled of soap. He drew in breath, let it out. He smacked his shiny pink lips in sleep.

I began to hum, just as I had hummed to Henry in my dream. And after a moment, he opened his eyes. They were two milky blue orbs, unfocused, fluttering. He couldn't see my face, but he could hear my voice, and he knew that I was there.

I could not hold fast to the baby in the dream, but with this one ... drawing him closer, I kissed him, once on each plump cheek.

"I shall call you Jack Henry," I told him. "Jack Henry Cullen Rycroft."

CHAPTER 29

When spring came, I was still living at home in Connecticut. Rehearsals for a new musical were slated to begin in June, but until then I wanted to spend time with my family and with my son. I wanted undivided time with Jack Henry, time to watch him take his first steps, to hear him laugh, to gaze at his tiny hands as they explored the soft plush of his teddy bear and the rounded contours of his wooden rattle. I loved to call out his name and see him turn to the sound of my voice, and to smile in recognition. He knew that I was his mother, and that I loved him.

Also precious were the times I watched Dad bend over Jack's bassinet, a look of pride and wonder on his face. Often, too, he held Jack in his arms and sang him lullabies while feeding him his bottle. "You know, Anna," he said to me once, "it's a marvelous thing to be a grandfather. And I'm so glad you decided Jack will grow up in this house. We'll all keep a good eye on him whenever you have to be on the road." Humming, he rocked Jack for several minutes. Then he added, "I'm going to do it right this time around, I promise."

Before my return to the theater, we had one more thing to do—Dad and me. We had to bury Henry. We wanted to give him the gift of a stone, to mark not his death but his life. Dad ordered a gravestone that had Henry's full name: Henry Richard Cullen. Beneath were the words "Beloved Son and Brother."

No birth date, no death date, and we didn't have a body to bury. But Dad intended to dig a hole in the distant yard beside the copse of trees, a small hole, one that would hold only a small hinged box, about the size of a hatbox. It would hold those things we associated with Henry: his baby quilt, his velveteen bear, and Dad's copy of *A Christmas Carol*.

We chose Sunday, May 21, as the day for the burial. It was also my birthday. Putting Henry to rest was my gift to myself.

We went to church that morning, then had a bite of lunch and a time of rest. Toward mid-afternoon, Dad built a fire in the fireplace for me, though the day was mild. He told me to stay right there and enjoy a good book while he went about the task of digging the hole. The younger children went with him to decorate the area about the grave with garlands of fresh flowers.

While I read in the library, Ellie, Betty, and Margaret bustled about the kitchen, preparing the birthday dinner and cake that would follow Henry's service. Jack Henry slept in his bassinet beside my chair. Every time I glanced at him, I felt a deep sense of satisfaction. That, and an unbounded gratitude that this little boy was mine. Second chances, I discovered, can come in wonderful small packages.

I had just reached a hand toward the bassinet when the library door banged open and startled me. Margaret stomped in and strode across the room, clutching the Sunday paper. One glance at her face told me she was furious.

"Did you see this?" she cried.

I held a finger to my lips and nodded toward Jack. "Don't wake him up. Now, did I see what?"

"He's ..." She swatted at the paper with the back of her hand. "He's gone and eloped!"

"Who, Margaret? Who are you talking about?"

"Frederick Mansfield! The rat! He's run off with one of the nurses at the sanitarium."

I shook my head slightly, trying to take it in. I couldn't speak, so I held out my hand to ask for the paper.

She gave it to me. I stood and moved to the hearth so I could read with my back to Margaret. I didn't want to let on that the news was a kick to the heart.

There it was, in large-point type: *Frederick Mansfield Elopes!* And beneath that, in smaller type: *Star of Broadway ties knot with nurse.* The article was brief but told more than I wanted to know. Freddy and a nurse had run off in the night, escaping the sanitarium under cover of darkness, as though they were playing a scene from a poorly scripted movie. The next day a marriage license was filed in the courthouse in Albany for a Frederick Mansfield and a Juliana Barnes.

All the years I had spent loving him had come to this.

I lowered the newspaper and gazed at what was left of the flames in the fireplace. The pain of the loss surprised me, catching me off guard. I had scarcely thought of Freddy for months, so what did I care if he was married? I was the one who had let him go, and for good reason.

After only a moment, the sting subsided. This was simply the final letting go. Maybe the hand that was writing my story was giving me a gift. It was, after all, my birthday.

I heard Margaret take a step toward me. "Oh Anna, I'm sorry," she said. "Maybe I shouldn't have told you. At least, not today. It could have waited."

"Never mind, Margaret." I turned around and smiled. "I'm glad you told me. And you know what? I'm sorry for this nurse, whoever she is. She's a starry-eyed fool." *Just as I was once,* I thought, though I didn't say that aloud.

Margaret's eyes widened. "She is?"

"Of course she is. Imagine running off with a no-good lush like Freddy. And she's a nurse at the sanitarium, for heaven's sakes. She should know better. But no, Frederick Mansfield is handsome and famous and charming and … and so hard to resist." I laughed lightly as I crumpled the newspaper into a tight wad. "Listen, Margaret, I give it six months tops."

"Six months? That's not very long, is it?"

"No, not very long."

"But …" She paused and looked about the room as though searching for the right words. Then she cried, "How awful! Not that I care a fig about Frederick Mansfield, but … well, I mean, you're right, that poor nurse. I hadn't thought about what she might be getting into. I only thought about that man running off and being happy with someone who isn't you while you're still … well, you know. But I'm sure you're better off than she is! I mean, I certainly wouldn't want to be divorced after only six months. You've hardly had time for even a honeymoon!"

Dear, sweet Margaret. I smiled at her again and shook my head. "No, nobody wants to be divorced after only six months. It's not much of a happily-ever-after, is it? All right, to make ourselves feel better, let's give her the benefit of the doubt. Maybe she'll have one good year, maybe two, if she can put up with him for that long."

Margaret's shoulders slumped, and she sighed. "Oh, Anna, it's just so—"

She was interrupted when Peter appeared in the doorway. "Dad says to come on, Anna," he announced. "Everything's ready."

I tossed the paper into the fire. The flames, rekindled, leapt up hungrily. In another moment, the news about Frederick Mansfield was turned to ash.

Jack fussed quietly when I lifted him from the bassinet, but he soon settled back to sleep against my shoulder. Margaret and I headed outside and moved across the lawn with Ellie, Betty, and Uncle Cosmo not far behind. Uncle Cosmo carried his violin in one hand, the bow in the other.

After we had all gathered about the grave, Dad cleared his throat, looked around the circle at each of us, and said, "Well, shall we begin?"

The granite stone, delivered and permanently secured a couple days before, was now trimmed with flowers: daisies, roses, baby's breath. Similar arrangements wreathed the small hole in the earth and were scattered about the lawn, the children's handiwork. Beside the grave lay the little pine box, its lid open so we could see the embroidered quilt, the small velveteen bear, and the book.

I nodded at Dad. He pulled a sheet of paper from his breast pocket and unfolded it. We all waited quietly, even the youngest. I could hear the leaves rustling in the nearby trees and the birds calling out one to another.

Dad looked at the paper in his hand, up at us, down at the box. "Henry," he began, "we aren't here to say good-bye, because you will always be with us. We're here simply to acknowledge your life, to proudly claim you as our son and brother, and to thank you for teaching us that every star, however dimly it shines, has a name. Your name was—is— Henry Richard Cullen. This stone is here to proclaim your name to the world, to tell the world that we love you, and to tell you we are grateful you came to be with us, however briefly."

He stopped, cleared his throat again, and looked at me. His eyes shone. My own burned with unshed tears. Still, we smiled at each other.

"Henry," he continued, "we will see you at the Pinnacle of the Stars. This time we'll come to you, and you will welcome us. We look forward to that day with expectation, hopefulness, and joy."

Dad folded the paper and tucked it back into his breast pocket. He held out a hand to Ellie, who gave him a small black Bible. He opened it to a page marked with a ribbon. "Anna, dear," he said, "would you be so kind as to read to us the words of Isaiah 40:26?"

I settled Jack more securely against my shoulder and reached for the Bible. My eyes were drawn to a passage underlined in black ink, which I read aloud:

> Lift up your eyes on high, and see who hath
> created these things: who bringeth out their
> host by number, and calleth them all by their
> names: by the greatness of his might, and
> strength, and power, not one of them was
> missing.

Oh yes, of course. I recognized the words that Marley had recited to me at the Pinnacle of the Stars. He must have offered the same words to Dad.

I closed the Bible and handed it to Ellie. Dad crouched down and started to lower the lid of the box. But before he had closed it all the way, he looked up at me and said, "I'm having second thoughts about burying the book."

I gazed at him curiously. "Why is that, Dad?" The book was, after all, what had brought us to Henry.

"Someone else might need it someday."

I paused in thought, then nodded. I held out a hand. "I think you're right. May I have it?"

"Of course."

He lifted the book from the box and placed it in my hand. Then he closed the lid and lowered the box into the hole. He stepped to where the shovel was stuck by its blade in the ground, pulled it up, and started stabbing at the little mound of dirt piled at the foot of the grave. The first scoop of dirt and pebbles hit the lid with a pattering sound. So did the second. But then the soil fell quietly, back into the hole out of which it had come, until the box was lost to view.

Finally, after the final toss, Dad tapped at the earth with the flat of the shovel. The patch looked desolate and bare compared to the rest of the yard, but we knew in time the grass would grow there again. Dad straightened and took a step back. He gave a nod to Margaret and then, as planned, each child laid a flower on the grave, saying, "For you, Henry."

When they had finished, I handed Jack off to Betty and asked her to take him back to the house. Then I turned to Uncle Cosmo. "Play something happy for us, Uncle," I said.

He had to think about that. I'm not sure Uncle Cosmo was used to playing happy songs. "What should I play?" he asked.

"How about 'Georgia Snow'? I haven't heard you play that one in quite a while."

His eyebrows met above his nose, but then he shrugged and said, "Why not?" He tucked the violin under his chin, lifted the bow and played heartily the song I had once so despised, but that now seemed happily appropriate.

While his notes filled the air, the music sent the younger children dancing and twirling about the yard. Inspired by their playfulness, we all joined hands and began dancing in circles in the grass. Suddenly, the day was filled with laughter, and even Uncle Cosmo was smiling—a real true smile of something like joy.

I don't know how long Uncle Cosmo played and how long we danced there by Henry's stone—maybe minutes, maybe hours. Time was inessential; only the moment mattered. And the music. And all of us together. And the joy of laughter.

At long last, Uncle Cosmo must have grown tired, because the music stopped, and Ellie began to herd the children toward the house, saying dinner would soon be ready. They whined at first, not wanting to go inside, but she enticed them with reminders of birthday cake and ice cream, and that sent them running across the yard.

Dad and I remained behind, looking at the stone. He said, "Well, darling, happy birthday."

"Thanks, Dad. It's been an unusual day, don't you think?"

"It certainly has. But everything's all right now, isn't it?"

"Yes." I nodded. "Everything's all right."

"Henry's at peace."

"At long last."

"But darling, are you?" he asked. "At peace, I mean?"

"Yes … and no. I just found out that Freddy ran off with a nurse and got married. I suppose you read about it in the paper this morning."

Dad nodded. "Yes, I did. And good riddance, I say. I'm just thankful he didn't run off with you."

I laughed lightly at that. "I agree. Still …"

When I didn't finish my thought, Dad said, "Still, today you are twenty-eight and unmarried, and you are wondering whether the right one will ever come along."

I looked at him with raised brows. "You read my mind. How did you do that?"

"I just know human nature," he said with a shrug. "But don't worry, darling. Life is filled with good gifts, and generally they come when you least expect them."

"I suppose you're right."

"I know I'm right. And I also know that being married to Frederick Mansfield would not have been a good gift."

I nodded. "I completely agree with you there."

I thought about the words Freddy had said to me the last time we were together, nearly a year ago: *You and I, Anna—we're not ordinary people. We will never live ordinary lives. We are far above all that.*

Frederick Mansfield had believed that the whole world was a stage built especially for him, and that of the story unfolding in history, he was somehow the star. He would never understand that without the Henrys of the world, and the Jack Henrys and the Tiny Tims, there would be no story at all, because they were the heart of the story, and no story lives without a heart.

"Dad?"

"Yes, Anna?"

"I wonder if old Marley could get through to Freddy somehow."

"If anyone could, it would be old Marley, persistent fellow that he is. But"—he paused thoughtfully a moment—"I'm not sure even he would have much success. It's possible for people to change, but not everyone chooses to. Freddy?" He shrugged. "Your guess is as good as mine."

"Well, I have someone else in mind for the book, at any rate."

"Who?"

"Jack, of course. Even a Tiny Tim might need to be given the tour, don't you think? Just to know where he fits into the story."

Dad nodded. "I hadn't thought of it that way, but yes, no doubt that's so. You can begin to read the story to Jack tonight. Old Marley will know when it's time to pay a visit."

"I'll do that. In the meantime, I'm sure Marley has plenty to do to keep himself busy."

"No question there," Dad said with a laugh. "So long as there are Scrooges in the world, the old chained chatterbox will probably never rest, poor devil."

I let out a sigh. "Maybe someday he can rest," I said. "Maybe someday he'll have completed his task and he can stop wandering the earth and haunting people."

"Yes. Maybe he will, someday." Dad smiled and offered me his arm. "Shall we go join the others?" he asked.

"Yes, I'm ready."

I took his arm, then hesitated.

"What it is, Anna?"

I thought I'd had heard the rattling of chains somewhere in the upper branches of the trees. I glanced upward, expecting, in spite of myself, to see Jacob Marley there, smiling down on us with something like satisfaction or maybe simply amusement. But there was no Marley, and perhaps the rattling of chains had been only my imagination … or a bit of undigested beef, or a blot of mustard, or a crumb of cheese.

I smiled. "It's nothing, Dad. Let's go."

Arm in arm, we walked across the lawn toward home.

If you enjoyed this book, will you consider sharing the message with others?

New Hope Publishers is an imprint of Iron Stream Media. Let us know your thoughts about any of our books at info@ironstreammedia.com. You can also let the author know by visiting or sharing a photo of the cover on our social media pages or leaving a review at a retailer's site. All of it helps us get the message out!
Twitter.com/IronStreamMedia
Facebook.com/IronStreamMedia
Instagram.com/IronStreamMedia

Iron Stream Media
derives its name from Proverbs 27:17,
"As iron sharpens iron, so one person sharpens another."
This sharpening describes the process of discipleship, one to another. With this in mind, Iron Stream Media provides a variety of solutions for churches, ministry leaders, and nonprofits ranging from in-depth Bible study curriculum and Christian book publishing to custom publishing and consultative services. Through the popular Life Bible Study and Student Life Bible Study brands, ISM provides web-based full-year and short-term Bible study teaching plans as well as printed devotionals, Bibles, and discipleship curriculum. For more information on ISM and LPC Books, please visit
IronStreamMedia.com
ShopLPC.com